IN DARKNESS AROUND US

An Anthology by
J. Wesley Buck

IN DARKNESS AROUND US

TABLE OF CONTENTS

IN DARKNESS AROUND US

POSSESSION

The incessant ringing of the phone brought Rachel from the shower with a large towel wrapped around her slim figure. She grabbed the phone and lifted it to her face.

"Dr. Estes." She listened for a moment as a look of surprise came to her face, quickly replaced by an angry frown.

"Christ! I'll be there as soon as I can." She closed the phone and returned it to the stand. Rachel dressed and gave her hair a quick brushing. She went down to the garage, got into her car and started the engine. She drove out of the underground garage and made the tires squeal as she turned onto the street.

I must concentrate on the man in front of me. I will have to follow him because I can't kill him here. There are too many people around. I must kill him! Why? I'm not sure, but he must be killed. Now he's turning down a heavily shadowed street, Empty Street. I have become the hunter. I follow him quietly, making certain he doesn't know I'm behind him. The buildings along this street stand dark and boarded up. The streetlights give cones of light surrounded by darkness. This makes it much easier for me to close on him without being seen.

I am only a few feet behind him now and the urge to kill is overpowering me. I close on him under the next streetlight. I grab him from behind. He turns and faces me. I see the terror come to him as he recognizes me. But I don't know him! My hands clutch his soft, warm throat. He is stronger than I thought, but no match for my strength. He struggles frantically, trying to get my hands from around his throat. It feels good to be squeezing the life out of him. I'm enjoying hearing him gasp for breath, seeing his eyes bulge and his face turning blue. His tongue is hanging out the side of his mouth and saliva spills down on my wrists. His arms drop limply to his sides and he hangs limp in my grip. I release him and he falls to the sidewalk. I'm elated! But I know there are others I must kill, ones I want revenge against. Not this night though. I must find a place to hide. I look around at the boarded up building and decide on one of them.

I must find a way into one. I'm tired and want to sleep. I know my next victim will come to mind when it's his time to die, and I'll know where to find him.

Rachel was very pissed off when she came through the door of the lab. Dr. Walter Childs and Chief of Security Aaron Mills were waiting in her office. Her oval face is capped by short, dark, blonde hair and inset with large brown eyes above a slim curving nose and lips that carried a hard frown. She stopped facing them.

"How the hell was he able to get out?" she demanded.

"We don't know," Mills replied. "He was able to evade, or deactivate, every security system in the building and the outer grounds."

"How long has he been gone?" Rachel asked.

"We don't know," Mills said. "It was only discovered that he was missing when the orderly took him dinner."

"Rachel," said Childs, a man with hazel eyes and white hair. "What are you worried about? He can't survive long without the special supplement injection."

"We don't know that for certain, Walter. We do know he's very dangerous," Rachel said.

"What can we do, Doctor Estes?" Mills asked.

"Call the police. Get someone over here who will have the authority to act."

Police Lieutenant Rick Archer was surprised at how young and pretty Dr. Estes was. He had expected an elderly woman in a lab smock.

"Dr. Estes, I'm Lieutenant Rick Archer." She noted his surprise.

"If the doctor bothers you, Lieutenant, Rachel will do."

"Then call me Rick. Now what's your concern about this man who left here?"

"Left here! That's an understatement," Rachel said. "He evaded and deactivated every security system in this building." Rick nodded.

"That's impressive," Rick said. "I saw some of the systems when I came in. But why is this man so important?"

"He's a clone with no memory or personality. But he poses a very real danger, Rick."

"How?"

"He's demonstrated on more than one occasion to be an extremely aggressive person."

"Lieutenant, I think Rachel is overreacting," Childs said. "He can't possibly live for more than seventy-two hours without a special injection." Rachel turned an annoyed look on Childs.

"I am not overreacting, Walter. We aren't certain he needs the injection." Rick held up a hand.

"Just how dangerous do you think this clone to be?" Rick asked. A light on the phone on Rachel's desk came on and began blinking. She lifted it to her ear.

"Dr. Estes." Rachel lowered the phone and handed it to Rick.

"It's for you," she said. He took it from her and put it to his ear.

"Archer." As he listened, his eyes locked with Rachel's as he nodded.

"I'll find out, Captain." He handed the phone back to her and she returned it to its cradle.

"Do you know a Donald Wells?" Rick asked. Walter and Rachel exchanged shocked looks.

"Yes," she replied.

"I think you should start telling me more about this clone," Rick said. "You both seem to know a man who was found murdered."

"Jesus!" Childs exclaimed. Rachel paled and went behind the desk and sat down. She turned her eyes up to Rick.

"I don't believe it's a coincidence, Rick," she said. "The clone escapes, a man is murdered, no coincidence," Rachel said, emphatically.

I awoke hungry and have a strong desire to kill. I'm going to kill the man whose face I see in my mind. I don't know who he is, only that I want very much to kill him. I want to do that more than eat. I pull myself out through the basement window and stand in the dark, empty street. He won't be around here, but I know where he is. I begin to walk.

It takes me time to get to his home. It's surrounded by a high brick wall with locked steel gates. I move along the wall looking for a way over. I must think of a way in. My hunger and urge to kill are beginning to engulf me. Only if I kill can I eat. I move back along the wall carefully searching for a way over. I move my hands over the bricks and think I can scale this uneven surface. I try climbing.

It took time, but I'm over the wall. I move from one shadow to the next that covers me. I see light in the patio doors and slip up to them and look in. There sits the man I must kill.

I watch awhile to make sure no one comes into the room. I press down on the door handle and the door silently opens. He turns toward me, surprise gives away to fear.

"You! But how? It's not possible." I walk up to him and look into his eyes.

"I'm here," I say, not knowing where the words come from. I clamp my hands around his throat. He struggles longer than the first man, but the end is the same. He couldn't break my grip. I let his lifeless form drop to the floor. Now he's dead, I can eat. I rip off his jacket and tear his shirtsleeve. I take hold of his arm famished. I begin to eat.

Rick and Childs walked into Rachel's office.

"What is it?" she asked, looking up from paper work.

"There's been another murder," Rick replied.

"Oh, no!" Rachel exclaimed.

"Rachel," Childs said, slowly. "There's a new factor involved. The victim's arm was devoured."

"What?"

"The clone ate the flesh from his arm, Rachel," Childs said.

"Walter, that means – oh God!"

"It means he can now survive without the injections," Childs said. Rick looked from one to the other confused.

"What the hell are you two talking about?" Rick asked. Rachel took off her glasses and laid them on the desk.

"We thought we had him under control, Rick," Rachel said. "We were giving him injections of a special supplement. He would need these injections every seventy-two hours in order to stay alive."

"And now?" Rick asked. He could see the pain and fear in her eyes.

"If he's devouring human flash, he can live without the injections," Childs said.

"What was in those injections?" Rick asked. Rachel quickly sucked in a breath.

"Fluids from the flesh of living animals," she replied. Rick sat down as the implications sunk in. He looked from Rachel to Childs.

"I think it's time you told me who this is a clone of," Rick said. Childs looked at Rachel and nodded. She looked back to Rick.

"Damon Hunter," Rachel said.

"But he died over a year ago," Rick said.

"And his clone has just reached the adult stage," Childs said. "We were to transfer Hunter's personality and memory into the clone."

"His brain and spinal cord are intact in a special solution in the lab," Rachel said. Rick got an enlightened look.

"That may explain it," Rick said.

"What?" Childs asked.

Both of the murdered men were members of the board of directors of Damon Hunter's company."

"But why would the clone be killing them?" Rachel asked.

"You tell me? Is there anything else I should know, Rachel?" Rick asked.

I am refreshed and hunger isn't a pressing necessity. The urge to kill is most compelling. I see the face of the man I will kill in my mind. I know where to find him and must go. I climb out the basement window as it was getting close to sunset. I must hurry if I'm to catch him where I know he will be.

I walk into the parking garage, see his car, and go to it. Naturally it's locked. I will wait for him to come to me, so I wait in the shadows. I hear the elevator stop, the door opens, and he comes out. He comes to his car, unlocks it, and opens the door. I move up behind him as he tosses his briefcase onto the passenger seat.
I grab him by the hair and smash his face against the top of the car. Blood spatters across the top of the car. I look around to make sure no one was attracted by the noise. It is time to eat.

Rachel and Rick sat in the lunchroom having coffee.

"Damon Hunter spent a million and a half dollars for the special equipment and research needed to clone him," Rachel said.

"How did someone with your looks get into this sort of work?" Rick asked. Rachel blushed and turned her eyes down. She wasn't used to hearing men say such things. She looked back at the solid built man with dark brown hair and hazel eyes.

"I was fascinated with bioengineering. Damon heard of my experiments in cloning and came to me. He wanted me to make a clone of him, and transplant his brain and spinal cord into the clone body."

"Did he say why?" She shrugged.

"I guess he wanted what he thought was immortality. I never asked. I was just glad to get the money for research."

"What kind of man was he?" Rick asked.

"I have no idea what his private life was like, Rick. But I had the impression he was a vindictive, cruel man," Rachel said, an idea coming to mind. "Maybe that's why his clone is showing such violent behavior." Walter came hurrying into the lunchroom.

"Lieutenant, you're wanted at the Hunter Building. There's been another murder."

"I'm coming with you," Rachel said, getting up from the table. "I feel responsible."

They walked into the brightly lit underground parking garage. A uniformed sergeant came over to them.

"The security guard found the body less than an hour ago," the sergeant said. "He was making his rounds but didn't see anybody." He looked at Rick and shook his head.

"It isn't a pretty sight, Lieutenant."

"How was he killed?" Rick asked. The sergeant grimaced and glanced at Rachel.

"You better see that for yourself," the sergeant said, turned, and walked toward the car. As Rick and Rachel followed him, he stopped and turned back to Rick with a look that was easy to read. Rick turned to Rachel.

"You better wait here, Rachel," Rick said. She shook her head.

"If I'm to be of any help, I have to see what happened to understand how the clone is thinking."

"Don't say you haven't been warned, Miss," the sergeant said.

They followed the sergeant to a gray Mercedes. The door on the driver's side stood open. The windshield, dash, and seat were stained with blood. The sight of so much blood made Rachel's stomach become unsettled. The body lay on a gurney in a bodybag. Rick went over to it and looked at the ME.

"Open it," Rick said. The ME unzipped the bodybag and pulled it open. Rachel choked, turned away, and vomited. Rick was having a hard time not doing the same.
The man's face was caved in, his throat had been ripped open like an animal had attacked him. Rick nodded and the ME closed the bodybag.

"What kind of animal attacked him?" Rick asked.

"A human animal, Lieutenant. There are human teeth marks on his throat." Rick looked at the ME with an incredulous look.

"How could a man do that?" That asked, trying to grasp a primitive way of death.

"Whoever did this was determined to kill. I might add, extremely vicious," the ME replied.

Rachel was quiet as they drove back to the lab.
There's been three murders," Rick said. "Each more savage than the last. I want you to tell me everything about this clone, Rachel." She glanced at him with a lost look.

"You know as much as I do, Rick. There must have been some kind of genetic memory passed to him. That's the only thing I can think of. The clone has no memory he can recall. It's like he's reverted to a primeval state." She was thinking, trying to understand it herself.

"You mean he's become a predatory animal?" She nodded.

"In simplistic terms, yes. But he's selective about his victims. He does have the capacity to learn while still being cunning," Rachel replied. "I would get the other members of Damon's board police protection. He's killing them for a reason, otherwise the killings would be random."

"I'll pass your recommendation to the captain. But I want you in solid with this case. You know more about this clone than anyone." Rachel turned her face to him with a determined look.

"I'll cooperate in any way I can, Rick."

I feel quite satisfied with myself, although I'm not sure why. I see the face of a woman in my mind and know she presents a danger to me. I don't understand how such a lovely woman could be a danger. I see her in a white lab smock, but can't make any link between her and a peril for myself. She will have to wait. I know whom I'm to kill next. I can see his face and know where to find him.

I climb out the basement window and make my way through dark alleys. I must be sure to avoid being seen by anybody. I come to the edge of the park and look over at his house. There are armed men at the gate. They must have thought he would be next and are there to protect him. It doesn't matter since there are only two of them. I hurry to the far end of the park, crouch down, and dash across the street. I stop behind some bushes and look back at the gate. I haven't been seen.

I climb the fence and drop into the yard, and head for the back of the house. Only one room showing light. That's where he must be. I glance quickly through the window and see him sitting at a desk.

I go to the next window and push on it. It's locked! I go back past the lighted window to the next window and push on it.

It rises quietly as I push on it. I climb through into the dark room. I open the door and peer out. The house is quiet. I go to the door that opens into the room where he is. I open the door quietly and step into the room. He doesn't suspect a thing. I suddenly have an overpowering compulsion to kill this man in particular. He turned suddenly, saw me, and his eyes widened in fear.

"My God! It's you. But you're dead." He cringed back in his chair as I walk over to him. Fear has kept him quiet. I eagerly proceed about my business.

Rick pulled to a stop behind a squad car parked in front of a two-story house. He saw Captain Abbot standing by the porch. Rachel and Rick went over to him.

"Christ, Rick! The man had his head chewed off and set on his desk," Abbot said.

"Uh," Rachel got out, barely able to control her stomach.

"Captain Abbot, this is Dr. Rachel Estes." Abbot gave her a hard look.

"So your creation has gone amok," Abbot said. Rachel shook her head.

"It's not my creation. It's Damon Hunter without a modern mind," she said, defensively.

"Would you like to go in for a look, Doctor?" Abbot asked.

"Not after what I saw in the parking garage." Abbot looked at Rick.

"This madman didn't let the police presence deter him," Abbot said. "What do you recommend, Rick?"

Put officers at their front porches and have an officer patrolling the grounds." Abbot looked back at Rachel.

"Where the hell can this clone be hiding, Doctor?"

"I have no idea," Rachel replied. "I don't understand how he can know where these men live, he has no memory."

Back in Rachel's office, she, Childs, and Rick were trying to outguess the clone.

"What can we presume to know about the clone, Rachel?" Walter asked. Rachel was lost in thought for a moment, then looked back at Rick.

"He's a very selective predator. He's been using his natural weapons, hands and teeth."

"Sooner or later he's going to pick up something and get the idea of a weapon," Childs said.

"You mean like a caveman picking up a rock?" Rick asked. Childs shook his head.

"No. Weapons, such as rocks and sticks, go back much further then the idea of the caveman, Lieutenant," Childs replied. "We're dealing with a very primitive mind in the clone."

"It has a mind empty of knowledge," Rachel said. "One that's functioning on instinct alone." Rick frowned.

"Then how is his instinct able to determine where his victims live?" Rick asked.

"A good question," Childs agreed. "But he is learning."

"If you say so," Rick said. "But for being a dumbass, he sure knows how to get to where he does his killing."

"What his motives are is unknown," Rachel said. "We don't know why he selected these particular victims. I know how this is going to sound, but I believe he's being controlled by something." She was trying to explain something she didn't understand.

"Why do you think he's killing Hunter's board of directors, Rachel?" Rick asked. She shrugged.

"I can only guess, but would say he has a deep hatred of those men, like Damon had. I'm at a loss to explain as to how it could have been passed to the clone."

"Isn't there someway we can set a trap for him?"

"I doubt it, Lieutenant," Childs answered. "We must take into account the mental level at which his mind is functioning."

"On such a primitive level, his instincts are greatly enhanced," Rachel added.

"If a trap were set, his instinct would alert him to danger," Childs said.

Give those men all the protection you can, Rick," Rachel warned. "Until he makes a mistake, or we can learn where he's hiding, their lives are in danger."

The face of the man I'm to kill flashes in my mind, and so does the girl in the lab smock. I feel uneasy with the thought of killing her, but I still sense she's a danger to me. I must kill the man first. I want him dead much more than the girl.

I don't know why, but I feel a greater urgency about killing him. I climb out the basement window and move down the deserted street.

It takes awhile for me to walk to his home. I see two armed men in a car by the porch and another coming in sight from the side of the house. He's stopped and talking to the others. He then proceeded around the other side of the house. I must be vigilant. I feel a strong sense of danger here.

I move down the street away from the house, keeping in shadow. When I know the two men can't see me, I cross the street and slip into the yard of the adjacent house and around to the back. I climb a wooden fence and drop into the back yard of my prey. I move from tree to shrub, getting closer to the house. I'm just about to look in the window when I hear someone coming. I crouch behind a shrub at the side of the house. The armed man walks past me. I slip up behind him and smash my fist against the back of his neck. He crumples quietly to the ground. I must move swiftly.

I look through the window at an empty room, then move to the next window. This room, too, is empty. I move to the back of the house and hear the back door open. I cautiously peek around the house. He's standing smoking a pipe. I slip closer to him, then grab his legs. He falls to the ground with a grunt. I'm on top of him when my hand finds a wooden handle; I lift it above my head.

Rick displayed his badge on his jacket pocket as he and Rachel went toward the rear of the house. An ambulance sat in the drive treating the unconscious officer. Abbot came up to them.

"You don't want to look," Abbot said. "The clone used a trowel on him and it's not a pretty sight. He must have been in a hurry tonight."

"Why do you say that, Captain?" Rachel asked. Abbot turned a grim look to her.

"He didn't take time for a snack. Goddamnit! We have to find a way to stop this madman."

"What can we do, Captain?" Rick asked.

"We have to trap him or kill the bastard."

"You can't kill him!" Rachel exclaimed. "We have to study him." Abbot glowered at her.

"Then you better come up with a way to trap the murdering son of a bitch or he's dead," Abbot said, in a hard tone, shaking a finger at Rachel. He turned and stomped off toward the front of the house.

Back in the office, they had a city map laid out on the desk. Red dots marked the location of each murder. Rachel used a ruler and made lines from each to see where they intersected.

"Nothing," Rachel said. "As you can see, they meet right in the center of the city. It would be impossible for him not to be seen there."

"I'm still going to ask Captain Abbot to have it checked out," Rick said. "Shit, Rachel! We've got to think one step ahead of the clone, if you want him taken alive."

"Let's start by thinking like a predatory animal," Childs said.

"What do you mean?" Rick asked.

"He's got to have a safe lair he can go to without being seen," Childs replied.

"How does he get past the police without being seen?" Rachel asked.

"One officer encountered him, Rachel," Rick said. "He's now paralyzed with a crushed spine."

"What area of the city could he hide in, Lieutenant?" Childs asked.

"Unused factory buildings, boarded up tenements, empty houses," Rick replied. "Hell, Doctor, there are numerous places he could hide."

"What about the only survivor from Hunter's board?" Rachel asked.

"He's surrounded by police," Rick replied. "The clone won't stand a chance at getting at him."

"He's done a damn good job of avoiding the police so far," Childs said.

"Walter, do you think he might start killing randomly?" Rachel asked.

"No," Childs replied, firmly. "It's not his pattern. I believe he feels endangered by the men he's killed."

"Well if he can't get at the last man, won't he just stay in hiding?" Rachel asked.

"That's a bad thought," Rick said. "But he's got to eat." Childs' eyes widened.

"What if he should feel Rachel is a danger to him?" Childs asked.

"Why would he think me a threat, Walter?"

"He might see you as his captor. He may think you're the only one who may be able to find out where he is, and lead the police to him."

I am going for the last man I have to kill. I move through the shadows and quickly get to his home.
I see armed men on the grounds, but I must find a way in. I can't go away! I study the situation, look over the grounds, but nothing comes to mind. I have no chance with those men around. I notice a tall tree and that one of its branches is close to an attic window. But can I get to it without being seen? I take my time and look the situation over very carefully.

In the next yard is a tree almost as tall. If I can get to it, I can up and jump into the one by the house, and get in through the window. I make my way cautiously to the tree. I climb until I can get out on a branch. I leap for the other tree. Success! I'm now on the path to the last of my prey.

"Rachel, Dr. Childs," Rick said, seating himself in the office. "I think I may have found part of the answer. I talked with a VP at Hunter's company. It seems the victims were the board of directors that were going to vote Hunter out as chairman. They knew he was ill, and they wanted him to have some time for himself."

"That wouldn't explain why the clone would feel endangered by them, Lieutenant," Childs said. Rachel got an odd look.

"I think the clone doesn't understand why it kills, Rick," Rachel said. "It's functioning like a computer program is controlling it."

I move slowly along the branch toward the window. The room is dark. I push up on the window and find it's locked. But I must get in somehow. I've got to kill the man inside.
I look down and decided it was far enough from the ground so its shattering might not be heard. I tense for a leap and launch myself toward the window. I cover my face just before I smash through the window. I lay on the floor listening. Silence. I am now in the attic of the home of my prey.

"The shoot on sight order won't be rescinded, Rachel," Rick said, putting the phone down. "The mayor and police commissioner issued it jointly."

"But we need him alive, Rick. I've got to discover how those memories were transferred from Damon Hunter to the clone." Rachel was desperate.

"Unless we come up with a way to capture him, Rachel, no one is going to listen." She gave him an annoyed, stubborn look.

"Then I can only hope Walter is right."

"What are you talking about, Rachel?"

"That the clone will come after me." This brought a look of irritation to Rick.

"He's evaded the police for over a week," Rick said. "Do you think he would be stupid enough to come back here?"

"No, not here. But he might try at my apartment."

"Rachel —"

"Please, Rick. I've got to try to save him."

I lay quiet for a few minutes. There's no undue excitement coming from inside or outside.
I get up and begin looking for the way out of the attic. It's a door that lowers from the floor into the hall with a telescoping ladder on it. Using it will be risky, but I must kill. I push the door down as quietly as I can. No one comes to see what it is. I climb down the ladder into the dark hallway.

There's no light showing under any of the doors. I feel my way along the wall to the stairs and slip down very quietly. I see a door with light showing under it. No wonder my entrance hadn't been heard. I move to the door, kneel, and look through the keyhole. I can see him and his wife. I have no reason to kill her. He's the one I want. I move down the hall away from the door. I'm going to make noise that will lure him out. I stomp my foot and wait. The door is opening, he's coming into the hall, and right toward me.

"It was only a thought, Rachel." She got her stubborn look back.

"If it's a correct assumption, Walter, it could prove the only chance we have of taking him alive."

"It's no use, Doctor," Rick said. "I've tried to talk her out of chancing anything so foolish."

"It would be very dangerous to try getting him to come after you," Childs said, pleading. Her stubbornness grew harder.

"I feel responsible for what's happened," Rachel said. "I grew the clone here."

"But you aren't responsible for his escape," Rick said, frustrated at her stubbornness.
"All the security systems can't tell us how he escaped or when. Christ! I couldn't get out of this building without being seen."
"Then how did he?" Rachel asked.
"That's a question I've been trying to answer since I was assigned to this case. You say he's got a primitive mind. Well he was modern enough to evade all of your security," Rick argued.

I let the body collapse slowly to the floor. I make my way down to the first floor and hide behind a large drape hanging at the window near the door and wait.
"Ed?" I hear his wife call out, then scream. The front door bursts open and the armed men come in and run up the stairs. When the last one goes up, I slip out the front door and make my escape into the darkness.
He was the last I had to kill, but I don't know how I know that. The face of the girl flashes in my mind. I sense only slight danger from her. Suddenly I know all about her. She would have to wait until tomorrow. I'm tired and need rest.

"Ed Marshall was the last of the men who served on the board when Hunter was alive," Rick said.
"Then we've seen the last of the murders," Abbot said. Rick rubbed his chin.
"There could be one more, Captain." Abbot gave him a sharp look.
"Who?"
"Rachel. Dr. Childs thinks he may try coming after her."
"Then why the hell aren't you with her?" Abbot asked, irritated.
"She feels that if he does come after her, it will be her only chance to get him back alive."
"I know you, Rick. You agree with her. So tell me what you have in mind."

I had needed to eat again, so I killed a derelict from the streets no one will miss. I have watched her apartment for days. Every evening she is dropped off by the same man. He looks familiar, but I don't know who he is. I did recall that her name is Rachel. She's a very lovely woman. How can she possibly pose a danger to me? I don't understand.

I do know that in the time I've watched her I've become strongly attracted to her. I think she helped me once. I'll go to her tomorrow night, after I get some new clothing.

Rachel opened the car door and turned to get out. Rick took hold of her arm and she turned her face to him.

"Rachel, it's been over a week since the last murder, and there hasn't been a trace of him. That makes me uneasy. He could show up at anytime, and I don't want to find you dead."

"Don't worry, Rick. I'll be fine." He pulled her to him and kissed her. She returned it with a passion that surprised him.

Damnit, Rachel! I'm in love with you. I don't want anything to happen to you." She caressed his cheek and looked into his eyes.

"Rick, I…"

"What?"

. I love you too. But my personal life has to be put on hold until this mess is cleared up." She got out of the car, went to the door, and let herself into the apartment complex.

I have made a complete transfer. I'm now whole again. I can go to Rachel and reason with her so I won't have to kill her. It's easy for me to get into the garage which is dimly lit. I go to the stairs and up to the second floor. I look into the hallway and see it's empty. I go to her door and turn the knob. To my surprise it's unlocked. I go in and hear her in another room I sit down and wait for her. Rachel comes into the room, sees me, and screams.

"Hello, Rachel." This surprises her.

"How do you..?" She started with an obvious question.

"How do I know your name? Surely you know I was at Ackridge Biotech Labs."

"I do. But you're a —"

"Clone. I shouldn't have any memories?"

"Yes," she replied, becoming curious. But I was becoming very interested in her.

"You could say I'm still at the lab." Her eyes go wide and her hand to her mouth, as understanding bursts in her mind.

"Damon!" she whispered.

"Correct, Rachel. With my new body in such close proximity to my brain, I was able to get some residual memories transferred into the clone mind. Then, gradually, I was able to transfer my personality."

"But how?"

"I'm not quite certain."

"Tell me something, Damon. Why the murders?"

"Those men were going to force me out of own company. I found out about it, but died before I could do anything."
I still feel the rage at their action.

"But they were thinking of you, Damon. They knew you were ill and wanted to have the time for yourself."

"It doesn't matter to me what their motives were. Their action against me was what I resented."

"So you had the clone kill them." I held up a hand.

"Enough, Rachel. I want you to know that before I died, I loved you very much. But an old man who is sick and dying has no right to tell a beautiful young woman that."

"I must say I'm flattered, Damon."

"Now I want to talk about us."

"What about us?" Rachel was suddenly feeling sick.

"Now that I have this strong new body, I can tell you that I still love you." She stood silent, not knowing how to respond to my words. With a conscious effort, Rachel got a grip on herself.

"What happened at the lab that caused the clone to escape?" she asked, buying time to get her thoughts in order.

"When I began to sense I was becoming aware in this body, I knew I had to get away from the lab. As you know, I had some unfinished business. I couldn't afford to have you testing the clone body."

"I see," Rachel said, understanding what he meant.

"I led the clone through the security systems. It was simple for me since I knew how they all functioned. It had been my company that had installed them." There was a knock on the door. I tensed, ready for whatever might come.

"Be very careful, Rachel," I warned. She opened the door and I saw it was the man who had been bringing her home. He came in, uninvited. He looked at me without showing any emotion. Rachel came and stood between us.

"Rick, I would like you to meet Damon Hunter." He quickly looked at her, surprise on his face.

"Damon, this is Lieutenant Rick Archer of the police." I had to nod.

"So that's where I've seen you before. You were at the scenes where some of my old friends met with violent ends."

"How?" he asked, looking at Rachel. She shook her head.

"This isn't possible," he said, looking at me.

"I'm not sure of the how myself, Lieutenant. But it certainly is real. I guess when you die with a burning hatred, you have a powerful motivating force to guide you."

"Then you committed those murders."

"I recall them only in flashes. I just guided the clone to them. It had no idea why it had such strong compulsions to kill. It didn't understand. I just channeled my hatred and it reacted as I wanted it to."

"When did you take full possession of the clone body?" Rachel asked.

"Only hours ago. It happened quite suddenly, my dear. I just became aware that I was in this body."

"That's amazing," she said.

"After all, this body is me." I saw him start to reach for his gun. I lept to my feet and we grappled, struggling. We twist around and fell over the coffee table. I'm much stronger and was quickly on top of him. I clamp my hands around his throat. This was a man who wanted to take away my freedom and my Rachel. I have no recourse but to kill him. I feel a sudden sting in my shoulder and look up at Rachel as she empties a hypo into me. I begin to feel weak and getting light headed. Now comes blackness.

Rachel, Childs, and Rick sat in front of Abbot's desk.

"What are they going to do with him, Captain?" Rachel asked.

"That's a good question, Doctor. From what he told you and Rick it's clear that the mind that now inhabits the clone, forced it into committing the murders."

"What does the DA's office say?" Rick asked.

"Plead him insane," Abbot replied. "It would be an open and shut case due to the mutilation of the victims."

"What jury would believe such a story?" Childs asked. Abbot shook his head.

"I don't know," Abbot said. "After he's put safely away, will we be able to talk with him, and do some studies on him?" Rachel asked. "After all, this is something unique, to say the least."

"I don't know why not," Abbot said. "As long as he's in secure restraints." The phone on the desk rang and abbot picked it up.

"Abbot." He listened then hunched forward.

"When?" Abbot slowly put the phone down. He turned a grim look on them.

"Hunter's escaped. He overpowered six guards," Abbot said, slamming his hand on the desk." How the hell can he have that kind of strength?"

"I wish I knew," Rachel said, clearly frightened. "That was one of the things we were hoping to find out. The sedative in the hypo was triple the normal dosage."

"And that knocked him for only an hour and a half," Rick said.

"Rachel can't go back to her apartment, Captain. She's certain to be his target now," Childs said.

"You're right, Doctor. But where can she go and be safe from this maniac?"

"She can stay at my apartment," Rick said. "Hunter doesn't know where I live." Abbot turned his eyes to Rachel.

"Are you willing to stay with Rick, Dr. Estes?" Abbot asked. Rachel hesitated.

"For Christ sakes, Rachel," Childs said, emphatically. "You don't have a choice." She nodded.

"All right, I'll stay with Rick."

Those puny shitheads! Thinking they could hold me. That synthetic steroid solution I had Rachel add to the amniotic fluid has really paid off. I must make plans for Rachel now that she's betrayed me. I'll just have to kill her. I'm going to have to be careful and move only at night. That will make it much more difficult for them to spot me. But tonight, I must eat.

Rachel was pacing and Rick sat on the sofa watching her.

"Will you sit down and quit worrying, Rachel?"

"I'm not worried, Rick. I feel safe here with you. I'm trying to understand how that clone could have developed superhuman strength." Rick stood and embraced her.

"It's hard to believe that such a beautiful woman can also be a first class scientist."

"My parents were understanding people. When they learned just how much I wanted into bioengineering, they spared no expense for my education."

"But you had to be very intelligent to know early on what you wanted." He saw the sudden expression of recall flash over her face.

"That's got to be it. Early on!"

"What is it, Rachel?"

"You must take me to the lab, Rick. I just remembered something that cloud could prove very important."

"Going out can be dangerous."

"I know. But if I can discover what the cause is, then I may be able to develop something to neutralize his strength."

It's dark enough to go hunting. I'm hungry and want decent food. I walk through foul smelling alleys, stepping close to the street to look for prey. Finally I see her, and she looks like Rachel. If it is, then she's bait for a trap. But I can see no one else on the street. I hurry down the alley and get ahead of her so I can get a good look at her. A block ahead, I look out as she walks under a streetlight. It's not Rachel. But the resemblance is amazing. She is coming toward me. I step into the dark of the alley mouth and wait. When she passes, I grab her from behind and she screams and struggles furiously. She breaks free and starts to run. I grab her head and give it a vicious twist. There's a loud crack and she slumps in my arms. But I won't be so merciful with lovely Rachel.

Childs and Rachel worked into the night, analyzing the amniotic fluid the clone was grown in. Rachel saw something through in the microscope.

"Walter, look at this." He looked into the microscope for a minute.

"I've never seen anything like it," Childs said, lifting his eyes from the microscope and looking at Rachel.

"I don't know what it is either, Walter. But Damon Hunter insisted I put in some liquid. Now we've got to see if we can analyze it," Rachel said.

The phone rang and Rick looked at the clock as he picked it up.

"Archer."

"Captain Abbot wants to speak with you, Lieutenant. Just press line two," the operator said. Rick pressed the connection.

"Yes, Captain?"

"I have some grim news, Rick. A young woman was found dead along a railroad embankment. Her breasts had been devoured." Rick frowned and shook his head.

"Christ! He's still eating flesh."

"Rick, the woman had a striking resemblance to Dr. Estes. The letter R was painted on her forehead in blood."

"We've got to get the son of a bitch, Captain."

"We're doing everything we can. But he just vanishes."

"I'll tell Rachel, and check with you later, Captain." Rick lowered the phone and stood.

He went to the lab, and Rachel knew from his expression he didn't have good news. He told her and Childs what he had been told.

"No!" Rachel exclaimed, her hand going to her head. She swayed on the lab stool. Childs grabbed her before she could fall.

"Do either of you have better news? You've been working all night."

"We've been able to isolate a strange compound," Childs said. "But so far, unable to identify it." Rick put his hands on Rachel's arms.

"I'll buy you a cup of coffee," Rick said, helping her off the stool.

I must figure out a way to get to Rachel. I know that damned detective wouldn't let her go back to her apartment.
It's clear he's in love with her. She could be at the lab, but that would be too risky. But if she's staying at the detective's place, maybe I can get her there. I must find out where he lives. Then, my dear, lovely Rachel, I have a little score to settle with you.

"Look at this, Rachel," Childs said, excited. She stepped beside him and put her hand on his shoulder.

"Look, and tell me what the structure resembles," Childs said. Rachel looked into the eyepiece, lifted her head, and looked at Childs.

"It resembles a steroid," she said. "But I've never seen anything like it." Childs nodded.

"It's artificial, Rachel. A synthetic steroid."

"That means the police will only be able to stop him by…"

"Killing him," Childs finished her sentence. "And that may not be easy, Rachel. You better tell the lieutenant."

"That's right, Captain," Rick said. "I don't fully understand all that Rachel told me, but it's going to take a lot of shooting to stop the crazy bastard, that much was clear." Rachel sat at the desk relieved, but exhausted. Rick hung the phone up and looked at her.

"You and Dr. Childs have done excellent work. You've put in long hours. Now we can go back to my apartment and you can get some sleep." Rachel stood and took off her smock.

At the apartment, Rachel was ready for sleep, but Rick wanted her to feel safe.

"I'm putting this revolver under the pillow, Rachel. If I'm called out, you'll feel better knowing it's there." It didn't matter to her. She collapsed on the bed asleep. Rick brushed the hair from her forehead, went in and made himself comfortable on the sofa. All he could do now was wait.

Around seven, the phone awoke Rick.

"Archer."

"Rick, we just got an anonymous tip about where Hunter's hiding. I want you in here," Abbot said.

"On my way, Captain." He hung up the phone and pulled his jacket on, looked in on Rachel and found her sleeping. He went out and made sure the door was locked behind him.

I watch him come out, get in his car, and drive away. My little trick has worked, and now Rachel is mine. I find the front electronically locked. Someone would have to press a buzzer for me to open the door. I go around to the back of the place and see a basement window. I knell and look in. It was dark, but I can see it's a laundry room. I use my elbow to smash a pane of glass, pick out the splinters, and unlock the window. I climb in on a washer and move to the stairs. Not a sound to be heard. No one heard the glass breaking. I go upstairs to the apartment I know is the detectives. I use my strength to force the door open, step in, and push it shut. The lights were on and I look around for Rachel. I find her sleeping in his bed and that enrages me.

"Rachel. Beautiful Rachel," I say. The sound of my voice startles her awake. She cringes against the headboard.

"What do you want, Damon?" It's clear she's close to panic.

"To repay you for your betrayal."

"I only done what I had to, Damon."

"Nobody crosses Damon Hunter. Besides, I won't let the detective have you. You belong to me." She recalled the gun under the pillow. She grabbed it, pulled it out, and aimed it at him.

"Now, now, Rachel. You shouldn't play with things that can hurt you." I moved too fast for her, and knocked the gun from her hands. It hit the floor with a loud thud.

"I'm the one thing you played with that can hurt you. I don't know whether I want to take you with me to keep as a pet, or…"

"Damon, I was only trying to save you. To get you back to the lab," she said, desperate.

"Or kill you, you lying slut."

"Your killing is over, Hunter," Rick said, from the bedroom door. He stood with his automatic aimed at Damon's back. Hunter turned slowly.

"Freeze, Hunter! I've got help on the way. He continued to turn until he faced Rick.

"On the way isn't the same as being here, Lieutenant. Only you are here. One puny man and no match for my strength. And you want to take Rachel from me. After what we've been through, I won't allow you to do that."

"I'll shoot, you crazy bastard."

"I believe it best if I kill you, Mr. Detective. Shoot if you want, but it won't do much harm to this body. Not with what it has in it." Damon was smiling confidently. He took a step toward Rick, and he pulled the hammer of the automatic back, clicking loudly.

"Don't take another step, Hunter." Hunter's smile turned demonic and he moved closer to Rick. The automatic roared and bucked six times. Hunter dropped, but he wasn't 'dead.

Abbot and four officers came rushing into the bedroom as Rick lowered his weapon.

"Better call an ambulance, Captain," Rick said, without looking at Abbot. "The son of a bitch is still alive." Abbot nodded to one of the officers and he pulled his shoulder mike to his face. Rachel leaped from the bed, raced to Rick, and pressed herself tightly against him, her eyes closed. He put his arms around her.

"Oh, God! I've never been so scared, Rick." They went out of the bedroom with Rick keeping his arm around her shoulders.

26

Hunter got to his feet and came after Rick. He hit his shoulder and Rick went down pulling Rachel with him. He knew what was coming. Two of the officers quickly drew their weapons and fired. There were enough shots fired for them to assume Hunter was dead. Abbot took Rachel's hand and helped her up.

"Cancel that ambulance. Call the ME instead," Abbot said.

"Damn! Six bullets in him and he still had a powerful punch," Rick said, rubbing his shoulder.

"How the hell did you know he would be here, Rick?" Abbot asked. Rick frowned.

"We never released any photos of Hunter," Rick replied. "So the only one who could have made the anonymous call was Hunter. I didn't think of it at the time, but I'm listed in the phone book." Abbot nodded.

"He had to get me out of the apartment so he could get to Rachel. Then it was a toss up between his love for her and his wanting to kill her. I was only a block away when it occurred to me the phone call was a ruse. That's why I couldn't explain when I called you, Captain. I had to get back here."

"Good thinking, Rick," Abbot said, and looked at Rachel. "Well, Doctor, you still want him as a laboratory specimen?"

"Christ no, Captain. He was an inhuman monster."

"Rick, take Dr. Estes to her apartment. You know how confusing these investigations can get."

"Right, Captain."

The ME was examining Hunter's body when he stepped quickly away from it.

"What's wrong?" Abbot asked. The ME looked at him with wide eyes.

"His goddamn hand moved."

INVISIBLE KILLER

Planetary Body 181 was a chaotic, arctic body. Raw wind buffeted the line of people with thick driven snow. The bullet-like flakes stung their faces through the coverings as they struggled toward the science station. They were here to study this frigid world. The shuttle pilot had landed them as close as he dared in the hard driven crosscurrents.

Once inside, they began recuperating from their ordeal. They were still new to each other, having just met at the starbase before coming to PB-181. It took three to push the door shut against the wind shrieking around the structure.

"Everyone make it?" Helena Carter asked. She was a redhead with gray eyes and a slim figure under the bulky clothing she began removing.

"I did," Tony Mendez replied. He was tall, solid, with an olive complexion that matched his jet-black hair and dark brown eyes.

"So did I," Nancy Sands echoed, pushing ruffled brown hair from light blue eyes.

"We all made it," Josh Wade said. "First thing we better do is check the reactor." He was short and stocky with sandy hair and blue eyes. Bill Mooney, Joan Keaton, and Alice Lindsey were too numb to speak.

The place was functional and their private quarters cozy. Two exterior cameras were the only way to see outside without leaving the station.

"What idiot installed this weak radio?" Bill Mooney asked, looking it over, and shivering. "This hasn't got the power to transmit outside this sort of atmosphere."

"What happens if we have an emergency?" Alice asked, pulling off the last of the thermal clothing.

"We'll have to take care of it on our own," Helena replied, confidently. They picked out their rooms and settled in for their six months of learning what they could about this world of wind and ice.

Eight days after arrival, they couldn't find Alice. Helena knew no one had left the station, so Alice had to be inside and they began to search.

Josh was going to the storage area, which was cooler than the rest of the station, when he found Alice dead. The lower temperature made it difficult to estimate how long she had been dead.

They assembled in the rec lounge to discuss what might have happened to Alice.

"What could have killed her?" Joan asked, her brown eyes expressing unease.

"Let's see if we can find out," Helena said. "Bill, get her medical history on the computer." He stepped to the computer and activated it.

"Show medical history of Lindsey, Alice F.," he said. The monitor displayed her medical history, including the last physical she had had at the starbase. Bill looked to Helena and shook his head.

"No problems," Bill said. "She was healthy." A puzzled look came to Helena.

"She had no condition that might account for her death?" she asked, unsure as to what should be done.

"None," Bill replied. Helena could think of only one thing as she turned a serious look on the other people.

"We've got to learn what happened to her," Helena said. Joan looked at Josh.

"Was there anything out of the ordinary where you found her?" Joan asked. Josh puckered his lips and shook his head.

"I didn't take a close look, but didn't see anything," Josh replied. "It looked like she had been walking and just fell. There's not a mark on her."

"We haven't the equipment to perform an autopsy," Helena said, feeling sad as well as uneasy. "Wrap her in a sheet and put her in cold storage."

Three days later, Nancy was found dead in her room. She lay by her bed and had no mark of violence on her. Whatever had killed Alice had struck again, and the people in the station were growing nervous. Helena paced rubbing her hands.

"We got to find the cause of these deaths," Helena said, glancing at each of them, her tone carrying urgency.

"What could it possibly be?" Tony asked. Helena shrugged and frowned.

"I don't know," Helena replied. "It's so baffling."

"Could it be some indigenous life form?" Josh asked. Helena shook her head.

"No. The planet was thoroughly scanned," Helena said. "No indigenous life was found." Josh got an annoyed look.

"It sure as hell wouldn't be the first time they missed something," Josh retorted.

"That's true," Helena agreed. "It's also true we would have an answer, if we could perform autopsies."

A week after Nancy's death, Joan was in the storage area getting equipment for her lab. Abruptly, everything started to spin and she put her hand against the wall for support. Everything went dark and she collapsed to the floor. A few minutes later, Bill found her and carried her to the lounge. She was alive, but unconscious.

It took some minutes to bring her around and Helena sat beside her when she opened her eyes.

"What happened, Joan?" Helena asked in a concerned tone. Joan rubbed her forehead and sat up.

"I don't know. I was getting supplies when I became dizzy, and now I'm here." Helena noted the bruise on her forehead where she had fallen. Helena stood and turned to Bill.

"Did you see anything?" Bill nodded at Joan.

"Only her on the floor," he replied. Helena turned to the people standing around.

"Damnit, people, it's important we find out what's happening," Helena said. "If Bill hadn't found Joan when he did, she might be dead. But from what?"

"How do you find something when you don't know what you're looking for?" Tony asked.

"I think it's an indigenous life form," Josh said, feeling this being the most logical answer.

"That's not an option, Josh," Helena said, firmly. "I'll not accept any alien life hypothesis. It's got to be something natural."

"Then what the hell could it be?" Josh asked, angrily.

"Not an alien life form," Helena said, in a firm tone.

"What if they did miss something in the scan?" Joan asked. "Or something that didn't want to be found?" Helena knew she had to get the situation under control.

"I doubt they could have missed something big enough to present a danger to us," Helena said. "And there's no report of anything like this happening among the construction personnel."

"Whatever it is, it only seems to strike when a person's alone," Tony said, feeling a growing fear. Helena gave him an annoyed look.

"What are you suggesting, Tony?" Helena asked. "That we all sleep in the same room?" Anger flashed on his face.

"No, damnit! I am suggesting that when anyone goes into the storage area, they should go with a partner. That's where Alice died, and Joan was attacked."

"What about Nancy?" Helena asked, trying to sound reasonable. "She wasn't in the storage area when she died."

"The only way to account for her is that whatever it is moves around," Tony argued. "But we know two attacks occurred in the storage area." Helena nodded when she saw the fear on their faces.

"All right," Helena said. "Nobody goes into the storage area alone. Agreed?" They all nodded.

Nothing out of the ordinary occurred over the next two weeks and this tended to restore a feeling of security among the station's inhabitants. Josh was alone at the monitors watching outside lights struggle against the murky glaze of the ever-blowing snow. He recorded data he read from the instruments. Everything began to spin as he became light headed. Josh attempted to keep himself upright in the chair, but slid to the floor unconscious, where they found him dead.

After removing Josh's body, they sat in silence.

"Three deaths in different parts of the station," Helena said, breaking the uneasy silence. "Joan was attacked, but saw nothing. We know two of the victims had to have seen what attacked them, yet neither put up a struggle. So just what are we up against?"

"If something was here, we would have seen it," Joan said, a tremor in her voice. "Or at least, heard it."

"She's right," Bill said. "We've been assuming   whether we admit it or not – that what's happened has been caused by a creature. What if we've been thinking from a wrong premise?" Helena gave him a puzzled look.

"You said nothing like this occurred to any of the construction personnel, Helena," Bill continued. "Did any stay in here?"

"No," she replied. "They stayed in portable prefabs during construction." Tony nodded.

"Then it has to be the station," Tony said. Joan got an incredulous look.

How could this station kill three people and attack me?" Joan asked. Tony got an annoyed frown.

"I don't know," he admitted. "But it's the only thing left."

"I see what you mean, Tony," Helena said. "Let's forget about this planet for awhile. We've got to solve this mystery." Tony looked pleased.

"We can start running tests around the station," Tony said. "We might come up with something."

After a week of multiple testing and retesting, the results produced nothing tangible. Helena was tired and frustrated.

"What are we overlooking?" Helena asked, trying to think of something new. Joan shook her head.

"We've run every test we can," Joan said. "We don't know anymore now than when we started." Bill's mind was running on another track.

"True," Bill said. "But what if we've been doing the wrong tests? We haven't tried searching for an invisible killer."

"What the hell are you talking about?" Tony asked. Bill leaned forward in the chair.

"Nobody has seen a damned thing," Bill replied. "Joan saw nothing. So whatever this thing is, it's invisible."

"That's ridiculous," Tony said, sarcastically. Helena had become interested in Bill's reasoning.

"Go on, Bill," she said.

"A virus or bacteria could have been missed in the scan. But if it were either, we would all be infected. Maybe this is a gas we're dealing with."

"I don't understand," Joan said.

"I do," Helena said. "And it makes sense. A gas that knocks you out quickly, but prolonged breathing it causes death."

"Exactly," Bill said. "It would explain why Joan didn't die. I found her before she had inhaled much of it. And all of the victims were face down on the floor."

"What sort of gas are you talking about?" Tony asked, becoming interested.

"A gas that's odorless, but poisonous over time," Bill replied.

Helena was getting into thermal clothing, preparing to go outside for a sample of ice beneath the station.

"Hand me the core laser, Tony," Helena said. He got it and fought to get the door open far enough for her to slip out.

Stepping outside, the wind-driven snow assailed her unmercifully. She struggled to the side of the station, placed the laser, and lased out a three-foot core of ice from below the station. She fought her way back to the door and slipped inside. She handed the core container to Bill.

"Free the core so we can run some tests," Helena said, removing the thermal clothing.

All were exhausted after fifty-one hours of grueling, fruitless testing filled them with frustration.

"All we've discovered is that the water from this ice has some peculiar chemical properties," Bill said. "Properties that could take a fully equipped lab a month or more to explain."

"I still think we're overlooking something obvious," Helena said, about to fall asleep.

"What's left?" Tony asked, rubbing his tired eyes. "We've done every damn test, and we've come up with nothing."

"If we don't get some sleep," Bill said. "We're not going to able to continue." Bill rubbed his eyes with his fingers.

"Bill's right," Helena said. "Let's get some sleep."

Twelve hours later, they were refreshed, having coffee, and discussing where to begin.

"Bill, will you wake Joan?" Helena asked. "We've got to continue with our investigation. A few minutes later, he came hurrying back into the lounge.

"Joan's dead." Bill was visibly shaken by his discovery as he led Helena and Tony to Joan's room. They found her lying half off her cot, her face against the floor. Tony turned a fearful look on Helena.

"What the hell are we going to do, Helena?" Tony asked, a trace of hysteria in his voice. "We can't stay here. We can't call for help, and we can't survive outside for very long." She glanced at Bill and knew he was thinking the same thing. Tony was beginning to lose it.

"Is there a way to modify the radio, Bill?" Helena asked. He shook his head.

"No. Its components can't withstand the necessary power boost without burning up." A wild look came to Tony.

"So we just wait to die?" Tony asked, his voice rising in hysteria that ended in a crazed laugh. Helena became alarmed.

"Get a grip on yourself, Tony," she said, sharply. He regarded her in silence for a moment then seemed to relax, and turned sullen. Helena looked at Bill.

"The answer is in this station, Bill. But where?" She stood wracking her mind for an answer as she heard the icy fingers of the wind playing around the structure. She turned and left it to the men to take care of Joan's body.

She went to the computer and called up the floor plan of the station. She stared at the monitor realizing the locations of the deaths held no pattern. She called up the data on the station's foundation. Studying it took her a few minutes to reach a conclusion. She looked up as Tony and Bill came in.

"Tony, Bill, I think I know the answer.

It took them half an hour to cut a piece of insulation from under the floor. They cut it in paper-thin slices and began testing it. Two hours produced nothing. Helena's shoulders slumped as she beat down her frustration.

"This has to be the answer," she said. "It's the only thing under the station."

"There's one other thing under the station, Helena," Bill said. New testing began using the water from the ice she had retrieved.

"We'll know in a few minutes," Bill said, warming a test tube of water. Tony looked skeptical.

"We've done this before," Tony said, snidely. Bill ignored him as he lifted the test tube, dropped in a slice of insulation, and stuck it under his nose, which he quickly wrinkled.

"A sour smell," Bill said. "But I'm having no reaction. He picked up another slice of insulation and dropped it in the test tube and reheated it.

"Now I'll try again," Bill said, lifting the test tube to his nose. He took a couple of breaths and dropped to the floor unconscious, the test tube rolling away from him.

Helena and Tony lifted him into a chair, and took a few minutes to revive him. He opened his eyes, rubbed his forehead, and had a glazed look.

"That's powerful stuff," Bill said. "It would make a hell of an anesthesia, and it doesn't have an odor."

Bill blinked his eyes. Helena pressed a finger against her lips as she worked out the solution to their problem.

"The ice under the station must give off vapor wherever there's a warm spot," she said. "That would explain why it seems to move around the station." But Tony had passed the breaking point.

"So we've solved the problem!" he exclaimed, loudly and derisively. "But it doesn't do a damned thing to help us. We're stuck here for another four months." Helena folded her arms and regarded him with a hard look.

"I know," she said, calmly. "But at least, we know what we're up against." Bill regarded her with an uncertain expression.

"We have no way of knowing where or when a warm spot will produce the gas," Bill said. "The temperature in here is constant." He suddenly looked down at his feet with wide eyes.

"Except where we are. Our body temperature is higher than the station's temperature."

"Then explain Alice's death," Tony demanded. "It's much cooler in the storage area."

"Her body heat produced more of the gas," Helena replied. "The gas kept forming under her after she fell." Bill got an urgent look.

"We've got to devise some means of staying alive until the ship returns," Bill said. Helena nodded.

"We know the gas accumulates at floor level," she said, considering an idea. "But it's the sudden updrafts that knock you out, presenting the real danger. The updrafts are going to be the problem."

"If we can devise a way to detect the gas, we should be able to avoid updrafts," Bill said.

"How can you possibly do that?" Tony asked.

The shuttle bucked in the frigid gale making it difficult for the pilot to land. Once down, he turned on the exterior lights and strained to see through the turgid white atmosphere. He pressed the communication activator.

"No one's here at the rendezvous, Captain," the pilot reported.

"Go to the station and see why they're late," the captain replied. "We were in contact with them only hours ago. And keep an open channel to the ship.'

"Yes, sir." The pilot got into the cumbersome clothing and left the shuttle. The wind almost bowled him over as he stepped away from the shuttle.

The raging wind smashed snow against his face mask stinging his bare skin. He had to force his body forward with each step. After a tiring struggle, he made it to the station.

He fought the door shut and bared his hands and face as he looked around, noting the place was silent except for the wind.

"Hello." Getting no reply, he began moving through the station looking in the empty rooms. He took his communicator from his pocket feeling spooked by the empty station.

"The place seems to be deserted, Captain. I'm continuing to search." Each room he looked in was as empty as the last, then in one of the labs, he found a man and woman unconscious. He checked their pulses and both were alive. He quickly lifted his communicator.

"Captain, I've found two people unconscious. I think they may need medical help."

"I'll send a med team down. Do what you can for them until they arrive." He got them both in chairs and worked with Helena until she began regaining consciousness.

"What's your name?" the pilot asked. She was still groggy and not certain this wasn't a hallucination. The pilot took hold of her arms and she knew he was real.

"There's a medical team on the way. You're both going to be all right." He turned his attention to bill, but it took longer to bring him around. Bill was just becoming conscious when the medical team arrived.

Helena and Bill lay in the sickbay relieved to be off PB-181. The captain stood between the beds with a look of respect.

"That's a hell of a story. How did you manage to stay alive?"

"If the pilot hadn't found us when he did, we would be dead," Bill replied.

"We were both hit by the same updraft," Helena said. "There was no one around to help us."

"It was Helena's genius that kept us alive," Bill admitted. "She modified an atmospheric analyzer to detect the gas so we could move before it reached a dangerous level." Helena had a puzzled look.

"I don't understand why the analyzer didn't detect the updraft that hit us," she said, feeling very lucky.

"Bill was able to do a slight modification to the radio. That was how we were able to contact you. He done it using less power than normal."

"Have you brought the others onboard?" Bill asked. The captain nodded.

"The bodies are on their way up," the captain replied. "What happened to the other man?
I was informed before leaving the starbase there were seven of you."
Bill and Helena exchanged sad looks.

"Tony went mad," Bill said. "He couldn't take the stress the gas threat imposed on us. He developed a paranoid fear of it."

"We tried to restrain him," Helena said. "He knocked Bill out, and shoved me against something that stunned me. By the time I got back on my feet, the door was standing open and Tony was gone." Bill nodded.

"At least he didn't die from the gas," Bill said. The captain slowly shook his head.

"The conditions on the surface make it impossible to search for his body," the captain said. "The wind would have covered him with snow in a short time."

"What do we do now?" Helena asked.

"Rest," the captain said. "You damned well deserve it after staying alive under those conditions."

"What about the planet study?" Bill asked. The captain got a slight smile.

"There's another team on the way. The powers that be want this planet studied, but damned if I can see why."

"They can't send more people down there to die," Helena said, concerned. The captain patted her hand.

"I've taken care of that," the captain said. "I've got a team down there covering the insulator with plastic."

"How can you be sure it won't leak through?" she asked.

"It's a special molecular plastic, Dr. Carter. It's sprayed on as a liquid. Once it sets, it forms a solid layer." Bill looked worried.

"One layer might not be enough," he said. The captain nodded.

"I thought about that. Three layers should be more than enough to contain your invisible killer."

PINE RIDGE ROAD

Neil Jamison sorted through the manila folders strewn over his desk. He put some in his briefcase and laid others aside. Linda Alsen, his assistant, came in with three folders.

"You'll need these for your presentation," she said, handing them to him. "These cover the specialized research you've done on angina pectoris." She was attractive with dark auburn hair and hazel eyes set on an oval face with sharply defined lips. She wore a smock over a navy blue dress that outlined her slim figure and showed off her well-toned legs. She was aware Neil didn't see a woman when he looked at her, only a highly qualified assistant.

"Thanks," he said, taking the folders and putting them in the briefcase. As he pulled the case closed, she felt deflated at his response. Yet she felt lucky to be going with him. She regarded a man with dark brown hair, gray eyes, who was slim, as befitted a man who spent most of his time in a lab and worked out in a gym. He rubbed his hands together, as he looked around the office his eyes coming to rest on her.

"Are we ready to go, Linda?" She nodded, keeping a neutral expression.

"All ready," she replied, slipping off the smock and hanging it next to her coat. He held her coat as she slipped her arms in the sleeves. They turned to the door and he held it open allowing her to step through as he usually did.

They went out of the complex to the parking lot and got in a light green Ford Taurus. As they pulled out of the parking lot, the first drops of rain spattered on the windshield. By the time they got on the interstate, the rain was drenching the area. The bright dazzle of oncoming headlights turned each drop into a multibeamed star.

"How far to the turnoff?" Linda asked. He glanced at her.

"About an hour. We should make it to Providence tomorrow morning." As they lapsed into silence, Linda wished she could get him to say more, but knew his mind was on his presentation. Neil's life was his work and there didn't seem room in it for her except as his assistant. She was satisfied to have some time alone with him, although she knew it would be a lonely time. They turned from the streaming flow of headlights onto a dark backroad that took them down a steep hill into darkness.

Nancy Vogel was packing to go with her husband to New York. She had short cut light brown hair, and soft blue eyes. She had retained her shapely figure after deciding she wanted no children by Ross. He was too self-centered, caring only about making money and had no interest in children. She felt he only wanted her around as a sexy trophy to take to parties and show off to others, who thought as he did.

"Are you ready yet, Nancy?" he called, impatiently, from the living room of their plush Boston apartment.

"I'll be right out." She closed the suitcase, picked it up, and went out of the bedroom that was a cold reminder of just how empty her life had become.

Ross looked at his wife's legs covered with dark hose showing below the miniskirt. He got his usual scowl.

"Aren't you a little old for such a short skirt?" he asked, derisively. She regarded him, considering his words. He was a handsome man with green eyes and jet-black hair. That was the exterior and gave no clue to the ruthless personality that inhabited his mind.

"Other men like what they see when they look, and have no trouble getting an erection." He turned from her angered at her words.

"I must look good to you too. If not, I don't think you would have kept me around as a decoration to show off to your friends." He turned back to her with an angry glare.

"Shut the hell up, Nancy." She got a cynical smile.

"Did I touch a sensitive nerve, dear?" she asked, sarcastically.

"Goddamnit, Nancy, I'm not continuing this conversation. Now let's go."

They sat as far apart as possible on the front seats. The car moved along the interstate through pelting rain. The only sounds were the beat of the windshield wipers and occasional growl of thunder. Ross slowed the car and turned onto the dark backroad. Nancy glanced at him.

"Where are you going?" she asked, surprised at the sudden change in their route.

"This is a shortcut," Ross replied, glancing at her. "It will cut about two hours off our travel time." She got an uneasy look.

"I hope you know where you're going." He turned an angry scowl on her.

"I know exactly where I'm going, Nancy." She regarded him with a hard frown.

"You always have, Ross."

Tara Roland was puzzled at her husband's sudden trip to Rio and kept glancing at him as they packed. He had kept his attache case beside him the whole evening and was packing hurriedly, something he didn't usually do. She pushed her shoulder length blonde hair back and turned brown eyes on him. She had a small nose set above narrow lips. He noticed her glancing at him.

"Come on, Tara, hurry up. We've got to be in New York tomorrow afternoon." She noted his brown eyes held a quiet frenzy and he kept brushing at his sandy crewcut. He was a solid built man, but Tara felt he looked somewhat diminished. He saw her still staring at him, stopped packing, and came to her putting his arms around her.

"Tara, darling, this is our chance for a better life." He pressed her against him and kissed her. She responded by putting her arms around him feeling something was wrong, but didn't ask what it was.

"I love you, Steve," she said, not wanting to pull away from him.

"And I love you," he said, kissing her forehead. "Now finish packing."

They hurried across the sidewalk to the red Honda through pelting rain. Steve started the car and drove through Boston to the interstate. As they sped along, Tara glanced at the speedometer.

"Slow down, Steve. What's the hurry? He glanced at the speedometer.

"Sorry, darling. I didn't realize we were going so fast. The turnoff is just ahead." She turned a puzzled look to him.

"What turnoff?" she asked, unsure of where they were going.

"It's a way to avoid the congested traffic, Tara."

"Are you certain it's safe?" He glanced at her with a slight smile.

"Don't worry, darling. We'll be in New York in the morning."

The trees bowed before the wind and rocked the car like a boat in a gale. The wind hurled the rain against the car pounding it mercilessly. Lightning cut the sky, ripping the fabric of darkness. Thunder followed, becoming the noise of the threads ripping. The two-lane road was devoid of traffic, as it had been since they had turned onto it. They had seen no farms, nor passed any small towns for three hours. All that was visible, along both sides of the road, was an impenetrable pine forest.

The surface of the road stretched ahead, forever outrunning the headlights. Neil was beginning to suspect they might be lost, and knew they needed to find someplace to stop before they ran out of gas. He knew he had taken the correct turn off the interstate, but was beginning to have doubt. He pulled the car off the road and put it in park.

"What is it, Neil?" Linda asked, wondering why he had pulled off the road. He had a sheepish look.

"Hand me the map, Linda, please." He turned on the dome light and lit a cigarette. He put it in the ashtray as he took the map from her. He moved his finger along the map as a violent gust of wind shook the car. He glanced at Linda, who had an uneasy look, then turned his attention back to the map.

"Damnit!"

"What is it, Neil?"

"This road isn't on the map. How the hell did we get on it? I know I made the right turn from the interstate." She got a slight smile.

"Are you saying we're lost?" He glanced at her with an annoyed frown.

"That's putting it mildly. If we were just lost we would be able to stop and ask directions. We haven't even seen a farmhouse."

"What are we going to do?" He shrugged, picked up his cigarette, took a drag and stubbed it out.

"Go on, and hope we find a gas station, diner, someone who can give us directions before we run out of gas. There must be a piece of civilization somewhere out here." He handed her the map, turned off the dome light, and pulled back on the road. A short time later, Linda saw a light off the road.

"That looks promising," she said, pointing. Neil pulled the car to a stop into a drive leading through the pines. In the lightning flashes and through the sheets of rain, they saw a mansion with warm glows in its windows looking like a beacon in the stormy night.

There were mortar stoned pillars on each side of the drive supporting an arch that bore Marsac House in shiny brass letters.

The car shuddered under the force of the wind gusts as it sped along the dark, empty road. Nancy was beginning to wonder if Ross really knew where he was going. They had seen neither structure nor light since leaving the interstate over two hours ago. When lightning lit up the landscape, all they saw were violently whipping pine trees.

"Are you certain this is the shortcut you meant to take?"

"I know where the hell I'm going, Nancy," Ross snapped, glancing at her. "We'll come to an intersection that connects with the interstate south of New York." She turned eyes back to the windshield and said no more.

A bright flash of lightning stabbed into one of the tall pines, sparks flew, and the stump ignited in flame. The top of the tree came crashing down across the road. Nancy screamed as Ross hit the brakes. The car skidded, slewing sideways on the wet blacktop stopping with an impact against the tree.

Nancy slowly lowered her hands from her face and looked at Ross with wide eyes. He looked back at her, his knuckles white from gripping the wheel. He turned up his collar and got out. He went to the tree whose branches were whipping wildly. The wind pushed against him as he went to the right side of the road. In the glow from the headlights, Ross saw there was enough room to get the car past the tree and lip of a ditch that was mud. He protected himself from the assaulting branches as he turned back to the car.

He climbed in, took out his handkerchief, and wiped the rain from his face.

"We can make it past the tree." Nancy looked at him, still not over their near miss. He backed the car away from the tree, swung to the right, and moved slowly, inching the car past the tree. The rear wheel began slipping on the muddy lip of the ditch and began to slide. Ross pressed the accelerator down hard; the car lurched forward, fishtailing. With tires squealing and smoking, it sped quickly down the dark road.

"There's lights," Nancy said, pointing. Ross stopped the car; leaned forward, and looked up at an arch that proclaimed the place was the Marsac House.

Tara was growing uneasy about Steve's decision to take this road. They hadn't seen a house since turning onto it. She glanced at him. His face was just visible in the glow from the dash, and she saw his expression held an intense desperation.

"Are you sure this is the right road?" she asked. He glanced at her as she turned her eyes back to the windshield.

"Look out, Steve!" she screamed. He jerked his eyes back to the road and hit the brakes.

The car came to a jarring stop when it slammed against a tree. He turned his eyes back to Tara, who sat with her eyes closed.

"Damn! That was close," he said, relief in his tone.

He got out and was pelted by wind driven rain stinging his face. He turned up his collar and went to the front of the car. He found a deep dent and the headlight hung out of its socket. He went to the far side and gauged the distance between the tree and the muddy water rushing through a ditch. Steve decided he didn't want to chance ending up in the ditch.

Getting back in the car, he wiped his face with the coat sleeve and looked at Tara. He put his arm around her and she regarded him with an uneasy expression.

"I'm going to push the tree aside," he said.

"Oh, Steve!" she exclaimed, quickly pressing herself against him. "Can't we just go back?" He rubbed her back gently.

"No, Tara, we can't go back." She pulled away from him with a baffled look.

"Why can't we go back?" He took her hands and regarded her solemnly.

"We've come too far. We need to find a gas station soon or we're going to be stuck. I should have thought to fill up before we left the city." He turned away from her, put the car in gear, and slowly pushed the tree out of the lane. He backed the car up, turned the wheel, and sped off. It was then he noticed the lights off the road.

"There's a driveway, Steve." He pulled the car to a stop, leaned over her, and looked up at the arch over the drive. A flash of lightning showed they were at the drive leading to the Marsac House.

"Are we going to ask directions?" Linda asked. Neil glanced at her with a hesitant frown.

"It seems we don't have a choice." He started the car up the drive and heard the tires crunching over gravel. The headlights lit up the lower front of the imposing house. He stopped the car near the front door. It was a stately place with a dark gray, ornate façade that projected an aura of wealth that was attractive and daunting. The glow from the windows appeared most welcome. Neil looked at the front door with a brass knocker the size of his head. He looked at Linda.

"I don't like this place," he said, feeling uneasy. Linda regarded him with a cocked eyebrow.

"We can go on," she said. He decided to do just that and put the car in reverse. The engine sputtered and died. He turned a look of disbelief on Linda.

"We're out of gas!" She got a slight smile.

"If we were teens on a date, I wouldn't buy that line. But seeing where we are, I have to believe you." He turned off the lights and ignition, dropped the keys in his pocket, and turned up his collar and got out into the cold, stinging rain. With Linda beside him, they hurried to the door. Neil made three wraps with the knocker and the door opened. Light spilled past a woman with short black hair and eyes. She had a gently sloping nose above full red lips. Neil was instantly captivated and stood facing the beguiling woman before him. He felt he knew her, but wasn't' certain. Linda looked at him wondering what was wrong. The silence lasted for a moment.

"Yes?" the woman asked, jarring Neil back to reality.

"We ran out of gas –" He got no further.

"You must come in and get warmed from the cold of the night," she said, enticingly. "I'm Vera Marsac." Her name sounded familiar and he was unable to understand his attraction for this woman.

"You can put your coats on the rack. I'll get coffee for the both of you." She moved off down the hall presenting an elegant figure, leaving Linda wondering about Neil's reaction. As soon as Vera's footsteps faded, she turned to Neil.

"What's the matter? I've never seen you act like this before." After seeing his response to Vera, she had a spark of jealousy come to mind. He, too, was unable to understand his reaction. He regarded her with a puzzled look.

"She seemed familiar, but I don't recall ever having met her." They walked from the foyer as they spoke stepping into a room with a large fireplace with a warm fire crackling in it.

It was like stepping into the past. The furnishings were Victorian, and the walls held the trophies of many big game hunts.
Above the fireplace hung the portrait of a nude woman seated on an Eighteenth Century turquoise French couch. Her figure, shapely legs and jutting breasts with dark nipples stood out as almost real. A small light at the bottom of the frame highlighted the painting. Neil stepped closer, glancing at the right hand corner of the portrait.

"This can't be."

"What is it?" Linda asked, stepping beside him. He glanced at her and pointed to the corner of the portrait.

"Is this a painting of the woman who let us in?" Linda stepped back and took a second look at the woman's face.

"I would say yes, although not as recognizable without clothes. Why?" He pointed to the corner of the frame. Linda leaned forward to see and quickly turned her head to Neil.

"London, 1889! It's not possible. The women we seen must be a descendant." Taking a closer look at their surroundings, they found the windows framed with red velveteen drapes, and all the furniture was from the same period as the portrait. They were standing in a replica of a Victorian drawing room. Neil noticed the windows, but as it was dark outside he didn't expect to see much.

The fire's warmth felt comforting as they awaited Vera's return. She came in carrying a silver tray with two cups of steaming coffee, and a matching cream pitcher and sugar bowl.

"This will warm you up," she said, placing the tray on a stand. "Cream or sugar?"

"Black, thank you," Neil replied.

"I'll have cream," Linda said, regarding Vera closely. After a couple of tentative sips, Neil sat his cup down and looked at Vera.

"Do you mind if I smoke?" he asked.

"Not at all," Vera replied. She turned to another stand and took a large glass ashtray from it and handed it to him.

"Here you are, Neil." He froze at her words. His brow furrowed and his eyes widened.

"Do you know me?" Vera nodded at Linda.

"I heard her call you Neil," Vera replied, and got an apologetic smile. "I hope you don't think me rude." Neil shook his head.

"It just surprised me. It seems I'm the one being rude. This is my assistant, Linda Alden. I'm Neil Jameson." Vera nodded to Linda with a slight frown and turned her attention back to him.

"We've been expecting you. Please make yourselves comfortable." This was a shock to both of them, and they exchanged glances.

"What do you mean, we were expected?" Linda asked, uneasy. Vera cocked an eyebrow.

"There are others coming later," Vera said, ignoring the question. "Enjoy your coffee and the fire." She turned and left without another word. Linda turned to Neil with a frown.

"You said she looked familiar. Will you explain what's going on, Neil?" He shook his head.

"Damned if I know. But I'm going to find out when she comes back."

An hour passed without an appearance from Vera. The unexpected bang of the knocker startled Linda and Neil. They saw Vera pass the drawing room to the foyer, the front door opened, and déjà vu. They heard words similar to theirs answered by Vera. They exchanged bewildered looks. Vera showed the couple into the room and hurried off.

The man was of medium height and build with green eyes and black hair. The woman had short brown hair, blue eyes, and a natural beauty to her face. Neil stepped toward them.

"I'm Neil Jameson and this is Linda Alden."

"I'm Ross Vogel and this is my wife, Nancy," he said, shaking Neil's hand. They took a few minutes to get acquainted before Neil asked the question uppermost in his mind.

"Are you expected?"

"Expected?" Ross asked, surprised. "Hell no. We got on that damned road and this is the only place we've seen." Neil and Linda got uneasy looks.

"That's what happened to us," Linda said.

"Vera said we had been expected, and that others would be coming," Neil said. Ross glanced at Nancy and back to Neil.

"What the hell's going on?" Ross asked.

"We've been wondering the same thing," Linda replied. Neil glanced at the portrait and felt drawn to that charismatic face. He pointed to it.

"What do you think of that portrait?" Neil asked. Nancy and Ross looked at it.

"It's a very good likeness of Miss Marsac," Nancy said, with a touch of envy in her tone.

"Take a look in the lower right hand corner," Neil said. They stepped to the painting and quickly looked at each other. They turned back to Linda and Neil.

"This is either a mistake or a joke," Ross said. Nancy stood quiet looking bewildered.

"The woman who showed us in can't be more than twenty-eight," Nancy said.

"Maybe so," Linda said, nodding at the portrait. "But it certainly looks like her."

It wasn't long before the knocker thundered again. Vera went through her routine as if she was reading from a script, and a third couple came into the drawing room. The woman had shoulder length blonde hair, hazel eyes, and a pretty face with a distracted expression. The man had a solid build with a sandy crewcut and anxious brown eyes. After the introductions, Vera returned with coffee for all. After filling each cup, Vera turned a glowing smile on them.

"My brother Seth will join you in a short while," she said, in a pleasant tone. "I know you're curious about Marsac House and my brother will answer any questions you may have." She left before anyone could ask a question. The six people looked at each other wondering what was going on in this strange house in the middle of nowhere. Linda directed Tara and Steve to the portrait. They, too, were bewildered when they saw the year, but none had an answer to the mystery.

Neil was smoking another cigarette and nursing coffee when they heard someone approaching. Vera came in with a tall, slim man with penetrating blue eyes and jet-black hair combed straight back. He held a cigarette in a holder and wore a silk maroon smoking jacket. He appeared to be an elegant Victorian gentleman. Neil quickly stubbed out his cigarette and went to him. Vera stepped in front of him, frustrating Neil.

"Neil Jameson, may I present my brother, Seth Marsac." She stepped aside and the man extended his hand in a gracious manner.

"I'm delighted to meet you, Mr. Jameson," he said, in a cultured voice. Vera proceeded to introduce him to the others, and all were impressed by Seth Marsac. Neil glanced at Vera and turned his attention to Seth.

"Vera told us we were expected," Neil said. "Can you please explain that?" Seth looked at his sister with a tolerant smile.

"I'm afraid you must forgive her," Seth replied, with an apologetic tone. "Vera has a flarc for the dramatic. You see, on nights like this we usually get two or three couples who have underestimated the length of Pine Ridge Road."

"That road isn't on the map!" Neil exclaimed. Seth nodded.

"When they put the interstate through, it intersected with the road," Seth said, spreading his hands. "But for some reason unknown to me, they failed to show it on recently printed maps." That sounded plausible to Neil, and the others accepted his explanation.

"I'm intrigued by that portrait," Neil said, glancing at Vera. Seth got a knowing look and smiled.

"Ah," he said. "Most people are. The resemblance is striking, but that is a portrait of Vivian Mortain. She was one of forbearers from the Victorian age." Linda looked from the portrait to Vera.

"The resemblance is uncanny," Linda said.

"It is most unusual," Seth admitted. "The women of our family have always carried a strong resemblance of their mothers."

"It's incredible!" Ross exclaimed, looking from the portrait to Vera.

"It's late and I know you must all be tired," Seth said, glancing at Vera. "Will you show our guests to their rooms." She nodded and looked at them.

"Please follow me," Vera said, starting for the far side of the foyer. Neil looked around as they went up the wide staircase. And marveled at the replica of a Victorian Manor House. The furniture must be worth a fortune, he thought. Seth the perfect Victorian gentleman, but Vera didn't fit. Their footsteps were muffled in the carpeted hallway.

Neil and Linda were shown into the same room. Neil wasn't aware of this until Vera pulled the door shut leaving them alone. He looked at Linda with an embarrassed look and started for the door.

"It's all right, Neil. We'll make do. He turned back to her feeling awkward.

"Sure you don't mind?" She could see this was uncomfortable for him.

"You seem more self-conscious about sharing this room than I do." He nodded, scratched his head, and wondered what he should do. The bed was a four-poster with a gild, ornate crown, and coral spread and canopy. A small stand with a lamp was beside the bed and a French armchair by the fireplace. Against the wall, on the far side of the room, was an Eighteenth Century French couch that matched the chair.

"You take the bed, Linda. I'll make myself comfortable on the couch." Neil sat down on the couch feeling out of place with Linda. She glanced at him with a disapproving frown.
It was a perfect setup, but he was concerned about keeping his proper distance. Since this place seemed Victorian, Linda felt Neil fit right in, she thought.

Nancy and Ross looked around the room Vera had ushered them into. It was as straight laced as the rest of the place, Nancy thought. It was identical to the room occupied by Neil and Linda, except the bed had an emerald spread to match its canopy.

"I wonder which room Queen Victoria is sleeping in?" Ross wondered, aloud, impressed with the furniture. Nancy gave him a scowl.

"I wouldn't know," she replied. "But this place has more style than those clone hotel rooms." He got a satisfied look.

"You're right, Nancy. But this isn't costing me a dime." She turned a disgusted look to him.

Tara sat on the light blue spread covering the bed and looked around what she considered a priggish room

"I wonder what movie set this furniture is from?" Steve asked, walking around touching the furniture. She looked around with an uneasy look.

"I've got a cold feeling about this place, Steve." He sat on the bed and put his arm around her.

"Nonsense, darling, this is a comfortable room. Let's get some sleep so we can get an early start. We have to be in New York tomorrow afternoon."

The storm continued with unabated fury throughout the night. The wind smashed rain against the gray mansion and howled in fury around its cornices. When dawn came, the rain had reverted to a steady downpour.

As they appeared downstairs, Vera was there to greet them with a bright smile and cheery disposition.

"I hope you slept well," Vera said. Nancy and Ross said they had, as did Steve, but Tara made no comment. Vera led them into the dining room and served them coffee and asked what they would like for breakfast.

Neil and Linda were last to come into the dining room that they found from the sound of voices.
Neil walked to the window and looked out. The rain seemed to be coming down harder than the night before. He was uncomfortable being around Vera.

She caused him to have thoughts he would just as soon not have to deal with. Not only were they distracting, he felt, but something was out of kilter here.

He turned and faced Vera. She looked into his eyes causing him to feel an insatiable passion for her. He thought she was the most beautiful, desirable woman he had ever met.

"Coffee," Vera said, handing him a cup on a saucer. The reaction of Neil didn't pass unnoticed by Linda, and it made her uncomfortable.

"Thank you," Neil said, taking it, and struggling against the attraction he felt. Linda saw the odd expression that came to Neil when Vera looked at him, and came over to them.

"How are we going to leave without gas?" Linda asked, ignoring Vera, who got an irritated look and moved away. Linda had never seen Neil act like this and it made her feel jealous. Neil usually had only one thing on his wind: his work. He glanced at her with a confused look.

"We can't simply rush off," he replied, abruptly finding himself making up an excuse to stay. "The nearest gas station is probably miles from here, and no one wants to walk through the rain." Linda glanced over her shoulder as she rubbed an eyebrow.

"What about the other cars, Neil? Surely we didn't all run out of gas." Neil frowned and nodded.

"I'll ask." He went to the table where the others were having breakfast.

"Excuse me," Neil said. "But could one of you give me a ride to the nearest gas station? I ran out of gas last night." The four quickly turned their eyes to Neil with expressions of disbelief.

"I ran out too," Steve said.

"So did I," echoed Ross. Seth heard them as he came into the dining room.

"I trust you all had a pleasant night," he said, glancing at each of them. Neil turned to him.

"Is there someway we can get to a gas station?" Neil asked, feeling an urge to get away from this house. Seth got a surprised look.

"Why on earth would you need to?" Seth asked. Neil glanced at Ross and Steve and back to Seth.

"We ran out of gas," Neil replied. Seth got a slight smile.

"Your tanks were filled during the night," Seth said. "But it's impossible to go anywhere."

"Why?" Ross asked.

"Two rivers, one north and one south of us, have flooded," Seth replied.

"I don't wish to alarm the ladies, but the road has been cut by floodwater. Of course you're welcome to remain here until the situation is cleared up."

"Do you have a phone?" Steve asked. "I need to make a call to a business associate in New York and let him know I won't be able to make it." Seth tugged on his ear.

"I'm afraid not. This area is too remote for them to consider putting a phone line," Seth replied. The six looked at each other, the women suddenly feeling apprehensive.

"I know your next question," Seth said. "Marsac House has it's own generators. It was from the generator fuel supply that your cars were refueled." Linda, Nancy, and Tara clustered as they listened. None of them cared for being isolated in this place.

"I have a fine library," Seth continued. "It's the only form of entertainment Vera and I have – except welcoming guests on stormy nights."

Back in their room, Linda stood facing Neil with folded arms.

"I don't like it here," she said, with a tremor in her voice. "Why are these people living in such a remote place?" Before he could reply, a loud crash of thunder felt like it shook the room. Neil looked at her, never having paid her any attention only her work. For the first time he saw Linda as a desirable woman compared to Vera. A strong compulsion gripped him. He had to get Linda away from this house.

"I have no idea why they live out here, Linda. But I get the feeling something's not right. It might be the isolation, but it makes me uneasy." Her arms dropped to her sides.

"Nancy and Tara don't like it here either. Counting you, that makes a majority that feel uncomfortable here." He got an annoyed look.

"We can't go anywhere with the road washed out." She gave him a dubious look.

"Are you certain that's the only reason you want to stay, Neil?" He stared at her, uncertain as to what she meant.

"You are aware of the effect Vera has on you, Neil?"

"Who? Oh! The name didn't register for a second." She couldn't believe what he had just said.

"Christ, Neil! Last night she looked familiar to you." Feeling uncomfortable, he averted his eyes.

"I was mistaken." He looked back at her as he thought of a reason to get away from the room.

"I'm going to pay a visit to Seth's library. Want to come along?"

"I'll wait here, Linda replied, confused. This was so unlike Neil.

"We've got to get away from this place, Steve," Tara pleaded. He gave her an irritated look.

"Damnit, Tara, you heard what Seth said. The road's under water." Her mouth fell open as her eyes widened.

"And you just accept his word for it?" Anger washed over his face.

"Well if you think the man's lying, why don't you go down to the car and see if it has a full tank of gas. If it does, then he's not lying about conditions of the road." Hot anger filled her.

"I'll do just that," she said, and quickly walked from the room. He stood staring after her bewildered by her action.

Tara was in the foyer pulling her coat on.

"Going somewhere?" Vera asked, in a cold tone. She startled Tara and sent a shiver through her.

"To get Steve's attaché case," she replied, uneasily. "He has some paperwork to catch up on."

"Here," Vera said, opening a closet. "You'll need this." She handed Tara an umbrella. Tara regarded it in surprise for a second then took it.

"Thanks." As she turned, she could feel Vera's eyes watching her. She opened the door, stepped out, and opened the umbrella.

She hurried to the car, climbed in, took the keys from her pocket and slid them in the ignition. She turned the key and stared in disbelief as the needle on the fuel gauge slid over to full.
She turned it off and removed the key and slipped the key ring back in her pocket. She reached over the seat and took hold of the attaché case.

Going back to the house, Tara felt more frightened than she had. Who could have filled the tank during the night? Surely not Vera! And Seth certainly didn't look cut out for that sort of work.

Nancy paced as Ross sat with an elbow on the chair arm holding his chin on his hand. He was pissed at her insistence on leaving.

"For Christ sakes, Nancy, will you stop that goddamned pacing." She turned to him with an angry glare.

"There's something screwy about this place, Ross." He regarded her without changing expression.

"What?" She got a helpless look and waved her arms.

"I don't know, damnit! It's just the odd feeling this house gives me." He dropped his arm and leaned forward with a cynical look.

"A feeling? Maybe you aren't satisfied staying someplace that doesn't cost me anything." Rage flashed through her and she focused angry eyes on him.

"You son of a bitch! I should have gone through with the divorce instead of letting you talk me out of it so you could keep a few fucking dollars in your pocket." He stood with a reddened face, clutching his hands at his sides.

"I don't want to hear this shit." He stomped across the room, went out, and slammed the door to emphasize his anger.

A few minutes later, a knock came on the door. Nancy opened it and faced Vera.

"May I come in?" Vera asked, keeping her eyes on Nancy.

"Yeah." Vera stepped in and closed the door. Vera's stare made her feel lightheaded as she stepped closer to Nancy.

"Why do you stay with such an uncaring man?" Vera asked, reaching out and gently caressing Nancy's cheek. Her hand went up and she pressed Vera's hand against her face. She felt helpless as Vera pressed her lips to Nancy's. Vera unbuttoned Nancy's blouse, pulled it off, and dropped it. Nancy was powerless to stop Vera as she unhooked her bra and pulled it down her arms dropping it on the blouse. She caressed Nancy's breasts, rolling her nipples to firmness between her fingers. Vera's hand went under Nancy's skirt and began rubbing between her legs.

Lying down on the bed, Nancy felt Vera's hot breath on her neck and was becoming aroused. It had been a long time since she had been in such a situation with Ross and it seemed like a pleasant division. Nancy stiffened as she felt the strong sting on her neck and became engulfed with euphoria.

Ross found Neil browsing through the shelves of books that lined three walls of the room.

"Find anything interesting?" Ross asked. Neil glanced at him with an excited expression.

"This is a fabulous collection," Neil said. "These books are original first editions, each worth a neat sum of money." That quickly got Ross' attention.

"Show me one," Ross said. Neil moved his hand along the books, stopped and pulled one from the shelf and held it up.

This is Charles Dickens' A Christmas Carol," Neil said, impressed. "Just look at its pristine condition. No dry, yellowed, flaking pages. And this binding could be brand new." Ross waved his arm around the room.

"How many of these are first editions?" Neil turned and looked along the shelves with an awed look.

"All of them," Neil replied. "There's a fortune in these books." This got Ross thinking about taking a few of them when he left.

"Ah, gentlemen. I hope you'll enjoy our library during your stay," Seth said, coming into the library. "And get as much delight from these volumes as Vera and I do." Neil shook his head.

"This is an amazing collection, Seth," Neil said, in praise. "There are countless hours of pure classical pleasure here." Seth smiled proudly.

"I'm glad you find them interesting, Neil." Seth suddenly lost his smile and got a serious expression as he recalled why he had sought them out.

"I'm afraid I have unwelcome news."

"What?" Ross asked.

"I heard on the weather monitor that this storm front has stalled over the coast," Seth replied.

"What's that mean?" Ross asked. Neil looked at him with a frown.

"It means the rain is going to continue and the flooding worse," Neil replied.

"Quite true," Seth agreed. "They have no idea how long the rain will persist, but they said the flooding will be more severe." Neil decided to see if he could get an answer to Linda's question.

"I'm curious, Seth," Neil said. "Why do you live in such an isolated area?" Seth got a slight frown.

"We used to have an apartment in New York. We were the Victorian specialists at the Metropolitan Museum.

After our apartment was burglarized for a third time, we decided to move out of the city. A friend of ours knew the gentleman who owns this house and we made an agreement to lease it. We feel much safer here."

Tara came into the room carrying the attaché case and drew a hard look from Steve.

"Why the hell did you bring that in?" She could see he was annoyed at her action.

"Vera saw me," Tara replied, mystified at his attitude. "I told her you had paperwork to catch up on." She started to put it on the bed and hit it against the post. It fell open, spilling bundles of hundred dollar bills onto the floor. Tara's eyes widened as she realized what her husband had done.

He moved quickly to retrieve the bundles and put them back in the case. He closed it and turned to her. She was looking at him as though she was seeing a stranger.

"You weren't going on a business trip," she said, bewildered. "You were skipping out of the country." He regarded her with a hard look.

"That's right, Tara. I gave my all for the firm for nine years, and they were going to downsize – kick my ass out on the street. So I took my chance to retire." He stepped quickly forward and took hold of her arms.

"Tara, I did it for us." His desperation was clear in his tone as he pleaded for her understanding. She looked at him with a steady gaze and shook her head.

"I thought I knew you, Steve. But I've fooling myself, living with a stranger." Her voice expressed hurt and humiliation. He held desperately to her arms.

"You've got to believe me. I did it for us, Tara." She stared at him. For the first time in their marriage, she didn't believe her husband.

Linda walked into the living room looking for a drink after leaving Neil lying on the bed reading. She found Seth there. He glanced at her and smiled.

"From your demeanor, I would say you need a drink."

"You're right, Seth, I do need a drink." He went to a cabinet, opened it, and looked over his shoulder at her.

"Name your poison, Linda."

"Bourbon straight and warm." He poured a drink and handed her one. He gave her a hesitant look.

"Pardon my personal observation, Linda, but I see a desire on your part to have more of a personal relationship with Neil.
But he seems unwilling to give it." She turned from him to the window and saw it was still pouring.
Seth had seen her dilemma clearly, but she hadn't thought it so obvious. She had been in love with Neil for sometime, but he remained dedicated to his work and seemed to have no time for a personal relationship. She looked down at the glass in her hand.

"Right again, Seth. I see how men look at me, but all Neil sees is an efficient assistant."

"You're quite an attractive woman, Linda. I can help you, if you like." She turned back to him.

"How?" Seth opened a drawer below the liquor compartment and took out a small vial filled with lavender liquid. Linda's eyes went from him to the vial. He held it between his thumb and index finger.

"This is a specially blended perfume," Seth said. "Famous, and not so famous, women through the ages have used this unique blend to get the men they wanted. It makes a man want the woman who wears this essence." He regarded her with a serious expression for a moment.

"But I must caution you, Linda, it will work only if Neil has feelings for you. Would you like to find to find out?" Her eyes narrowed.

"What's the catch?" Seth relaxed and smiled.

"No catch, Linda. I don't like seeing two people who care for each other unhappy." He held out the vial to her, as she reached out, and he laid it in her hand.

"Use it sparingly and get close to Neil. But be prepared for passionate lovemaking should it have its desired effect."
He put his glass down and walked from the room. Linda turned back to the window and took a drink, glancing at the vial. Neil was the man she loved the one she wanted.

When Ross returned to the room, he found Nancy lying on the bed nude.

"I've been waiting for you, love," she said, in a sexy voice. He regarded her with a puzzled look.

"What the hell is wrong with you?"

She turned and sat up on the bed.

"I want to make love. It seems the most exciting thing to do in this boring place." Ross only half heard her.
His mind was on how to get his hands on a few of those first editions. He sat down and Nancy got up and walked provocatively to him, knelt down, unzipped his pants and began stroking him with her mouth. Ross thought her behavior odd, knowing this wasn't like the Nancy he knew.

The more she moved the more aroused he became. He began to undress with her help. She took his hand and pulled him toward the bed. She lay back and spread her legs. He entered her and began a heavy thrusting. He kissed her throat, getting soft moans in response. Ross was giving his wife what she had been wanting.

Tara found Linda still nursing her drink, staring out the window. Tara saw the wet, gray day as she looked toward the window.

"I need a drink," Tara said.

"The bar's open," Linda said, pointing to the open liquor cabinet. "Help yourself." Tara poured a stiff drink and took a sip. Linda noticed the lost expression Tara had.

"You look upset." Tara glanced at Linda.

"How can you have been married to someone for ten years and remain blind to what they're really like? Then suddenly find out he's a stranger, someone you never really knew." Linda shook her head.

"I can't say, Tara. I've never been married." Tara turned a hopeless expression to her.

"You're lucky."

"I wouldn't say that. I've worked with Neil for three years and he never paid any attention to a woman – until last night." Tara got a knowing look.

"He finally got amorous?" Linda got an annoyed look.

"Not for me. Vera!" Tara's eyes widened.

"Vera? I guess she is an attractive woman in an odd sort of way." That made Linda's mind up.

"Excuse me, Tara. I've got to talk to Neil about something." She put down her unfinished drink and left.

Linda stopped outside the room and looked at the vial in her hand. She took the cap between her fingers, opened it, and brushed it along both sides of her throat. She hesitated to open the door, wondering what had overcome her. To believe in a love potion was silly, but she wanted to believe. It was time she learned the truth about Neil.

Linda went in and sat down on the bed beside him. After a few minutes, his eyes lifted from the book to her face.

"Something wrong, Neil?"

"You're beautiful," he said, putting his hand against her cheek. His hand went behind her head and pressed it forward until their lips touched. The years of denied emotion erupted in an explosion of passion.

Late that night, as the storm's fury rose once again, Neil went downstairs for a drink. Vera was sitting on the sofa reading; her legs crossed showing a lot of desirability. Neil had a hard time keeping his eyes away from her.

"I was wondering if I might get a drink? He asked, making a lame excuse to look at her. His afternoon with Linda had convinced him he wanted no woman other then her, but doubt crept into his mind as he looked at Vera. She put the book down and came to him, regarded him with a slight smile, then put her hands on his face and pressed her lips on his. She lowered one hand and found a way into his pants and began fondling him. Neil's reaction was immediate.

"Let's go to my room, Neil." He started to say no, thinking of Linda, but Vera looked into his eyes and he was helpless to refuse. He felt an irresistible urge to possess this most desirable woman. She took his hand and led him upstairs.

She took him into the room and closed the door. Vera took off her dress and he saw she wore nothing underneath except a garter belt and dark hose. She undid his pants and they dropped.
She took hold of him as she pressed against him. But something – a blurred image – came through the wall and distracted Neil. A hideous creature with a malformed face and one large yellow eye came toward him.

"You have been chosen to become one of us," it said, in a guttural voice. It was coming for Neil and he couldn't move because Vera was holding him. He felt cold fear explode in him.

Neil jerked into a sitting position, sweating, heart pounding, breaths coming in quick succession. His sudden movement awoke Linda, who lay beside him.

"What is it?" She asked, putting a hand on his shoulder. He couldn't answer because the fear was still real in his mind.

"Neil?" She sat up and put an arm around him. He glanced at her and wiped the sweat from his face.

"A bad dream," he said. "Just a bad dream." He lay back down and kissed Linda. She put her head on his shoulder and put her arm over him. Linda knew they had to find a way to get away from this house.

A blinding flash of lightning followed by a blast of thunder had Tara sitting up in bed She could see someone sitting at the foot and quickly reached over and turned the lamp on. It was Seth.

"What are you doing here?" Tara asked, suddenly frightened.

"You have become disillusioned with your husband, Tara." She glanced at Steve's sleeping form. The talk wasn't disturbing him. She looked back at Seth.

"I don't know what you're talking about," she said.

"Come with me, Tara," Seth said, in a commanding tone.

"No!" Seth's eyes took on a strange yellow glow and Tara couldn't resist. She pushed the covers aside and stood. She had on a short black negligee. Seth stretched out his arm and offered her his hand. Tara put her hand in his and they left the room.

The carpet muffled their passage through the hallway. Seth opened the door and Tara went in. She shivered as his hand slid under her negligee and she was vaguely aware that the room contained only a Grecian couch before the fireplace that produced the only light in the room.

She sat down, and Seth pushed her down until she lay on her back. His hands moved over her breasts in such a way as to make her want him. She moaned softly and closed her eyes as his hand moved lightly up her leg and opened the negligee. His finger suddenly made her feel like she was on fire. She opened her eyes and saw Seth as a tall, bat-winged man standing over her. But her only interest was in his enormous erection. Tara took hold of it and pulled it to her. When he entered her, the pain was unbearable, but was quickly followed by a rapture that gushed through her.

The next morning, Steve found Neil alone in the dinning room with a cup of coffee and cigarette. He approached hesitantly, not certain what to say.

"Neil can you take a look at Tara? I know you're in medical research but she needs a doctor." Neil's brow furrowed as he looked at Steve's worried expression.

"What's the problem?"

"You better see for yourself."

Tara lay semiconscious. When Neil saw her he became alarmed as he examined her. He found she had a fever and was delirious. Steve pulled the cover off his wife. Neil stood, shocked at the blood soaked bed under her. He gave Neil a grim look.

"No wonder she's so pale," Neil said. He was no medical, doctor but surmised Tara had suffered a miscarriage.

"How long has she been pregnant?" Steve got a surprised look.

"Tara's unable to have children," he replied, confused that Neil had drawn such a conclusion. Neil looked at Tara.

"It appears she's had a miscarriage," Neil said. Steve shook his head.

"That's not possible," Steve said. Neil looked from Steve to Tara and shook his head.

"Look, Steve, we don't want to alarm the others, so let's keep this to ourselves. If anyone asks about Tara, tell them she's not feeling well." Steve looked at his wife with a deeply concerned look. Steve nodded.

Neil was more than a little concerned at Tara's loss of blood. If she hadn't been pregnant, he could affix no explanation for it.
He took a drink of the now cold coffee as Ross came in with a worried expression.

"Something wrong?" Neil asked. Ross regarded him for a moment with a hesitant expression.

"It's Nancy," Ross replied. "She's burning with fever." This came as a shock to Neil and he felt it was no coincidence.

"Want me to take a look at her?"

"Would you, Neil? Please.

Neil's examination of Nancy revealed some of the same symptoms Tara was suffering, although she hadn't lost any blood. Neil lifted her eyelid and saw her eyes were rolled up. He looked at Ross.

"Has she had any unusual bleeding?"

"Only on her neck." Neil rolled her head to one side and examined two small circular wounds. He had never seen anything like them. He stood, took a deep breath, and made up his mind.

"Tara seems to be suffering from the same thing," Neil said. "But in her case, she's lost a lot of blood." A helpless expression came to Ross.

"What can we do, Neil?" Neil rubbed his chin, considering their situation.

"Flood or no flood, we've got to try to get these women to a hospital."

The rain was driven savagely against the windows as Neil explained, as best he could, the condition of the women and the urgent necessity for getting them to a hospital.

"You can try, Neil," Seth said. "But with this rain, the flooding has become much worse."

"I've got to try, Seth." He patted Neil's shoulder.

"You're a good man, Neil. You can take any of the cars with the assurance they have full fuel tanks."

Steve hurried through the rain carrying Tara covered with her coat. He climbed in the backseat and took the coat from her face. Although wrapped in a blanket under her coat, Tara was shivering violently and rolled her head from side to side mumbling incoherently. Ross came out with Nancy and climbed in beside Steve and pulled the door shut. Neil looked over the seat at the faces of the women. It seemed to him they were suffering from the same malady, but he had no idea what it was. Linda came running from the house and got in beside Neil. He started the car and turned down the drive splashing through deep puddles, and turned onto the road.

Fifteen minutes later, Neil stopped the car. They sat on a hill looking down on a vast plain of gushing, muddy water. There was no way through the brown water as some of the tallest pines were half submerged. Neil got a sick feeling as he gazed at the impassible deluge.

"Goddamnit, Neil, we just can't sit here," Ross said. "Let's try the other direction." Nancy mumbled words none could make out. Neil turned the car and drove back the way they had come.

They were now moving against the wind and rain inundating the windshield defeating the purpose of the wipers. They beat furiously but couldn't clear the windshield forcing Neil to a crawl.

Three quarters of an hour later, they looked over what they had faced earlier. Linda turned frightened eyes to Neil as he glanced at her.

"There's no way out," she said, with a shudder. She saw by his expression that he felt trapped too.

"There's something wrong in that house, Neil," Linda said. "I don't know what it is, but being there is like being caught in a nightmare." The men glanced at each other realizing they felt the same.

"Like it or not, it's the only place we can go," Neil said. "We can't keep these women out here. There, at least, they'll have warm beds." Again, Neil turned the car and headed back for Marsac House.

Before they reached the house, Neil stopped the car and turned in the seat regarding Ross and Steve with a grim look.

"When we get back, stay in the rooms with your wives," Neil said. "I'll have Vera bring your meals to you. Linda and I will see if we can locate any medication that might help. Don't leave your wives alone, no matter what."

"What are you going to do?" Linda asked. Neil got a desperate look.

"Try and take care of these women. And find out what's going on in that house."

After dinner, Neil stubbed out his cigarette and looked at Seth and Vera, who held drinks. Neil picked up his drink, noting Linda taking a stiff drink from hers.

"I feel helpless to cope with those women's illness," Seth said, with a concerned look. "I wish there was more we could do for them."

"Linda and I will do what we can," Neil said. "I had some antibiotic samples in my car. I don't know how much that will help, but it's all we have right now." Linda had been watching Seth and felt he was genuinely distressed.

"If you hear anyone moving during the night, it will be Neil or me checking on Nancy and Tara," Linda said.

"Of course," Seth said, nodding. "Feel free to go anywhere in the house. Keep them comfortable until we can get them help."

"Thanks for understanding," Neil said.

"If you'll excuse me," Seth said. "I'll go to my room."

"Thanks again," Linda said. Seth nodded to her and walked off followed by Vera. Linda put her glass down and looked at Neil.

"What now?"

"You check upstairs and I'll look around down here."

Linda began checking rooms and found Nancy sleeping with Ross dozing in a chair at the foot of the bed.

The same condition prevailed in Tara's room. Linda opened the door of the next room stepped in and turned on the lamp. She looked around a room that was exactly the same as the others, except for the color of the spread and canopy. She turned the lamp off and went to the next room.

At the sixth room, Linda was wondering why there were so many bedrooms. This thought was distracting her when she opened the door. She stepped in and reached for the lamp when someone grabbed her arm followed by a blow to her head. Linda went spinning into unconsciousness.

Neil was going through a medicine cabinet when he heard someone behind him and turned. He faced Vera who regarded him with wanton expression.

"We didn't finish making love last night, Neil."

"What?" he asked, uncertain of her meaning. Vera locked her eyes on his and Neil fought desperately against wanting her. She stepped closer, unzipped his pants and slipped her hand in.

"Come along now," she said, as though talking to a child. He felt compelled to go, but he didn't want to. He was unable to break the control Vera exercised over him.

In the living room, she unbuttoned her dress and pushed it off. Neil remembered the garter belt and dark hose enclosing her finely toned legs. He realized it hadn't been a dream that had awoke him. Vera sat down on the couch and spread her legs. She pointed at Neil and drew her hand down. He moved to stand in front of her. She lowered her hand as he dropped to his knees. She put her hands on the sides of his face and tilted it back so she could look into his eyes with a satisfied smile. Neil knew what she expected as she leaned back and pulled his head between her legs. Vera closed her eyes and slowly gyrated her hips.

This was what she had been wanting and decided Neil was good enough to keep. All thought of resistance had been purged from his mind and Vera made certain he enjoyed himself.

She had him stand, stripped him from the waist down, knelt before him and amused herself for a few minutes. She lay back on the couch and he entered her. It had been a long time since she had had a man who made her feel good. But the thought of Linda was struggling in consciousness, and was the one thought Vera couldn't control. Still the rain poured on Marsac House.

Linda came to and found herself on a table with straps holding her wrists, ankles, and one just under her breasts holding her down. The table was forked so that her legs were spread. She was surprised to find herself nude. She looked around as much as the restraints would allow. When it appeared she was in an operating room, a nauseous fear gripped her, but she fought it. Most of her fear was caused by not knowing what to expect.
Linda had no doubt who had brought her here as she listened to the stillness surrounding her.

It began to feel as if she had been on the table for hours when she heard someone come into the room. She tried to turn her head far enough to see who it was, but the straps prevented that. Whoever it was remained out of sight, said nothing, and this brought her fear to the surface again.

"Who's there?" There was no reply, but something skittered across the floor that sounded like an animal. She caught a glimpse as something ran under the table and everything became quiet again.

As she lay waiting for what she didn't know, her tension grew. The longer she was there the more hopeless she felt her situation became. Linda had no idea where in the house she was. That meant if Neil were looking for her he would have no idea where to look. A cold dread filled her as she heard heavy footsteps come into the room. Vera stepped beside her with a mixed expression of antagonism and triumph. She cocked an eyebrow and smiled.

"I want you to meet my last lover," Vera said. "Come out here, Vincent." Vera leaned down looking under the table.

"Come on now, you don't need to be shy in front of Linda." From under the table came a two-foot tall, misshapen form in a black robe. It looked up at Linda who saw a pathetic, mouse-like repulsive face.

"This is Vincent," Vera said, patting its head. "He used to be strong, virile, and handsome as a god." Linda gave her a disgusted look.

"That pitiful thing?" Vera ignored her sarcasm.

"He used to make wild, passionate love to me, but grew complacent and began to take me for granted. That's when I grew bored with him, and this is his punishment."

"That's sick!" Linda exclaimed, shocked, but felt no doubt Vera spoke the truth.

"Now I have a replacement for Vincent," Vera said, with a look of superiority and snickering smile.

"Neil now belongs to me. I haven't had a man as good since Vincent. I not only seduced him, but I control him."

"I don't believe you," Linda said, vehemently. Vera looked at her and snapped her fingers. Neil came in and stood beside Vera, his eyes dull as if he had no life in him.

"Your own eyes must convince you, Linda. Accept it. Neil's mine!"

"What have you done to him?" Linda now felt a heady desperation. Vera's smile returned.

"I gave him what he wanted. Something you couldn't, or I wouldn't have been able to take him so easily."

"You're going to kill me." Vera looked shocked.

"Oh, no, dear Linda. I wouldn't do that." It was obvious Vera was enjoying herself immensely.

"Later I'll let you see just how well I've trained him."

"You're a disgusting bitch! The sharp sting of Vera's hand burned across Linda's cheek producing blood at the corner of her lips. Linda turned a look of pure hatred on Vera.

"If you have Neil so well trained, why not let me fuck him?" Linda challenged, in a steady voice. Vera's shoulders stiffened and her frown turned cold.

"He's mine! I'll share him with no other woman." Linda got a cynical smile.

"Why not? Afraid I'll out fuck you?" Vera's hand struck her face again. Linda's eyes narrowed, her voice expressed unbounded rage.

"You're lucky I can't get my hands on you." Vera laughed lightly and walked from the room. Linda glanced at Neil as Vera came back in.

"I hope you enjoy the show, Linda." Vera snapped her fingers and Neil followed after her like a puppy.

The helpless rage that engulfed Linda couldn't be channeled. She could only lie and suffer with her anger and frustration.

She tried slipping her hand through the strap but it was tight and only chaffed her wrist. Quiet returned and she now had no hope of Neil coming for her. Linda felt only growing despair.

She heard someone running toward the room. The door burst open and Ross came in with a wild look.
His eyes were red and puffy, his face a pasty white. He seemed to have difficulty focusing on where he was.

"Ross! Can you unloosen these straps?" she shouted, desperately hoping she would be freed. He looked around as if he hadn't heard her.

"I've got to find that blood-sucking bitch!" he shouted. His words were slurred and he seemed incoherent.

"What are you talking about?" He looked but didn't seem to see her. He pointed to his neck where two small wounds trickled blood.

"I stayed with her! I thought I was protecting her. I wake up to find her drinking my goddamn blood. I'm going to find her and kill her."
He stumbled back out the door and was gone.

"Ross, wait!" she shouted. She was now totally frightened as she realized from his words and wounds what was wrong in this house. But she was strapped to the table, vulnerable to Vera's every whim.

Seth walked quietly into Tara's room, clenched his fist and drove it hard against the side of Steve's head. The chair fell over spilling him onto the floor. Tara's light blue eyes snapped open, then closed. Seth turned to the bed, walked over and looked down at her pretty face. He sat down and put an arm on each side of her. He bent down; feeling it was time to make her his. He didn't see her eyes snap open, her mouth widen or reveal long fangs.

Tara waited until Seth was about to penetrate her throat and struck. It was fast, ferocious, and took with such surprise that he had the side of his throat ripped out before he could get away from her. He rose clumsily from the bed, staggered backward, his hand pressed against the bloody remains of his throat. He collapsed at the foot of the bed, blood spilling and forming a pool under him.

Tara pushed the blood soaked cover from her and got out of bed. In a hunched animal walk, she went to the unconscious Steve and rolled him on his back. Gently, she rubbed her hand against his cheek and turned his head exposing his throat. She made a mewling sound and glanced furtively around the room. She brushed at his hair then viciously sank her fangs into his throat.

The one idea Neil was focusing on was Linda. He didn't know it was the perfume Seth had given her that kept his mind centered on her. It was beginning to break Vera's control.
He had to strain to keep Linda's face in his mind, and the longer he held it, the more Vera's control eroded. It was taking time, and he was desperate to save Linda. Neil, too, now understood the secret of Marsac House.

He struggled to regain self-control and made a tremendous effort to free his mind. It was the most mind-wrenching thing he had ever done, but his concentration finally snapped Vera's influence. Now he had to find Linda.

The passageways Vera had taken him through remained vague, but he recalled enough to find his way back to Linda.

Linda tried frantically to free her hand, but only succeeded in rubbing her wrist raw. Vera's return surprised her with a wild looking Nancy.

"I've brought you a treat, Linda," Vera said, pleasantly. "My pet is going to lick your crotch."

"No! Don't you dare," Linda screamed, helplessly. Vera gloated as she stood over her looking at the hunched Nancy.

"Show her how pleasurable it is, my pet. But don't hurt her. She'll be a source of amusement." Nancy moved her head between Linda's legs.

"No!" Linda couldn't even struggle, only close her eyes and try not to think of what was happening. Then she heard Vera.

"I prefer Neil's tongue." It was a boast that infuriated Linda. She fought against what Nancy was doing, but it was beginning to have an effect, and Linda couldn't help becoming aroused. When Vera seen what was happening, she broke into raucous laugher. It was the bitterest sound Linda had ever heard.

She began to concentrate on hatred of Vera; her face, laugh, everything about her had to be hated intensely. As Linda's' arousal grew, she heard the door burst open followed by the voice of Neil.

"I'm free of you, Vera." Vera stared in shock as she saw it was true. He had broken her control. When Neil saw what Nancy was doing, he moved beside the table and shoved Nancy's head back. She stumbled and sprawled on the floor. She was quickly back on her feet in a hunched pose. Vera glared angrily at him.

"You may hurt him, my pet." Nancy began moving toward Neil. He looked around for a weapon and found only a long surgical knife.

"Don't come any closer," Neil warned, holding the blade in front of him. Nancy never took her wild eyes off him as she closed on him. She rushed at him and he jerked the knife up and her momentum drove her onto it. She staggered back emitting a shrill, unearthly howl. She fell to the floor fighting fitfully to pull the blade from her.

The action took Vera by surprise, giving Neil time enough to free Linda's wrists and almost the strap over her torso. Vera, driven by rage, moved on Neil. He had no weapon, and had to move quickly to avoid her. Nancy lay bleeding, an eruption of blood on her lips with every exhalation.

Linda quickly freed the strap over her and sat up. She freed her ankles, got off the table and picked up a stainless steel tray. She moved behind Vera, lifted the tray, and released her rage as she brought it down. There was a loud metallic clang as the tray impacted with Vera's head. She dropped to the floor and lay still.

"Come on!" Neil grabbed her hand as she stared at Vera and dropped the tray. It seemed she had no feeling left in her.

"Linda!" Neil shouted. "We've got to get the hell out of here."

He pulled her along as they ran through the dimly lit passageways. They moved through numerous turns and bends that led upward until they found themselves on the ground floor. They stopped panting by the front door. Neil turned when she wouldn't go any further.

"What's the matter?" She gave him a helpless look and spread her hands.

"I'm naked! I can't go out like this. I've got to get dressed." Neil nodded.

"We've got to be quick," he said, and they headed for the stairs.

In the room, she jerked the suitcase from under the bed, opened it, and took a blouse and skirt out. She slipped them on as she pushed her feet into a pair of flats. They rushed back downstairs to the foyer and began pulling on their coats.

"Going somewhere?" Vera asked, smiling.

The storm was again increasing in fury with lightning licking hungrily across the sky and thunder a continuous roar. Neil grabbed a small golden statue of an Egyptian oblisk from a stand and wielded it like a knife.

"That's such a puny weapon against me," Vera said, in a soft, sexy voice. She started toward them opening her arms for an embrace.

"Get to the car, Linda," Neil said, tossing her the keys and never taking his eyes from Vera. She continued her slow, provocative walk toward him.

"What about you?"

"Goddamnit, Linda, just get to the car." He hoped his tone would move her. Neil kept backing away from Vera and heard the door open. He continued backing toward it.

"You want me, Neil. I know that." Vera's eyes were taking on a yellow glow and he felt their power working on his mind. She was slowly eroding his will to resist as he stepped outside in the rain. Vera kept draining his will by keeping a steady gaze on him, and he couldn't look away.

"It's me you want, Neil. Not Linda." Her voice now had a tone of desperation and it loosened her grip on his mind.

"Stay with me, Neil." She was now quite close and opened her dress making him conscious of each step backward. She was almost against him and put her arms around his neck.

Linda pulled the car up and opened the door.

"Get in!" Linda screamed. She felt a flood of fear as she saw Vera's lips touch his. With a superhuman effort, he broke the kiss.

"No!" he shouted, as rain ran down their faces. He shoved the oblisk above his head and lightning was quickly attracted to it. It danced on the statue for a full minute causing the gold to melt under the brilliant blue aura that also enveloped Neil and Vera.

Laura screamed as their fiery corpses fell back through the door. The fire clinging to them ignited the carpet, and the fire spread rapidly. Linda could only watch in despair as flames lit up each window in both floors of Marsac House. Flames erupted in orange towers through the roof causing it to crash down into the interior pushing out part of a wall and strewing debris over the rain soaked lawn. the inferno raged through the entire structure before the rain began having any effect. There remained only a smoking, smoldering ruin standing in the downpour.

Reality struck as a brutal shock. Vera had won! She had taken Neil from her. As tears filled her eyes, Linda put the car in gear and turned down the drive. They flowed as she thought of Neil being lost to her. It was a truth her mind fought against. She began to invent ways he might have survived, but knew there was no hope.

IN DARKNESS AROUND US

An incredibly bright light, and peculiar noise awoke Linda. She lifted her head from the wheel where she had cried herself into an exhausted sleep. The car sat on the hill at the edge of the great flood plain. She sat back and looked out, not quite certain where she was. A rapping came on the window and she saw a highway patrolman looking in. she lowered the window and was hit by the icy spray the helicopter was blowing. The officer had his hand clamped over his hat staring at her amazed.

"How did you get here, Miss?"

"We got lost." It was the only thing she could think of.

"Who was with you?" he asked, raising his voice to be heard.

"Neil Jameson." When she spoke his name, her eyes filled with tears.

"Come on, Miss, we'll get you out of here." He helped her out of the car and into the helicopter.

When she told her story, she had enough presence of mind not to mention Marsac house. If Neil had been with her she could have passed it off as nothing more than a bad dream. She told them they had been trapped on the road by the rising water and Neil had gone for help. They accepted her story.

Linda was driven to her apartment in a police car. As she walked up to the door, the rain was finally tapering off. She woke the super who let her into her apartment. Sitting on the sofa with a warm robe pulled around her, she stirred a spoon of creamer in the coffee. She was safe and dry, but remembered the people who perished at Marsac house. She felt empty at the loss of Neil, more so because she knew he had loved her. To lose him after learning that was almost unbearable. It was the worst pain she had known in her life, but knew she had to go on living. Go through life carrying the emotional ache. She thought of Nancy and wondered how the other people in that evil house had died. Linda shuddered as she knew she never wanted to find her again on Pine Ridge Road.

IT'S THE THOUGHT THAT KILLS

Joe Montgomery stepped off the bus holding his one small piece of luggage. He took a deep breath, as he felt secure looking around the small nameless town. He would stay overnight and move on tomorrow morning. He walked along the sidewalk marveling at the serenity of the town. Joe went into a café and ordered dinner.

As he ate he looked out the plate glass window at the center of town. It would never find him here, he felt. He paid the woman at the ancient manual cash register and wondered how many like it remained in use.

He walked leisurely from the café to the hotel and took a room for the night. The old elevator creaked and groaned as it lifted him to the third floor. Walking down the hall, Joe felt comfortable that it wasn't the Ritz. He slipped the key in the lock, turned it and opened the door. He stepped into an out-of-date room and realized the whole town seemed to be frozen in the past, but he felt completely at ease here. He laid the key on the nightstand, put his suitcase in the chair, and stood looking out the window he had just opened. Warm fresh air washed into the room as he listened to the sounds from the street below. He was tired and decided to turn in early. He couldn't get over how completely safe he felt it would never find him here. Never! It wasn't quite dark when Joe climbed into bed. He was calm as a sense of security filled him in the ancient hotel room.

His eyes snapped open. He was wide-awake looking at the luminous dial of his travel clock on the nightstand. It was almost two-thirty. At first, Joe wondered where he was, then recalled arriving late the previous afternoon. But he couldn't recall why he had come here. He rolled on his back and stared at the ceiling that changed from black to orange. The blinking neon sign outside the window flashed making the ceiling alternate between color and darkness. He sat up becoming wet with sweat that quickly soaked his T-shirt. A cold fear began to grow in him. It had followed him! It had found out where he was. But how?

Joe glanced around the room at the antiquated furniture that disappeared when the orange light flashed off. The curtain was a rising wraith as the soft breeze lifted it and dropped it limply when the wind deserted it. He sat up on the bed, his feet resting on the cool linoleum.

He pulled off the wet T-shirt, mopped his face, and dropped it beside him. He went into the bathroom, pulled the towel from the rack and wiped his upper torso. He took the suitcase from the chair and laid it on the bed. Opening it, he took out a T-shirt and an awful dread abruptly filled him. This caused him to move faster.

He pulled the T-shirt over his head and jerked it down tightly, quickly pulled his shirt and pants on and pressed his feet into his shoes. A feeling of desolation grew in him, making him feel a great sense of loss he couldn't understand. Finally he was dressed.

He went to the door as a sense of its nearness sent a flash of terror through him. He cringed against the wall breaking out again in a cold, fear-inspired sweat. He was being driven to get away from his room. He had to go! He must escape. Slowly, Joe opened the door slightly and put his eye to the crack and looked into the hallway. A dim yellow glow inhabited the eerily silent hallway. Only the flaking green paint of the walls were to be witness to his exit.

Joe pulled the door open far enough for him to slip out, then pulled it closed. He stood looking from one end of the hall to the other. The rundown hallway was empty, filled only with its silent embrace. He knew it was here. Who? He only knew it was someone who gave him reason to fear them greatly. He moved to the exit and pushed the door opened, and listened. The silence seemed very loud in his ears. The torment came, probing his mind. Joe panicked. Furiously, he flung the door open causing it to hit the wall with a loud bang. But he didn't hear it as he was sprinting down the stairs creating a cracking repercussion throughout the groaning wooden steps.

He came to a stop, slammed his back against the wall, and looked anxiously up the stairs. The cool wall helped calm him. It felt good. He stood by the ground floor exit listening to the echoes of his flight fade away. He was panting from his frantic descent, his breath gasping loudly in the stillness. His heart was beating so hard he thought it would burst from his chest. It took a couple of minutes to catch his breath.

Joe cautiously pushed the exit door open and surveyed the murky alley. It was devoid of sound and movement, but filled with a beckoning darkness. He slipped past the door and let it close with a slight click. He began making his way slowly through the darkness toward the light of the street that was his escape route.

He came to a sudden halt when he heard it. The sound of slow, deliberate footsteps moving toward the mouth of the alley.

Nearer and nearer the steps came. Louder and louder they grew. Joe was afflicted with paralyzing fear. He began to perspire heavily in the cool night air. He tried desperately to push himself through the wall his back was pressed against. Agonizing torment ate at his mind and unreasoning terror filled the pit of his stomach.

The cop moved across the mouth of the alley walking his beat with slow deliberate steps. Joe's fear was alleviated in a great rush of breath. He began moving along the cool brick wall until he could look into the street in both directions. Patches of aureate light filled the sidewalk in square puddles, but the emptiness of the street made Joe feel isolated. He wended his way past storefronts that had display lights on while others were obscured in profound gloom.

He found himself standing across from the small city park. It was shadowy, abyssal, and seemingly endless. He heard the leaves rustling softly in the cool night breeze. Joe hesitated; noting the park didn't look to be a very inviting place. He was aware that it was closer than it had ever been, and felt he had no choice. He raced across the street and was quickly swallowed by the infinite darkness that was the park. As he ran he thought he could hear the trees call his name. He had to get through the park. It felt much too dangerous here. He sensed this peril and increased his pace.

Joe slipped and fell hard on the dew covered grass and lay stunned for a moment. He gasped, filling his lungs with fresh air. The dew cooled his hot, sweaty face as sweat began to sting his eyes. He pulled his hand over his face wiping away the sweat. He clearly heard the voice and it terrified him, making him go rigid.

"Joe Montgomery. Do not flee. We must meet."

"No, Oh, no," he cried, galvanizing himself into action. He leaped to his feet and desperately raced off on his infinite journey through the somber park. Where had the voice come from? This stopped Joe abruptly. He turned around looking for the source of that voice. He was alone and felt despair then abandonment, and he didn't know why.

"Do not flee," the voice repeated. He clenched his hands and sought the voice.

"What the hell do you want from me?" he said, lifting his arms in a helpless gesture. Then terror filled him once more. Joe ran. He kept running until he burst from the park.

IN DARKNESS AROUND US

He stood on a street that glared with harsh streetlights. He hastened past windows with colored neon signs flashing.

He didn't know how far he had come or where he was. All he was certain of was that he had escaped the voice. He had had to if he wanted to live. He stumbled against a mailbox and leaned against its cool metal surface, a minor comfort. He was still panting and had to rest.

"Joe Montgomery, it is urgent that we meet," the voice said, insistent.

"No, goddamnit! Leave me alone. Just leave me alone," he shouted, into the night, his eyes searching frantically for the source of the voice. There was no one to be seen and he stood alone. Again he raced off, away from the demanding voice.

Overwhelming terror propelled him along streets, around corners, but always through a strange darkness in his mind. Joe eventually had to slow down and became aware of his surroundings. There were shadowed buildings standing in harsh yellow light lining both sides of the street. He didn't see houses but malevolent faces glaring at him, wishing him harm. What is this thing? His mind demanded. But he had no idea of what it was or where. He knew he had never heard the voice speak to him before. That meant it was much closer than it had ever been. His torment returned in a torrents. He pushed himself away from the mailbox and ran for his life.

He lost all concept of time and distance, not knowing how long he had been running. He knew he couldn't stop because it might catch up with him. He stumbled and fell, and was grateful to be down. The dew-covered grass again soothed his hot, sweaty face. He wiped sweat from his stinging eyes as he sucked cool air into his burning lungs. The smell of the grass seemed to comfort him, ease his fear. Joe didn't understand why, but he was beginning to feel safe again.

"Are you all right, Mister?" asked a voice, out of the darkness. Joe started violently and began crawling away on his stomach, his hands pulling and feet pushing. He rolled over and sat up against a tree. A man stood under the nearby streetlight watching him with concern.

"Are you okay?" the man reiterated. Joe emitted a frightened yell, leaped to his feet, and fled into the now dying night.

He was totally exhausted, but his nightmare was over for the present. But Joe knew it would be back and felt he could relax. It had never bothered him in daylight.

He got his bearings and headed back for the hotel desperately needing rest.

He went to the mouth of the alley feeling at ease as he neared the hotel exit.

"We meet at last, Joe Montgomery," said the voice, triumphantly. He quickly glanced around in the pink blush of dawn. There it was! It stood by a wall and he could clearly see the image of his nightmare. He looked around, his eyes coming to rest on a piece of metal pipe. Rage now took over as he hefted the pipe for attack.

"You son of a bitch!" Joe exclaimed, savagely. "Now that I can see you, I'm going to kill you." His anger was a raging flood in his mind, pushing out fear. He recalled all the terror filled nights it had pursued him, haunted him. Now it, too, clutched a piece of pipe. Joe charged it as it began coming toward him. He neared it lifting the pipe and brought it down in a hard arc. But it was swinging its pipe at him. Joe was faster and he smashed its head in. There was a piercing crack and his enemy fell shattered into a thousand sparkling fragments that tinkled lightly on the floor of the alley.

The silence of early morning returned to the alley. Joe felt triumphant, then was overcome with a feeling of impending doom. An agonizing pain erupted in his head. He dropped the pipe and pressed his hands against the sides of his head trying to push the pain out. But it was unrelenting. He couldn't understand what was happening to him. The afflicting pain dropped him to his knees as it grew more intense. It glowed brightly in his mind like an exploding star. He pitched forward, face down on the alley floor, moaned once and lay still. When he had smashed the image in the mirror he had killed himself.

Above the alley in the brightening day, hung a blue glowing disc.

"It has occurred again," thought one of the two gray aliens. "Every observer we have sent to this planet has had their minds destroyed. Why do they so quickly lose their ability to communicate with us?"

"Unknown," the other alien thought. "But they always return to this place.
And this is where their greatest denial of their origin happens. This makes the fourth observer to die on this primitive world."

"We must leave this planet of madness," thought the first alien. "It is a planet of insanity for any of us who walk on its surface." They began working the controls. The disc ascended slowly through the brightening sky until it was no longer visible from the alley.

THE DEVIL IN EDEN

He began his search in the seedy bars near the spaceport. He needed to be certain he chose the right man, one who was greedy and had a disregard for the authorities. A man like that could be trusted to keep silent. He believed he had now found the captain he was looking for. He had been in this vile smelling bar for the past two nights watching one particular captain. He made a casual remark to the bartender.

"Why that's Captain Malcolm. Haven't you heard about him?" The man shook his head and regarded the bartender with interest.

"He's gotten away with some of the biggest smuggling deals ever," the bartender continued. "The authorities were never able to prove a thing. Malcolm's as smart as a fox." That was more than a good enough endorsement.

He approached the table where Malcolm sat. When he stopped, Malcolm turned hard black eyes on him.

"Captain Malcolm, I was wondering if we might discuss some business?" Malcolm sucked on his lip as he regarded the man standing before him and nodded.

"I'll listen," Malcolm said. He pulled the chair from the table and sat down.

"I must leave Earth, Captain. I need to do so quickly and without the authorities knowing." Malcolm was quick in his appraisal. This man didn't lack wealth. His nails were manicured and his suit expensive. His black wavy hair was neatly trimmed and his blue eyes looked cold.

"It's clear you're no criminal. So why the secrecy?" He glanced around quickly.

"I'm a scientist. I've developed a device I can no longer test here without fear of discovery. If the authorities find out, they will take my device." Malcolm puckered his lips and narrowed his eyes. The story sounded plausible, but Malcolm wanted to know nothing about the device.

"What are you willing to pay?"

"Name your price, Captain." Malcolm scratched his head. This man was desperate to get away from Earth. Malcolm felt the risk minimal, and stated a sum, expecting an argument.

"I can have the money here tomorrow afternoon, provided we can leave tomorrow night." This was no problem for Malcolm. His ship would finish loading early the next morning. Malcolm extended his hand.

"We have a deal," Malcolm said. "Make certain you're not followed." The man looked relieved.

"The authorities don't yet know of my device, Captain."

The following afternoon, Malcolm sat in the bar waiting for his passenger who arrived with a suitcase and long green metal box. He sat down facing Malcolm, took an envelope from his jacket pocket and handed it to Malcolm. Malcolm opened it and looked at the crisp bills that made the envelope bulge and quickly stuck it in his pocket. The man looked surprised.

"Aren't you going to count it?" Malcolm shrugged.

"I trust you. You want away from here too bad to do anything foolish." The man nodded with a satisfied expression.

"Has my equipment been loaded?" Malcolm nodded.

"This afternoon."

"When can we leave, Captain?"

"There's a shuttle standing by to take us to my ship," Malcolm replied, with a twisted smile.

Malcolm's ship was leaving Earth orbit within an hour. Once away from Earth, the man told Malcolm he wanted to disembark at an obscure outpost in the Vega system. Malcolm was only too happy to comply as it meant a much shorter diversion from his planned course. Malcolm last saw the man when he left the ship at Riley's Station. It would be awhile before he discovered his passenger had been Gamel Spata, who was wanted for experimenting on people and murder.

The owner of Riley's Station was glad to sell his small ship to Spata. The money provided him a tidy profit. After purchasing the ship, Spata had to find an assistant who knew how to work specialized computers, was unknown and expendable. He quickly found his man in Clay Adden, who fit easily into Spata's plan. They left the station without revealing where they were headed. Spata could now continue with his research without fear from any authority.

By the time the authorities became aware of Spata's work after he was gone. In his lab, they found a man and woman dead, and two women comatose.

An immediate alert was put out for Dr. Gamel Spata. Escaping as he did, he left behind enough evidence that gave the authorities some idea of the device he had created. But the two things the authorities wanted were out of their hands: Spata and his machine.

Lou Tanner held his daughter, brushing blonde hair from her forehead.

"I'll be back as soon as I can, Honey," he said. Her small blue eyes looked sadly at him and she put her arms around his neck and pressed her cheek against his, giving him a tight hug.

"I'm going to miss you, Daddy," she said, in her six-year-old voice. He kissed her on the cheek. Trisha had become his life since the death of his wife. He put her down but held onto her hand and turned to his sister. She had been taking care of her since Wanda's death.

"Do you know what your assignment is, Lou?" He shook his head.

"All I know, Marty, is that I have to report to Admiral Hall."

"Then you could be sent right out?"

"It's possible." He bent down to Trish and she looked steadily at him.

"I have to go now," he said, and kissed her forehead. He released her hand and turned to leave.

"I love you, Daddy." Lou smiled at her.

"I love you too, Honey."

Kelly Martin lifted his eyes from the orders he had just received.

"I've been promoted, Dana, and transferred to the Staff Command School as an instructor." She got a slight smile as she brushed copper hair from her ear. She kept her gray-green eyes on him and nodded.

"You've earned it, Captain. Congratulations." He gave her an odd look.

"They're giving the Gemini to Lou Tanner." This was a shock to Dana. Standard procedure called for her to assume Martin's command. As his exec, it was the usual way promotion came. She looked perplexed.

"Do your orders say why?" He shook his head.

"Not a hint." He saw her disappointment, but there was nothing he could do.

"They must be sending Lou on a special mission. It's the only thing I can think of."

"Don't worry, Captain, I'll do my duty." Her words were sharp with disappointment.

"But there's no regulation that says I have to like it."

The crew assembled to bid their captain farewell.

"I want to thank you for your loyalty to this ship and to me," Martin said. "Do the same for your new captain. You're probably wondering why Commander Morton isn't getting command. I don't know. But I know Lou Tanner and he's a good man, thinking of his people first." He paused, moving his eyes over the crew.

"Good luck to you all," Martin concluded, turned, and boarded the shuttle. The crew came to attention and filed off the hangar deck.

Lou pinched the creases on his trousers and ran his fingers along them so they stood out sharply. Erect, he looked at his vague reflection in the polished marble façade of the HQ building. He pulled his blouse down tight, stretching the wrinkles out. He smoothed back his dark brown hair and studied himself through gray eyes. His black uniform, with light blue piping and silver insignia of rank, was as neat as he could get it. Now it was time to see the admiral.

Lou stepped into the anteroom as the door shut quietly behind him. Sitting at the desk was a most attractive redhead with brown eyes. She looked at him with a glowing smile.

"Captain Tanner reporting to Admiral Hall." She spoke into the intercom, then slipped from the chair in a calculated move. Her skirt slid slowly up her thighs. Lou didn't mind the view, and it was obvious she wanted him to look. He liked those long, shapely legs and the promise they offered.

"The admiral's expecting you, Captain." Her voice was sexy and fit her. She stepped to the door of the admiral's office and leaned toward Lou so he got a good look down her perfumed cleavage. When she opened the door, he had to look away and enter the admiral's office.

Admiral Hall was a solid built man with gray hair and piercing blue eyes. He sat with hands folded on the desk regarding Lou as he stepped in front of the desk and came to attention.

"Captain Tanner reporting, sir."

"Sit down, Captain." The admiral gestured to a chair. Lou sat down and felt this chair was here purposely because no one could get comfortable in it.

"Captain, you're being sent on a special mission. You'll take command of the Gemini immediately on boarding." Lou sat up straight.

"That's Kelly Martin's ship, sir."

"It was, Captain. Martin's been promoted and transferred."

"Excuse me, Admiral, but shouldn't his first officer be taking command?" Hall puckered his lips and nodded.

"That's the standard procedure. But this mission overrides procedure." This sparked Lou's curiosity.

"What's the mission, sir?" Hall leaned back and put his arms on the armrests.

"Two weeks ago a freighter strayed into an unexplored region of space. As it passed a Class G star, it picked up an unknown signal and recorded it. When the freighter made spacedock, the captain turned the recording over to Fleet Security."

"What sort of signal, sir?" A scowl came to Hall.

"One unusual enough to have the top brass at Fleet Command send the research vessel Hudson into that sector." Lou's curiosity grew.

"All communication with the Hudson ceased abruptly three days ago." Hall paused keeping his gaze on Lou, watching his reaction.

"You, Captain Tanner, were selected as the best officer to search for the Hudson." The admiral's voice carried an uneasy undertone that Lou didn't miss.

"Sir, a search and rescue mission could be handled by Gemini's first officer." Hall slowly shook his head.

"There's more to it than just finding the Hudson. In a routine examination of that recorded signal was matched to that of Dr. Spata's mind-warping machine." Hall's tone was grim, and he made certain by inflection, that Lou understood would be going after Spata. Lou felt cold as he nodded.

"I understand, sir." Hall leaned forward and rested his arms on the desk.

"Spata's machine is dangerous, Captain. It was unfortunate that Spata fled before he could be taken into custody."

"I'm aware he evaded arrest, sir, but I'm not too clear about the working of his device."

"That device," Hall said, tapping his finger on the desk for emphasis. "Could tap into a person's subconscious and create hallucinations that convinced the person it was real.

The terrible thing is that it breaks minds. That machine is a control device, and a damned illegal invention."

"What do I tell the crew, sir?"

"The crew is to know only that you're searching for the Hudson. The name Spata might make some of them nervous, if they know of him."

"How can a person defend against the device, Admiral?"

"You can't. At least, that's what the experts think."

"You don't believe it, sir?"

"The records found in Spata's lab showed the device worked well when the subject was unaware of what was happening." Hall paused with a frown.

"I think if you know what you're up against, you have a certain measure of defense. That's why you were chosen for this mission. Your record shows you think clearly under stressful conditions. Should you find Spata..." He spread his hands.

"You'll probably find the situation more than stressful."

"How can the crew be protected, sir?"

"Knowing what they're up against may prove their only defense."

"Anything else, sir?" Hall nodded.

"You can inform the crew about this mission at your discretion, Captain. A shuttle's standing by to take you to your command. The ship's officers' files are in the shuttle's computer. Familiarize yourself with your division officers. You may have to rely on them more than any captain ever has." The admiral stood and Lou got to his feet. The admiral extended his hand and Lou shook it.

"Good luck, Captain."

As Lou came out of the admiral's office, the redhead gave him a sexy smile. Lou grinned as he went to the desk, put his hands on it, and leaned toward her.

"When I get back, Sugar, I'm going to look you up." She caressed his cheek with a light touch.

"You know where to find me, Captain. But don't take too long. I don't like long waits." She put her hand to her lips and blew him a kiss.

Boarding the shuttle, Lou was handed a red sealed envelope by the pilot. He was shown to a seat forward where he had access to the computer. He opened his orders and found little different from what Hall had told him, with the exception of Spata.

He laid the orders aside and accessed the list of Gemini officers. The monitor showed a photo and personnel record of Dana Morton. As Lou read through the files, he knew he was getting experienced officers. Kelly Martin had been the best captain in the fleet, and had made a reputation with a tough, well-trained crew. Lou was satisfied, but felt uneasy. There might be animosity on Morton's part since she should have gotten the command. But, he thought, the admiral must think her unable to handle anything like spata and his device.

Lou turned his attention to the Hudson. There had been no distress call; its communications had just ceased. Efforts to reestablish communication had proven fruitless. The Hudson's last reported position, along with the coordinates of the star, had already been downloaded into Gemini's computer. He looked out the windscreen at the long, tubular shape that was Gemini. Not very glamorous, he thought. But it's a military patrol vessel. The shuttle moved easily into the hangar bay and bumped down lightly. They waited as the airlock was cycled.

Lou stepped from the shuttle and saw the crew assembled, and the attractive exec approaching.

"Captain Tanner, I'm Commander Morton," she said, in a formal tone.

"Commander," he said, stepping off the ramp. "I don't stand on ceremony. If you would please dismiss the crew and have the division officers assemble in the ready room. Then we'll get this mission under way."

"Yes, sir," she said, and turned back toward the crew.

The officers were assembled when Lou came in and started to stand.

"As you were," he said, quickly, moving to the head of the conference table. They reseated themselves and turned their attention on him.

"I'm Lou Tanner." He got no further.

"Your reputation precedes you, Captain," Dana said, in a tight tone. Lou saw the resentment in her expression, but her demeanor showed an efficient officer. Lou understood her resentment, but he was the captain.

"Commander, we need to get something settled. I didn't ask for this assignment. As a matter of fact, I asked Admiral Hall why you weren't given command. He chose not to reply." Lou's uneasiness had deserted him and he had taken command.

"The admiral briefed me on the mission and told me I was to command it." Lou put his hands on the table and leaned toward her with a steady gaze.

"Am I clear, Commander Morton?"

"Yes, sir," she replied, softly. He stood and glanced around at the other officers.

"I'm at a disadvantage since it seems you know all about me. I know each of you only from your service records."

"If you've seen our records, Captain, then there's nothing more you need know about me," Dana said. Lou looked back at her with a cocked eyebrow.

"Under the circumstances, I feel there's a great deal more I need to know, Commander." His voice was level and that brought a puzzled expression to her.

"What would that be, Captain?" He knew he had to get this under control.

"How will you react in a crisis taking orders from an officer you resent? I prefer to know before we find ourselves in such a situation." She stared at him for a moment.

"I'll do my duty, sir." Her tone was firm, and she kept her eyes on him as he nodded.

"I'll be counting on it, Commander." The people watched the sparks fly between them. He looked away from Dana and all attention focused back on him.

"Three days ago, all communication with the research vessel Hudson abruptly ceased. We're to proceed to its last reported position and search for her." Lou saw the perplexed expression each got.

"It could be something as simple as equipment, but we've got to investigate." He stressed his last words.

"Excuse me, Captain," Rob Daniels said. Lou nodded to the thin, blue eyed, black haired communications officer.

"Go on," Lou urged.

"The Hudson has the facilities to overcome almost any sort of equipment failure, sir."

"I know," Lou said. "But we have to consider every contingency. Don't you agree, Commander Morton?" she raised her eyes to meet his.

"Yes, sir. What you overlook could very well be the answer you're looking for." Lou nodded and turned his eyes to Tavala Cinn, the science officer. She had hazel eyes, auburn hair, and slender lips.

"What's known about the sector where the Hudson was last reported, Lt. Commander Cinn?" Lou asked.

"Only what the freighter recorded, sir," Tavala replied. "They sent a probe in but it disappeared."

"Are there planets around that star?" Lou asked.

"Yes, Captain," Tavala replied, with an excited gleam in her eyes. "The freighter reported a small solar system." Almost everything about that sector is unknown, and I don't like unknowns. I prefer to have minimal data before I make a recommendation."

"I appreciate that," Lou said, feeling good about his assessment of these officers.

"Commander Drake, how soon can the Gemini leave Earth orbit?" Lou asked, turning his gaze to the chief engineer. He had sandy hair, blue eyes, and soft facial features.

"Anytime, Captain. I've had the main drive on standby since we were informed you were coming onboard."

"How long to get to the designated sector?"

"That, sir, depends on much you want to distort spacetime."

"At max," Lou said.

"Four days," Drake replied, with no hesitation. "But it will mean pushing the main drive hard, sir."

"Our orders are not to waste time," Lou said. "Locating the Hudson is the highest priority to the brass."

"You won't just be pushing the main drive, Captain," Dr. Gwen Lewis, chief medical officer said. "You're going to be pushing a crew that hasn't had leave in over six months." Her hair was raven, capping pale gray eyes and full lips, set on an oval face.

"I'm sorry the crew hasn't had leave, Doctor," Lou said. "But I know this crew will do well. They've been serving under the best captain in the service, so I know they'll give more." Lou turned his attention to his security officer, Lori Feller. She had soft brown eyes, dark blonde hair, and a pixie-like nose set on a pretty face.

"Lt. Commander Feller, we've no idea what we might encounter in that sector, so I'll leave it up to you to make certain your people are ready for anything." Lou was thinking about Spata's device.

"We'll be ready, sir," Lori said, and nodded at Tavala. "I've learned a lot from Tavala. However, there's a difference between us. I've got to act on a situation as I see it. I can't afford the luxury of waiting for data."

"I understand that," Lou said, glancing around the table. "If there's no questions, let's get underway." He watched as they filed out, and felt guilty that he hadn't mentioned Spata.

As the Gemini headed for its destination, Lou was feeling at ease in his new command. He took time to familiarize himself with the ship and crew. It wasn't long before he was on a first name basis with his officers. All, that is, except Dana. Her attitude toward him remained cool.

Lou came into sickbay and found an idle chief medical officer.

"How's the crew holding up, Gwen?" She shrugged.

"Better than I expected, Captain. When this mission is over, I'm going to insist the crew be given a thirty day leave." He nodded with a serious look.

"And damned well deserved after such a lengthy tour." She cocked an eyebrow.

"I'm glad you agree, Captain."

"This crew is the best in the fleet. Kelly Martin seen to that. That's why I expect so much from them." She got a relaxed smile.

"They certainly seem to be giving you their full effort."

His next stop was Lori. She was training her people, and he was impressed with her thoroughness. After watching for a few minutes, he went over to her.

"Take a break, people," she said, when she saw Lou, and turned to him.

"You're doing a fine job, Lori."

"Thank you, Captain." She tilted her head and gave him a questioning look.

"I get the impression there's more to this mission than just locating the Hudson, sir." Quite perceptive, he thought. Since it had been left to him to tell the crew, it seemed the time to tell Lori. She needed to know more than the others. He glanced around and saw they were alone.

"Ever hear of Gamel Spata?" A look of unease came to her as she nodded.

"He may be responsible for whatever happened to the Hudson, it may not. But that's what the evidence indicates."

"A friend of mine was one of his experiments. She's never regained consciousness."

"I'm sorry," Lou said, folding his arms.

Lou was in engineering to see how the main drive was holding up. The engineering crew was efficient and he admired at how smoothly they functioned. He stopped beside Charles.

"How's the drive holding up?" Charles looked pleased.

"Surprisingly well, Captain. Operating at maximum for this length of time, I expected some difficulty." He turned a proud look to Lou.

"I said the Gemini would get us to our destination in four days, and she's doing it. A damn fine ship, sir." Lou nodded, impressed.

"You have a crew to match, Charles."

"Indeed, sir. But they're pretty tired." Lou expressed surprise.

"That's hard to believe watching them work." He patted Charles shoulder.

"They'll get leave when this mission's over." Charles smiled.

"They've more than earned it, Captain."

Returning to the bridge, Lou decided it was time to brief the others on their priority mission. Dana, Tavala, and Ross followed him into the readyroom.

"It's time you were told the real mission we're on," Lou began. "The Hudson wasn't in this sector by accident. It was checking to find out if Gamal Spata is in that system." Dana leaned back emitting an audible breath.

"If that's true, Captain, we could be in for a nightmare," Dana said. "I read about those mind snapping experiments of his. Now he's had eighteen months to improve his machine."

"That's why Tavala has to be alert for any odd power emanation," Lou said. "Ross, I want you to keep a scan for that frequency." Tavala looked bewildered.

"I've never heard of Spata, sir," Tavala said.

"Not many people have," Lou said. "He developed a device that penetrates the subconscious and produces illusions so real the victim believes they're real."

"Why wasn't he arrested, sir?" Tavala asked.

"By the time the authorities found out what he was doing, he had left Earth," Dana replied. "He left two people dead and two comatose. No one's seen or heard about him for the past year and a half."

"Is it certain he's in that system, sir?" Ross asked.

"That's what the Hudson was investigating," Lou replied. "It was searching for the source of that odd frequency produced by Spata's device."

"If they found Spata, the crew could be dead, Captain," Dana said. Lou nodded with a grim look.

"That's possible," Lou said. "And we can't take a possibility like that lightly, because the same could happen to us."

Lou made certain Gwen and Lori heard the recording of the briefing. He would be depending on Gwen to counter any effect of Spata's device on the crew. The intercom by his arm sounded.

"Captain."

"Can you come to the sickbay, sir?" Gwen asked.

"I'll be right there." He got out of the seat and looked at Dana.

"You have the bridge, Commander." She gave him a relaxed look.

"Please, Captain, call me Dana." Lou nodded, surprised.

"I'll be in sickbay, Dana."

"Yes, sir."

When he entered sickbay, he found Gwen with a troubled look.

"What is it?" She regarded him in silence for a moment as if getting her thoughts organized.

"What do you expect me to do against Spata's mind twister, Captain?" Her voice carried concern.

"Admiral Hall told me Spata used his device on people who weren't aware of what he was doing. He believes if a person knows what to expect the effect will be reduced." Her frown deepened.

"That's not what the experts think, Captain. It doesn't answer my question." Lou shrugged.

"Whatever you can, Gwen." A furrowed brow joined her frown.

"Do you think what Dana said about him perfecting that device, is true sir?" Lou nodded.

"More than likely." She closed her eyes, opened them, and inhaled deeply.

"Captain, we have no way of knowing how that device might affect a mind now."

"That's what we may face. We'll have to deal with events as they occur."

As he headed back to the bridge, Lou was considering what Gwen had said. By the time he stepped on the bridge, he knew it was time to brief the crew. They needed to know the danger they might face. Dana stood and he took the command seat and turned to Ross.

"Open the ship's PA," Lou said. Ross nodded.

"Done, Captain."

"This is the captain. Our mission is twofold. First, we're to search for the Hudson. Second, there's evidence Dr. Gamel Spata may be on one of the planets in that system." He paused, wanting to be certain they knew what they might be getting into.

"For those of you who don't know about Spata, I strongly suggest you access the ship's computer for the pertinent details. Should we find Spata, we're to take him back for trial. That's all."

"Do you think we'll find him, Captain?" Dana asked. Lou had been wondering the same thing.

"I don't know, Dana. If we do, taking him back might not be easy."

They had dropped to sublight, and were approaching the star's system. Lou waited until they were closer before asking for readings. He turned the command seat.

"What's out there, Tavala?" She glanced over her shoulder.

"Four planets, Captain. The second from the star is Class M." Lou cocked an eyebrow and absently rubbed his ear.

"What about the others?"

"Dead rocks, sir." Lou turned the seat to the two-man console in front of him.

"Let's get a closer look at planet two, Alan."

It took time to maneuver through the asteroid crowded system into sensor range of the second planet.

"Any trace of the Hudson, Tavala?" Before she could reply, the helmsman pointed to the screen.

"There she is, sir." Lou turned his eyes to the screen.

"What are you getting from the Hudson, Tavala?" She busily checked over her console.

"It's in a standard orbit, sir. But I get no life signs." Lou turned the seat and faced her.

"There's no one onboard?" he asked, stepping behind her and looking over her shoulder.
What he saw on the scanners verified what she had said. He stepped beside the command seat and activated the intercom.

"Shuttle bay, prepare a shuttle," Lou ordered. He turned to Dana.

"You have the bridge. I'm going over to the shuttle." She stepped close to him and shook her head.

"I can't permit that, Captain. It's my duty as first officer you don't take needless risks. I'll go to the Hudson." He knew she would continue to press her point, and nodded.

Very well. Take a couple of security people with you." she shook her head again.

"I would rather do this alone, sir. Until we know more, we don't need to risk lives."

"All right, Dana. Stay in contact."

"Yes, sir." As she left the bridge, Lou watched her with respect and knew she would make a fine captain.

Dana used the thrusters to lift the shuttle as the airlock hatch opened. When she exited the Gemini, she saw the Hudson below her. It was two large spheres connected by a central tube with civilian call letters emblazoned on the front globe and registry numbers on the rear globe. Dana made a slow orbit around it, looking it over.

"I don't see any external damage, Captain," she reported, noting the Hudson's shuttle bay hatch was open. "I'm going on board."

"Take a sidearm when you leave the shuttle," Lou said, over the radio.

"Yes, sir." Dana jockeyed the shuttle into the Hudson and set it down. Making a comlink with the Hudson's computer, she began the cycle in the airlock. She felt the vibrations of the ship's machinery as it began to function. She watched the pressure gauge as the hatch closed and the atmosphere became standard.

As the shuttle hatch opened, a gust of icy air rushed over her evoking a shiver as the hatch locked in position. Stepping off the ramp, she felt insignificant in such an immense place. The first thing to get Dana's attention was that all of the shuttle's were gone and the ship almost quiet. Dana lifted her weapon as she moved away from the shuttle. Her footsteps echoed eerily in the titanic bay.

"It appears the Hudson was abandoned, Captain. All the shuttles are gone. I'm going to the bridge."

"Be careful, Dana."

"You can count on it, Captain. A deserted ship this size is very disquieting and not a little intimidating." It felt odd to Dana to be walking through a ship and seeing no crew, hearing no voices. The sound was the automatic machinery. She came to the elevator in the forward sphere and took it up to the bridge.

Dana was aware that the only thing remotely alive on this ship was its computer. The elevator stopped and the door slid open.

"I'm on the bridge, Captain."

"We've been keeping a sensor lock on you, Dana. See if you can find why the ship was abandoned," Lou said. Dana was glad to hear his voice as she lowered the communicator. The emptiness of this ship made loneliness seem like a physical presence and did nothing to quell her apprehension. She stepped to the voice command of the computer.

"Computer, show log entries for the past twenty-four hours." Dana was conscious of how loud her voice sounded in the stillness. The computer held no log entries for the past seven days.

"Computer, show last log entry." She spun around quickly, expecting to see someone. The weapon was becoming slippery in her hand, so she slipped it in her belt. Dana had never felt such discomposure.

The last log entry was eight days old. But there was nothing but routine reports of the ship's status. There wasn't a hint as to why the ship had been abandoned. This mystery about the Hudson's missing crew made Dana uneasy.

"The last log entry was made eight days ago, Captain. There's nothing about where the crew went or why." Dana was getting a strong sense of unreality.

"I'm getting the hell out of here, Captain."

"You've done all you can, Dana," Lou said. "Come on back."

Her return to the hangar deck felt almost like a dream. Dana was relieved when the shuttle hatch closed behind her. She quickly set the Hudson's airlock cycling. It seemed to take so long that she began to think it had malfunctioned. And this was one place she didn't want to be stranded. Finally the hangar bay hatch opened, and Dana left the Hudson behind. She was looking forward to getting back to the Gemini where there were people. Being alone had frightened Dana.

Lou was becoming edgy about the situation. He told Lori and Gwen to meet Dana and him in the readyroom. They were going to have work out how they could find the answer to the Hudson's abandonment. Especially under such bizarre circumstances.

"Tavala, how long will it take to get an overall look at the planet's surface?" Lou asked, as he started for the readyroom.

"Two orbits should give us a clear picture, sir." Lou nodded.

"Let me know when it's finished."

Sitting in the readyroom, Gwen and Lori picked up on Lou's uneasiness when he came in with Dana. If Spata was behind the abandonment of the Hudson, they were going to have to be alert for any unusual occurrence on the Gemini.

"Was there any record as to why the Hudson was abandoned?" Lori asked.

"Not a clue," Dana replied. "All the time I was there I felt a weird sensation. It was like being in a dream, and I felt I was being watched."

"What could have happened to the crew?" Gwen asked.

"They have to be down the planet," Lou replied.

"And if Spata is down there, Captain?" Lori asked.

"Would any of you care to make a guess about that?" No one was willing to speculate.

"I want some answers before I send anyone down," Lou said. Dana, sitting to his right, was wanting to say something. Lou could tell by her troubled expression.

"You have something to add, Dana?" Lou asked. She turned a confused look to him.

"I don't know how to explain it, Captain, or even if I believe it myself now." He saw she was struggling for words she couldn't find.

"Just give us your impression," Lou urged. She took a deep breath.

"Everything aboard that ship was too damn normal, Captain! Except for the missing crew, everything was correct. It was like – like it was ready for inspection."

"Do you think something was influencing you?" Gwen asked.

"I can't be certain," Dana replied, and looked back at Lou. "Captain, I don't think there's a ship in the service that correct. I mean, it was textbook perfect." Dana was trying hard to convey what she had felt and found she was unable to do so. Lou looked at Gwen, then back to Dana, making up his mind.

"Dana, Gwen, we're going to sickbay. Lori, you can return to duty."

They remained silent as the elevator descended.

"What have you got in mind, Captain?" Gwen asked.

"If something was affecting Dana's mind, maybe a neuroscan might show something."

"The captain's right, Gwen. The sensations I felt on the Hudson weren't mine."

They walked into sickbay and Dana stepped onto the examination panel. Gwen went to the computer and told it what she wanted done. The aura from the panel surrounded Dana's head. The scan was made as Gwen watched the readout on the monitor.

"There's nothing, Captain," Gwen said, turning to him. "Since we know nothing about that machine, I have no idea what I'm to look for." Lou considered her statement. They were the bare truth. He nodded.

"Let's get to the bridge, Dana."

Lou and his officers had just assembled.

"Report, Tavala," Lou said.

"The planet has an Earth-like atmosphere and similar gravity. There's plant and animal life. There's no sign of civilization, but…"

"Go on, Tavala," Lou urged.

"There are five shuttles parked down there, Captain," Tavala said.

"Human life readings?" Lori asked.

"Yes. I mean, no. I don't know what I mean. Captain, this is very confusing for me," Tavala said, tensely.

"How so?" Lou asked.

"I'm not certain of the readings I got. I'm not certain if they're true. Somehow I feel as if I made them up." Tavala was desperately trying to explain what she meant.

"It was the sensors' behavior! Captain, I know they were being affected by something." Lou glanced at his officers. They needed answers. So far, they hadn't been successful in getting them from orbit.

"Dana, Lori, we're going down to the planet," Lou said. "Lori, I want you to brief your people about the peculiar situation. If any of them begins to feel they're being acted on, I want it reported immediately. That will be the only thing we have to work with."

"But, Captain –" Dana began.

"I'm going down, Dana. I've got nothing to worry about. I'll have you and Lori to protect my ass."

The shuttle pilot flew through the atmosphere without encountering much turbulence. When they neared the coordinates of the Hudson's shuttles, they saw them.

Set her down here," Lou said. The pilot touched the ground with a light bump. The hatch opened and the security teams moved out.

After a few minutes, they reported all clear. Dana and Lori exited the shuttle followed by Lou. It was a precaution Dana had insisted on. They were quick to enjoy the vista around them. The fresh beauty of a world untouched by man.

Green rolling hills interspersed with copses of many colored trees. The sky was azure with white clouds drifting leisurely. The breeze carried new, exotic fragrances to their nostrils.

"Welcome to Eden," Lou said. Nearby were fruit trees with small furry creatures eating the fallen fruit.

"Does this feel anything like being on the Hudson, Dana?"

"No, Captain. This place is beautiful and tranquil. It's a captivating world. As you said, Captain, this could be Eden." Dana was filled with elation as she looked around. She got understanding looks from her companions. Lou relaxed a little, satisfied with Dana's answer.

"Call in the security teams, Lori. We've got to get to those shuttles."

"Yes, sir," she said, and complied. Lou lifted his communicator and opened a channel.

"Tavala."

"Yes, Captain?"

"You have us on your sensor?"

"Yes, sir. I'm reading the nine of you clearly."

"Stay with us," Lou said. "We're starting for the shuttles."

"Right, Captain. I'll follow you all the way."

As they walked, they became even more charmed by this new world. But each was aware that unseen danger lurked here. They had begun with a quick pace, but soon became cautious. As they emerged from a copse, they saw the shuttles parked in a row. Lou didn't see anyone around them, and didn't like that. The shuttles seemed too obvious. Lou was certain it was a trap. He turned to the nearest security man.

"Crider, check ahead," Lou said. "If you begin to feel strange, get the hell back here. Understood?"

"Yes, sir." Crider moved away from them, his weapon ready in his hand. What happened stunned Lou. One second, Crider was walking in a crouch, the next second, he just wasn't there.

"What the hell!" Lori exclaimed. Lou glanced at the others. He didn't know what had occurred and this was no time to try to find out.

"Tavala."

"Yes, Captain."

"Did you get Crider's disappearance on your sensor?"

"His what, sir? I'm reading all of you normally. What happened?"

"Damnit!" Lou exclaimed. "Come on. We're getting the hell out of here." They turned back to the shuttle at a swift pace.

The shuttle climbed through the atmosphere and saw the blue sky change to the black of space. The pilot took them into the Gemini and set them down lightly. Lou took the landing party to the readyroom. He summoned his other officers. As they arrived he assigned them to interview the security teams.

A half-hour later, the security teams were dismissed, and the officers seated themselves in the readyroom.

"Report, Dana," Lou said.

"They saw the same thing we did, Captain."

"But Crider didn't vanish from the sensor until some minutes later," Tavala said, firmly.

"And I want to know damn well why. We have a mystery on our hands that's becoming more mysterious. We are sadly lacking data. So let's get moving and come up with some answers," Lou said. "Ross, I want you to send a report to the nearest base. Inform them our investigation is continuing."

"Right away, Captain," he said, and left the readyroom.

"Is it possible that some kind of invisibility shield at work down there, Charles?"

"I don't think so, Captain."

"Then how did Crider manage to vanish right before our eyes?"

"Captain, Crider showed quite normally on the sensor after you said he vanished," Tavala said. "Three minutes later, his signal faded." Dana decided there might still be a chance to get to the shuttles.

"Captain, let me take down another team. If we approach from a different –"

"You don't get it, do you, Dana?"

"I don't understand, sir."

"The shuttles are a lure. I'm not going to risk anyone until we have some damned answers."

"We can send a security team to the Hudson, sir," Lori said. "There might be department logs that never got put into the main computer before the ship was abandoned. If so, they may have some of the answers we need."

"Good idea, Lori. Assemble your team. Follow the same instructions as on the planet," Lou said, emphatically.

"Don't worry, Captain," Dana said. "Once they get on the Hudson they won't want to stay long." Lori gave Dana a disconcerting look.

The pilot deftly brought them into the Hudson. While they waited for the airlock to cycle, Lori stood before her team.

"Let's do this job quickly and efficiently. Find the department terminals and copy all logs from the past ten days. If any of you start feeling weird, you and your teammate get back here." The shuttle's hatch opened and they filed out. They felt some edginess at being on such a colossal ship with no crew; everything seemed to be normal. No one wanted to work alone.

In under an hour, they were glad to be climbing back on the shuttle. Lori looked around the hangar bay and shivered. Now she understood what Dana had meant. Yet Dana had been here alone. Something Lori was glad she hadn't had to do that.

The pilot lifted the shuttle and moved it out through the hatch.

"Commander!" the pilot shouted. Lori stuck her head in the cockpit.

"What is it?"

"I don't know! It was a real weird sensation. It's gone now, Commander." Lori went back to her seat. They landed back on the Gemini and exited the shuttle. The bay was deserted. Not a person was in sight; no one manned the critical stations. Only the hum of machinery could be heard. Lori looked around with a tingling sensation. The others were staring wide-eyed.

"Where is everyone, Commander?" someone asked. Lori had no idea what had happened.

"Damnit! This isn't possible," Lori said, lifting her communicator.

"Captain."

"Yes, Lori?"

"We're in the hangar bay, but no one is here," she said, a little unnerved.

"I'm not surprised. You're still on the Hudson," Lou said, feeling uneasy.

"That can't be, Captain! We just returned to the Gemini."

"Lori, get your team the hell off that ship now," Lou ordered.

They quickly returned to the shuttle. As soon as the airlock hatch opened, the pilot took them out.

There was the Gemini above them, just as it had been on their imaginary return trip. Lori couldn't believe they had all experienced the same illusion. Spata! It had to be that bastard's doing, Lori thought. She hoped they had found some answers.

Lou waited for the discs to be reviewed. He had given the job to Gwen, Lori, and Tavala.

"Captain, you better come down to the lab," Tavala said, over the intercom.

"I'm on my way. Dana, you have the bridge." Lou got to the lab quickly. He knew from Tavala's tone that they had found something.

"What was on those discs?" he asked, walking into the lab. Tavala gave him a confused look. Lou could see disquiet in Lori and Gwen's eyes.

"Look for your self, Captain," Lori said, slipping a disc into the viewer.

Lou was amazed. He was looking at the Hudson's crew in a mad panic. They were running for the shuttles like the devil was after them. Lou closed his mouth and looked away from the viewer.

"What caused that? I didn't see anything like an emergency."

"The log from engineering indicated that one of the ship's engines had exploded," Gwen said.

"That's impossible! There's no damage to the ship," he said.

"That's true, Captain," Lori said. "But all the people of my team had the illusion that we had returned to the Gemini too."

"Someone, or something, is using our minds against us, sir," Tavala said, in a shaky voice. "That must have been what happened to the Hudson's crew."

"It must be Spata," Lori said. "That's the only answer, Captain."

"Is there anything we can do to block this mind control, Gwen?" Lou asked.

"I don't know what, Captain. We don't know the potential of Spata's machine or even if it was the cause of these two events. Without more data, I can't say."

"If we can determine what happened to Crider, we might have some idea of how it works," Tavala said.

"I'll go down and investigate, Captain," Lori said.

"No," Lou said, emphatically.

Dana went to Lou when he returned to the bridge.

"Something just occurred to me, Captain. People were affected by something on the Hudson and the planet. But only our sensors seem to be affected by it." It was true, he thought. No one on the Gemini had experienced any illusion. He turned to the intercom.

"Lori, Tavala, come to the readyroom," Lou said, and turned back to Dana. "Come on, I think you may have something. Adam, you have the bridge.

In the readyroom, Dana told them what she had told Lou.

"Any idea why only our sensors are affected, Tavala?" Lou asked.

"I can only assume it's our distance from the planet, sir. Our orbit is higher then the Hudson's." Lou nodded.

"That means Spata's machine is limited in range, Captain," Lori said. "It can only brush our sensors. But that's enough to keep us from finding out anything."

"Could it be that the sensors on the Hudson are giving true readings?" Lou asked.

"That's an intriguing idea, sir," Tavala said. "But one that's worth checking out."

"Good," Lou said.

"But I'm not going to the Hudson alone," Tavala said. Lou had to smile at that.

"Lori, get a team together and take Tavala to the Hudson. Let's see if we can't start solving this mystery."

"Remember, concentrate on what you're doing," Gwen said, giving the only advice she could to the team. "It might help you to hold onto reality." She watched the shuttle leave from the enclosure at the rear of the bay. It was bizarre to Tavala walking through this huge ship and seeing no people, except those that had come with her. They moved quickly to the elevator and up to the bridge. Staying close together made them feel safer.

Tavala went to the sensor array and began taking readings, noting the captain had been right. It took some minutes to run the data and recheck it. Now she had a more complete picture than the Gemini's sensors had shown.

"Come on, Lori," Tavala said. "I have what we came for. Let's get off this ghost ship."

They stepped out of the elevator and walked quickly toward the hangar deck. But something wasn't right!

They couldn't find their way back. The passageway seemed to turn and branch, making them feel they were getting nowhere.
They passed nothing familiar, and Tavala had an idea. She stopped and turned to Lori, noting the expressions of alarm on each of the team.

"We never left the bridge, Lori," Tavala said. "This is an illusion. Everybody picture in your mind that you're still on the bridge." They all closed their eyes and focused on what she had said. When they opened their eyes, they were on the bridge. Tavala looked at Lori.

"We're going to have to make a strong effort to focus on where we're going," Tavala said. "If we don't, then some illusion is going to fill our minds." Lori turned to face the team.

"All right, people, you heard Tavala. Now let's really get off this spooky ship," Lori said. She was more than ready to go. They had no trouble getting to the hangar bay, and all felt an easing of tension as they boarded the shuttle.

Tavala was leaning forward, her hands clasped together on the table. The others were taking their seats.

"Let's have your report, Tavala," Lou said, leaning back in his chair.

"I counted forty-three human life forms around the shuttles, Captain. I know the Hudson's crew is forty-two, so the other has to be Crider."

"What's blocking our sensors?" Dana asked.

"An illusion. But the beam that produces it is quite weak," Tavala replied.

"Meaning what?" Lori asked. "We couldn't see those people when we were there."

"It can't affect us in orbit," Tavala explained. "But it's impossible to pinpoint the beam's location from here. If you want to find its source, Captain, it's got to be done on the planet."

"How was Crider able to disappear?" Dana asked.

"He didn't," Tavala replied. "Your mind was made to believe he had. It's quite likely all of you disappeared to him."

"But by concentrating, you were able to overcome the illusion?" Gwen asked.

"Yes," Tavala replied. "How we were able to experience the same illusion, I have no idea."

"Could Spata's machine be the cause of these illusions?" Ross asked.

"I don't think there's any doubt now," Lou answered.

"How do we locate it?" Charles asked. "Even on the surface you're going to need some way to detect it."

"I believe I can modify a communicator, Captain," Tavala said. "With Charles' help, one can be modified for that one frequency."

"Then let's get to work," Lou said. "We not only have to find that machine, we have to shut it down."

"What about Spata?" Dana asked.

"If we find him, we bring him back," Lou replied.

Lou had been anxious to get started. Tavala had told him it would take some hours for her modification. Gwen came on the bridge and stopped by Lou.

"Captain, I've been going over some of the data Tavala brought back," Gwen said. "I found something disturbing. I thought you needed to know before you send anyone down."

"What is it, Gwen."

"From what I've determined, the closer one gets to the source of the beam the more disruptive it will become to their mind. It may be impossible not to have an illusion, or become comatose."

"Any suggestions, Gwen?" She nodded.

"But I need time to test it." Lou didn't want to wait any longer than necessary, but knew Tavala wouldn't be finished for another couple of hours.

"How much time do you need?" Lou asked.

"Less than two hours, Captain. I'm going to ask Lori and a couple of her people to volunteer."

"Okay, Gwen, you got two hours. Let me know the results when you're finished."

Lori was glad to help and asked two of her people to volunteer. Gwen explained what she had in mind as she gave each of them an injection and sent them to the Hudson. They returned reporting success.

"I have the results, Captain," Gwen said, into the intercom.

"I'm on my way, Gwen."

Lori and her two volunteers were waiting in sickbay when Lou came in.

"Okay, Gwen, tell me about your test and its results."

"Every time a person has been affected by an illusion, they've been under stress," Gwen explained. "I gave Lori and these two volunteers an injection of tranquilizer and sent them to the Hudson. They were there for almost an hour and experienced no illusion, Captain." He gave her a dubious look.

"You're saying that a relaxed person is less susceptible to that machine?" Lou asked.

"That appears to be the case, Captain."

"No matter how close they get to it?" Gwen hesitated.

"I believe so, Captain," Gwen replied. "With a strong enough dose, I see no reason it shouldn't work." Lou rubbed his cheek.

"You don't sound sure, Gwen."

"I can't be, Captain. I don't know how that damned machine works. All I've done is cut the risk somewhat." Lou turned to Lori clasping his hands behind his back.

"What do you think, Lori?" Lou asked.

"It worked on the Hudson, sir" she replied. "We're willing to try it on the planet." Lou thought it over, and knew there was risk in any mission, and there was the Hudson's crew to consider. There was no telling what Spata might be subjecting them to.

"Okay, Lori. I'll have Tavala meet you in the hangar bay."

"I think Tavala should remain here, Captain. There's no need to risk more people," Lori said.

"She's the only one who knows how to work the modified communicator," Lou argued.

"She can give me a crash course," Lori said, stubbornly. Lou conceded.

"Very well. But I want you to stay in continuous contact with the bridge. Understood?" Lori nodded.

"Yes, sir."

Lori quickly mastered the modified communicator as Tavala explained its function. As soon as the shuttle landed, Lori was out of the cockpit standing before her four volunteers.

"Inject yourself," she said, pressing the injector against her arm. They moved out of the shuttle and Lori took out her communicator.

"We're ready, Captain."

"Proceed," Lou said. Lori lifted the sensor, activated it, and began scanning. It didn't take long before she had a strong bearing. Once she had a fix, they moved away from the shuttle.

The device was leading them to the machine. Things began to go awry. Two of her team vanished.

"Two of my team just vanished, Captain."

"Take your second injection," Lou ordered. The disappearance of her people unnerved Lori, but she obeyed the order. They went on along the path the sensor was showing.

"Captain, there's a cave about twenty yards ahead of us. The sensor is indicating that's where the beam is located," Lori reported. "We're moving on –" Lori's voice was abruptly stilled. Lou was out of his seat standing beside Ross.

"What happened?"

"Unknown, sir. Her channel is open but she's not responding." Lou stepped over to Tavala's sensor panel.

"Do you still have them?"

"Yes, sir. All five just stopped moving."

"Can you show me where that cave Lori spoke about is?"

"It would be about here, Captain," Tavala said, pointing to the screen. Lou now faced a dilemma. He didn't like losing people, but would have to risk others if he wanted to save the people on the planet. He quickly made up his mind.

"I'm going down."

"Captain, I can't –" He gave Dana a hard look.

"Don't argue, Dana. I'm leaving you in command," Lou said, sternly.

"Yes, sir."

"If I won't risk my ass, how can I ask anyone else to. Understood, Dana?"

"Yes, sir. He turned to the intercom.

"Sickbay."

"Yes, Captain?"

"Meet me in the hangar bay, Gwen. Bring a couple of stiff doses of tranquilizer."

"I'll be right there, Captain."

Gwen was waiting when Lou arrived in the bay.

"Have you ever given yourself an injection, Captain?"

"No."

"It's quite simple." She showed him the procedure.

"Thanks, Gwen," he said, slipping the injectors into his shirt pocket.

Lou entered the shuttle and took the pilot's seat as the hatch closed. He took the shuttle down in a steep descent. It wasn't long before he saw the other shuttle and landed beside it.

The hatch was opening as he went back and began concentrating on why he was here. He decided to wait until he was closer to the machine before using the tranquilizer. He walked quickly along the path the security team had taken, keeping his mind on Lori.

Strange images began to invade his mind, and he pressed an injector against his arm. The effect was almost immediate, and he felt at ease. He lifted his communicator.

"I've taken the first injection, Dana, and it's working." He went on until he saw Lori and the other team members lying on the ground.

"I found them, Dana." Lou went down on one knee and pressed his fingers to each of their necks. They were unconscious with steady pulses. He looked around for the cave and saw it. He stood and walked toward it, stopping just outside. He started to use the second injection, but changed his mind, deciding it was too soon after the first one.

"I'm going into the cave," Lou reported. He walked cautiously into the dimly lit cave. A huge dragon confronted him, and he recalled reading a story about dragons to Trisha. When he thought of that, the dragon shot flame at him. Lou moved into the flame and the dragon vanished.

The light was brighter when he stepped into a large cavern. There were three large electronic consoles against one of the walls powered by a small nuke. Lou was sitting in the shuttle with a strong urge to flee. Lou forced his mind back to reality. He went to the consoles and searched for a way to shut them down. He quickly found the power switch and reversed it. He breathed a sigh of relief. This had been easier than he had anticipated. He looked around the cavern and saw the body of a man lying beside a table.

He went over and looked down at what was left. Lou wondered if he was looking at the body of Gamel Spata.

He came out of the cave lifting the communicator.

"Dana."

"Yes, Captain?"

"The machine has been deactivated. Lori and her team are unconscious. Send Gwen down to tend to them."

"On it, Captain." He went back to Lori and saw she was coming around.

Lou knelt and slipped his arm under her shoulders and lifted her to a sitting position. She lifted a hand to her head as the other two began regaining consciousness.

"Can you tell me what happened, Lori?" She opened her eyes, saw who was holding her, and whipped her arms around his neck. She pressed her face against him. This surprised Lou, but he didn't mind.

"It's all right, Lori. I shut the machine down." He spoke in a soothing tone as he rubbed her back.

"Can you tell me what happened?"

"It was like having my mind slowly turned off, Captain," Lori replied, distressed. It was a few minutes before she took her arms from around his neck. Lou helped her to her feet as a shuttle landed some yards away. He helped her over to where Gwen put an arm around her and helped her into the shuttle. Gwen's assistant helped the security man as the woman made it slowly on her own. He saw the other two security people coming toward the shuttle supporting each other. They were pale but appeared to be all right.

Gwen finished her examinations and turned to Lou.

"They're going to be fine, Captain." He felt relieved and his communicator beeped.

"Yes?"

"I've been in contact with the Hudson's captain," Ross said. "They're okay, except for nightmares. And Crider is with them, Captain."

"That's good to hear, Ross. Tell them to return to their ship and prepare for departure." Lou lowered his communicator and looked at Gwen.

"I found something I want you to take a look at."

"Lead the way, Captain." They went to the cave where Lou pointed to the body. Gwen knelt and took a few minutes to examine it. She stood and turned to Lou.

"Whoever it is has been dead at least a year. You think it might be Spata, Captain?"

"We can't be certain until you run a DNA test, Gwen."

"I'll send a medical team down to get the body," she said, as they walked from the cavern.

Lou and his officers sat in the readyroom with the Hudson's captain.

"What are we going to do about that mind-busting machine, Captain Tanner?" Captain Lawrence asked. Before Lou could respond, the intercom sounded.

"Captain," Lou said.

"That weird frequency has come back on line, sir," said a bridge technician.

"Inform the Hudson to move farther from the planet," Lou said.

"Captain, my people suffered hell on that planet," Lawrence said. "That machine done the most bizarre things to their minds. And now the goddamned thing is operating after you shut it down. What can we do?"

"Any explanation, Tavala?" Lou asked.

"None at present, Captain. But this reactivation is creepy." Lou leaned forward, resting his arms on the table.

"We've got to destroy that machine," Lou said.

"How, Captain?" Dana asked. "Now that it's functioning again, we can't risk taking the ship close enough to use the onboard weapons."

"We've got to determine how that machine reactivated itself," Lou said.

"Maybe Spata hid out," Dana said. "And he turned it back on." Lou nodded and looked at Gwen.

"Have you made an ID on that corpse, Gwen?"

"No, Captain. He's an unknown. If it had been Spata, the ID would have been easy."

"Then Spata must be down there," Lori said.

"Then why can't our sensors detect him?" Tavala asked.

"Because he isn't down there," Lawrence replied. "Some of the tests we were able to complete indicated that he built those machines with very advanced artificial intelligence, composed from his own brain."

"Oh, God!" Tavala exclaimed. "If that's true, Captain, we won't be able to use the same tactics twice." Lou frowned.

"That puts us back to square one, Lou said, annoyed.

"I would say we're a couple of squares behind number one," Dana said. "We're facing a totally different situation now, Captain." The intercom sounded again.

"Captain."

"Sir, that frequency is rapidly increasing in power," the tech reported.

"It's reaching out for us, Captain," Tavala said, nervously.

"Take the ship into a higher orbit," Lou ordered the bridge. "And tell the Hudson to do the same. Come on, Dana, we're needed on the bridge."

Tavala was at her console when she saw something appear on a monitor she couldn't believe. She stared wide-eyed as the signal stabilized.

"Captain," she said, a little too loudly. "You better get Gwen up here to verify what I'm seeing."

"Sickbay."

"Yes, Captain?"

"Come to the bridge, Gwen." He and Dana went over to Tavala.

"I need verification of this reading, Sir," Tavala said. Dana glanced at Lou after they saw the monitor. What they saw made no sense to them.

Marge came on the bridge and over to Lou.

"What is it, Captain?"

"Take a look at this monitor," Tavala said. "Tell me what I'm reading is wrong. Marge studied the pattern on the monitor for a moment.

"Christ!" she exclaimed, looking away from the monitor to Lou. "Captain, we really have a problem now."

"What is it, Gwen?" Lou asked.

"This sine wave," she replied, pointing to the monitor. "It's a human mind functioning on a conscious level." Lou didn't quite understand what Gwen had said.

"What does that mean?" Dana asked.

"Damnit!" Lou exclaimed, harshly. "It means, Dana, that Spata has managed to transfer his mind into that machine."

"How far can he project power that could prove a danger to us?" Dana asked, apprehensive.

"Boosted by that machine, there's no way to tell," Tavala replied. It was going to take the resources of both ships to find a way to stop Spata. But no one had any idea of how it could be accomplished. Two things they all agreed on was that the machine had become an even more dangerous adversary, and it had to be destroyed. Dana had been considering an idea, wondered if it might work.

"Tavala, is there a way we could rig a shuttle to self destruct?" Tavala glanced over her shoulder.

"What do you mean, Dana?"

"We could guide it down by remote piloting and straight into that cave. But will the explosion be enough to destroy that machine?" Tavala thought for a few seconds and nodded.

"It can be done," Tavala replied. "But we can't be certain the machine won't affect the guidance system. But it's worth a try."

"Let's go talk to the captain," Dana said. "Adam, you have the bridge."

They stopped before Lou's quarters and Tavala pressed the door signal.

"Enter." They went in and faced Lou.

"Captain, we have an idea that might solve our problem," Dana said. "We would like your opinion about it." She told him about the plan to use the shuttle.

"It sounds good to me. It's more than anyone else has come up with. Contact Captain Lawrence. He should be able to help with this."

A short time later, Lawrence and his Chief Science Officer John Handley stepped from the shuttle. Lou, Dana, and Tavala were waiting to meet them. They went to the readyroom where Charles and Lori were. Once seated, Lawrence began.

"Captain Tanner, what your people propose may be our only chance to destroy that machine."

"I only hope it works," Lou said. "What can you do to help?"

"On the Hudson, we have about a hundred pounds of tritex explosive," Handley said. "And a prototype guidance system that can only be activated by voice command. My voice." Tavala looked Lou with hope.

"Captain, that might prevent any interference with the shuttle's flight," Tavala said. "We can transfer a chip of his voice into the remote flight control unit."

"I want to do the piloting, sir," Lori said. "I got a little score to settle." Lou nodded.

"The job's yours," he said.

"I suggest we move the ships into a higher orbit," Lawrence said. "We have to be far enough from that planet so the machine can't possibly affect us."

"Maybe we can fool it into believing we left," Dana said. "It might give us some advantage."

"I agree," Lou said. "We'll move the ships into a stationary orbit about a quarter of the planet's diameter. Now let's get this mission underway."

Both ships took up their new positions. Techs from both crews worked feverishly turning a shuttle into a missile. Lou kept noting that Lori had been giving him odd looks for the past couple of days. She definitely had something on her mind, but until she said something, there was nothing he could do. He had an urgent mission to accomplish.

In two days the shuttle had been stripped except for what would be necessary for its flight. It seemed they now had the means to destroy the machine along with Spata's mind. Lori sat at the remote piloting station on the bridge, and had taken the shuttle out of the bay and began maneuvering it. She dropped it in a shallow dive through the atmosphere. She kept her eyes on the monitor looking at what the shuttle's forward camera was seeing. She skimmed it along just high enough above the surface to avoid hitting anything.

The black mouth of the cave appeared on the monitor. Lori pushed the shuttle to its top speed. About a quarter of a mile from the cave, the shuttle erupted in a ball of boiling orange flame. Lori turned to Lou. Her eyes wide with shock and her mouth open.

"Goddamnit! He knew!" Lou exclaimed, slamming his hand on the armrest.

"I wonder if he knew what we were doing all along?" Tavala asked, shaking her head. Lou ran his hand through his hair wondering what they could do now? They had used the only viable option they had, and it had failed. The only thing that could be done now was bring in a heavy cruiser and have it blast the hell out of that cave from orbit. Lou pressed the intercom.

"Engineering."

"Yes, Captain?"

"The missile failed, Charles. Let's get the hell away from this planet."

"We're as good as gone, Captain." Lou turned the seat.

"Ross, contact the Hudson. Tell them we're leaving and for them to accompany us."

"Yes, sir."

From the time she had gotten over the shock of the shuttle's sudden destruction, Lori had put her head down on her arms and hadn't lifted it in ten minutes. Lou stepped behind her and gently clasped her shoulder.

"It wasn't your fault, Lori. You done a damn fine job of remote piloting" The intercom sounded.

"Captain."

"We're not going anywhere, Captain," Charles reported. "The Gemini is being slowly pulled down to the planet."

"The Hudson reports the same with her," Ross said. Now they couldn't even run! What was the solution to this damn problem? Lou wondered. He called a conference, inviting Lawrence and Handley to sit in.

"I never believed anything could become so powerful so fast," Tavala said.

"Our main problem is that we're being pulled down," Lou said. "What can we do about it? And how long have we got to do it in?"

"I estimate about twenty-six hours, sir," Tavala said. "Before we're in a fatal position."

"I sent out a report," Captain," Ross said. "But I can't be certain it got through."

"What the hell does the damn thing want?" Handley asked.

"That's what we've got to determine," Lawrence said.

"Tavala, is there anyway to communicate with it?" Lou asked.

"The only thing we have to work with is that sine wave, sir. It never varies, so I see no way to communicate with it."

"What about telepathically?" Dana asked.

"That's much too risky, Dana," Gwen said. "It might take your mind and leave you a vegetable." They came to one consensus: nobody had an idea of how to free the ships from the grip of the monster machine.

Lori had been thinking of trying something. It would be worth the risk if it could free the ships. It would appear harmless enough so that the machine should suspect nothing.
But she would have to talk to Lou first. She would need his personal assistance. The door signal sounded.

"Enter." Lori walked slowly in.

"Captain, I have something in mind that might free the ships," she said, obviously ill at ease. "But I'll need your cooperation."

"I'm interested in any idea that might get us away from here. Tell me about it." She took a deep breath and braced herself.

"The tranquilizer worked, to a point. I think I know something that will prove better."

"Go on."

"Sex!" Lori blurted out. Lou had no idea of how to respond, so he just stared at her.

"Captain, Spata's mind is in that machine. But psychologically, it's still a man's mind."

"And?"

"It will still be male oriented. And a man's desire for sex can't be turned off."

"I don't understand, Lori."

"Very well, Captain, I'll make it blunt. I have always put my career over everything else," she said, her voice revealing her nervousness. "Now I need your help so I can go down and destroy that machine." She could tell from Lou's expression that her idea still evaded him.

"Is that as clear as you make it?" She regarded him for a moment. She was used to taking risks, but talking to the captain like this was very unsettling. Lori took another deep breath, let it out slowly, and calmed herself.

"Captain, I don't want to die a virgin." Lou stared, wasn't certain of what she was saying.

"I want you to make love to me. I – I haven't had any experience at it." Lou sat speechless. Lori continued.

"Unless I can know that pleasure, I won't be able to convince Spata's mind it wants me." Lou didn't know what to do. Lori realized she was going to have to motivate him. She bent down and kissed him. It was a sudden fiery experience for them both. Lou wasn't thinking, he was reacting to her passion and his loneliness.

Later, Lou called a special assembly. He let Lori tell them about her plan.

"So if I can get Spata's mind concentrated on me, the ships might be able to break free," she concluded. The readyroom was filled with an awkward silence. They knew she was offering to give her life to save them. Dana had a strong suspicion that Lori had just had her first sexual encounter. And was equally certain that it had been with the captain.

"Any comments?" Lou asked. They all sat quiet.

"What about you, Gwen?" She raised her eyes to meet Lou's.

"I had been thinking along that line, Captain. But I thought we were dealing with a machine. Lori's plan makes sense."

"Do you have something that can stimulate Lori's mind so that her conscious will be sexually oriented?" Lou asked. Gwen raised a finger to her lower lip and rubbed.

"I believe so, Captain."

"Then let's get Lori's plan in motion," Lou said.

Lori swallowed hard when she landed the shuttle. She had gotten a lot closer to the cave than she thought she would That meant the machine could sense when something was dangerous. Lori went through the shuttle to the open hatch, gave herself an injection, and proceeded with her mission.

As she walked toward the cave, she kept thinking of how wonderful it had been with the captain. She was hoping this would be the only thought the machine would be able to sense. Lori walked boldly into the cave, and on into the cavern where the machine sat. She faced the machine, with the thought of disappointment that Lou wasn't here to fulfill her desire, her want.

She felt Spata's mind enter hers. Her sexual fantasy was so real she almost lost herself in it. But she began to concentrate as she slowly moved her hand to her waist and lifted her blouse. Lori's hand closed around the weapon.

Spata's mind was far too occupied with her fantasy to sense the danger she posed. She forced her eyes open, raised the weapon and squeezed the trigger. The blue pulses flashed and exploded one of the consoles. Lori felt Spata's sudden fear, followed by vicious hate. She fired at the second unit. It, too, exploded in flame and smoke. Just as she fired at the third, she began losing consciousness. But she could feel Spata's mind dying. Her last thought was that he had killed her.

"It had been over an hour since Lori had left. There had been no contact with her, and Lou wasn't waiting any longer.

"Dana, you have the bridge. I'm going after Lori." She could see the subtle difference in Lou, and it confirmed her suspicion about Lori and him. She wasn't about to try and stop him.

"Yes, sir."

Lou pushed the shuttle through the atmosphere and past safety limits. He sat it down near Lori's shuttle. He leaped out before the hatch had fully opened, and raced for the cave. He found her lying on the ground. The cavern was filled with a smothering brown smoke and the crackling of circuits burning out.

He had to keep waving his hand in front of his face to keep smoke from his face. He picked Lori up and hurried back outside. There came a heavy explosion from the cave that knocked Lou down. He scrambled back to Lori and checked her pulse. It was slow and steady. He carried her to the shuttle, strapped her in, and lifted off. He had to get her to sickbay quickly.

"I'm worried about her, Captain," Gwen said, voicing her concern. "Lori's been in a coma for two days, and there's nothing I can do."

"She's a tough woman, Gwen. I believe she'll be all right." But he was worried too. She had done a good job on Spata and his machine. But what had he done to her?

The Gemini and Hudson were headed home. On the third day, Lori began to revive. The intercom sounded.

"Captain."

"You better come to sickbay, Captain," Gwen said.

"I'm on my way. Dana, you have the bridge." Dana smiled to herself. She had never known anyone like Lou, and knew she would serve under his command again, if asked.

Lou stepped off the lift and proceeded at a quick pace. When he went into sickbay, he saw Lori was sitting up. He felt greatly relieved as he went to her.

"I'm certainly glad to see you're up." Lori motioned for him to bend down. When he did, she slipped her arms around his neck and softly pressed her lips to his. After that kiss, Lou was confused.

"Thank you very much, Captain," Lori said, keeping her arms around his neck. He glanced at Gwen, and saw she was having a hard time to keep from smiling. Lou looked back at Lori.

"Thanks for what?"

"For showing me there's more to life than a career, and for one hell of a sexual fantasy." Lou took her arms from around his neck, stood, and ran his hand through his hair; Lori took hold of his hand.

"Well I am the captain. I have to be there when my crew needs me." He looked at Gwen.

"I expect this to be kept confidential, Gwen." She smiled at him.

"Of course, Captain. I may need your personal attention before we get back to Earth."

ENTITY

He stood staring at her, immobile, sitting stoop shouldered on the bed. It seemed impossible, but there she was. Dr. Boyd put his glasses back over his eyes and looked at Dr. Carson.

"She was in this condition when they found her?" Carson nodded, regarding him with a troubled look.

"I don't ever recall having seen anyone in such a deep catatonic state. What could have produced such a state, Dr. Boyd?" Boyd looked at the unmoving woman on the bed.

"Whatever it was must have been sudden and traumatic," Boyd replied. "Tell me about her." They turned away from the door and began walking along the corridor.

"Dr. Karen Hersh, along with four others, were excavating ruins on Rigel Four," Carson began. "When the supply ship returned three weeks ago, they found her in her present state. There was no trace of the others."

"That's it?" Boyd asked, surprised at the scant data.

"That's all we know at present," Carson replied, glancing at him.

"And she hasn't responded to therapy?" Carson shook his head.

"She hasn't shown any reaction to therapy. That's why I decided to consult you, Dr. Boyd. You have a reputation for being able to penetrate the minds of catatonic patients through your hypnotic technique. Only if you succeed will we learn what happened to her and her missing companions."

For the past hour, Boyd had tried to get into Karen Hersh's mind. His method had been without results. She sat on the divan, laconic, staring with dull, empty gray eyes. She had light blonde hair pulled back in a ponytail. Under normal conditions, she would be an attractive woman. But without makeup and enfolded in the dull brown hospital robe, she looked very plain.

Boyd finished his notes and pushed his glasses up on his forehead. He placed his elbows on the desk and rubbed his face. He didn't know what more he could do for her.

"Are you really interested in what I have to say, Doctor?" The abrupt sound of her voice in the quiet office caused Boyd to start violently. He turned his face to her.

Karen Hersh was no longer the plain woman of a few minutes ago. She was beautiful. Her hair had the sheen of silk and hung loosely to her shoulders. Her lips were red and alluring, her face a blush of life, and her eyes seemed to glow. He was at a loss to explain her transition.

"Very much," Boyd replied, puzzled. "I'm very interested to learn what happened on Rigel Four, Dr. Hersh." She smiled.

"Then I must begin with our arrival. The transport Star Quest went into orbit around Rigel Four and soon had us disembarked. Our team consisted of Nigel King, Larry McMasters, Donna Wilson, James Hord and myself. An engineering unit had constructed our base, and it was very comfortable. It was air conditioned naturally, and our private quarters were delightfully furnished. Once we settled in, and our supplies stored, the Star Quest left Orbit and we were isolated.

"The next day, we began our dig. Nigel had a survey map and showed us where to start. Believe me, working in that heat was anything but comfortable. The temperature was such that it almost seemed to broil you in your own perspiration.

"Eight days after we began, we had cleared the front of a lone structure. It stood about fifteen meters tall and was constructed from what appeared to be black and white marble. The front was very ornamental, carved with strange alphabetical symbols. Nigel worked day and night to decipher them. But it wasn't until Donna discovered another panel of symbols on the side of the chamber that he had the key. It proved decisive to his success.

"Nigel then became very evasive, and wouldn't tell us anything about what he had translated. He abruptly had us move our dig away from the chamber. After that, Nigel seldom spoke to any of us. We knew he was studying something intensively, but didn't know what it was.

"As we excavated more ruins, there seemed to be a consistent pattern to the inscriptions on them. We couldn't translate them and Nigel wasn't talking. He was the philologist we were archeologists.

"We saw less and less of Nigel. Not only wasn't he speaking to us, he seemed to be deliberately avoiding us and we had no idea why. It was James who seemed to have found the answer when he discovered the first chamber had been opened. It could only have been Nigel who had opened it, but we couldn't locate him. He just wasn't to be found. There was nowhere for him to go on that desert world.

"It was Donna, reading Nigel's notes, that gave us a bit more of the puzzle, but its significance was lost on us.
She gave me the notebook and I read the translation. It was from the first chamber and was the inscription over the door. It read: This is the eternal tomb of Kohemteek, master of evil. If ever freed, he will consume all life.

"I found this rather curious, for we had learned from the ruins that this had been a highly scientific civilization. But what I had just read sounded like an ancient curse. We had found no trace of Nigel, and never saw him again.

"We kept our dig advancing and discovered even more inexplicable clues. All the ruins we had so far excavated seemed to form a circle around that chamber. It made no sense to us. I don't know why Larry began reading Nigel's notes, but he found the symbol Kohemteek was on all the pillars surrounding the opened chamber. It seemed this advanced civilization had been obsessed with Kohemteek.

"Then we discovered some of their historical records. It took all of us working together three painstaking days to translate them using the notes Nigel had worked out. Those records told us that Kohemteek had been a great leader who had ruled with benevolence and justice. This was a master of evil?

"The record then related the fall of a great meteorite. Kohemteek had personally went to find it. When he returned, he was a completely different person; his personality had been altered. He became a brutal despot, enslaving and murdering his people. He was eventually overthrown in a violent, bloody revolution. Kohemteek was captured and entombed in the first structure we had uncovered. I thought then I knew what was meant by 'he will consume all life.' We didn't believe the story. It sounded more like legend than reality.

"It was Larry who seemed to prove the validity about a meteorite altering personality. At least, that was what I thought at first. We were excavating a large ruin when we discovered it had an underground room. It took five days of hard work to break into it.
You can imagine our surprise when we realized that complex of ruins had been built over a meteorite. We felt it must be the one referred to in the altering of Kohemteek's personality.

"Larry was the only one who went down into the room. He looked it over, described it along with giving its dimensions.

But we had to leave it to someone with the expertise to study it. After that, Larry began to change. He had been the most outgoing person among us.

He became moody, irritable, and finally unapproachable. So we just left him alone. He kept to himself, sullen and distant. I hadn't the faintest idea what he might be going through. I noticed his behavior was the same that Nigel had displayed, but Nigel hadn't been near that meteorite. We couldn't make any sense of what was happening.

"We found more records that told of Kohemteek's long reign as a benevolent ruler. He had been the one who had turned these people into a race of scientific geniuses. Then came the most stunning discovery of all. Kohemteek wasn't a native of the planet. The people had no idea where he came from but his appearance had been prophesied. There was no record of his past, and if our translations were correct, he was believed to be immortal. Again, that seemed more like myth than reality to us.

"For the next few days, we excavated no ruins with his name on them. This only reinforced our belief that he was only a mythical character. Then we discovered some much older records and these made no mention of Kohemteek, but Koamtour. The prefix Ko-, in their language, referred to leaders, Doctor.

"Koamtour, though much more ancient, seemed to be a nonentity. His name was in the records, but always in an isolated way. It seemed Koamtour had been their leader, but he built nothing and had no association with people. It was very confusing for us.

"A week later, James found a lone record in what we assumed to be a religious vault. It turned out to be quite illuminating. Now we learned that Koamtour wasn't a person but a prophecy of a fuyure ruler. A great leader who would raise their civilization to great heights, bring them scientific enlightenment, and glorify their quest for knowledge. This future ruler would be Kohemteek. That one record began to change our thinking about him being a mythological person.

"We became so wrapped up in our work that it must have been a week before we realized Larry had vanished. We had no idea what had happened to Nigel, and now the same could be said for Larry. The planet is nothing but desert, Doctor. There was no possible place they could have gone. We weren't able to search very far from the base because if one lost sight of it, there was no landmarks to guide you back.

If you went out too far, you were surrounded by desert in every direction all the way to the horizon. It could give you no reference point making it easy to become disoriented. We assumed this must have been what happened to Nigel and Larry.

That provided an explanation for their disappearance. It was then I began having disturbing dreams. Dreams that tormented my mind while I slept, and couldn't recall on waking.

"Then came the night of the sandstorm. I'll never forget the angry howl of that wind. We were sitting with drinks discussing the day's dig. James' head suddenly snapped backward, dropped his drink, and his hands went back as though he was trying to grapple with something. Donna and I lept to our feet dropping our drinks. At first, I thought he was having some sort of seizure because we could see nothing behind him. We were both very frightened because we had no idea what we could do to help him. James began to scream horribly. And before our eyes he faded from sight. We could still hear him screaming, but it seemed distant as though he was in a cave.

"Donna was jerked around and her clothing ripped to shreds like she was being attacked with invisible claws. Now I watched her struggling against empty air just as James had done. I began to see a vague milky outline in front of Donna and saw what she was fighting Whatever it was turned to me. The last memory I have is of those horrible orange, reptilian eyes glaring hungrily at me." She leaned back and regarded Boyd for a moment.

"Well, Doctor, that's what happened on Rigel Four. The story's complete, except for one detail." Karen Hersh stood and walked to the desk.

Carson opened the door and stuck his head in and found the office empty. He pulled the door shut and turned to the orderly sitting by the door looking at a magazine.

"Has Miss Hersh been returned to her room?" Carson asked. The orderly put down the magazine and stood with a puzzled look.

"No, Doctor. She's still with Dr. Boyd," he replied, nodding at the door. Carson cocked an eyebrow and shook his head.

"There's no one in the office," Carson said. The orderly got a dubious look.

"That's impossible. I've been here since I brought her down. And no one has came out."

Carson turned the knob and pushed the door open. The orderly looked around the office, noting there were no other doors or window. He stepped into the office.

"What the hell is going on?" he asked. He turned completely around looking into every corner of the room. This didn't make sense! He felt a threatening presence and without warning his clothes were suddenly shredded as if by invisible claws.

SUDDEN IMPACT

There had been no warning. The astronomers had missed it just as they had missed others. A chunk of rock about a half a mile wide lit up the southwest blazing a path to Earth at 2:53 A.M. local time, October 18. It impacted in Southern California west of the Colorado River, instantly vaporizing the town of Blyth. The shockwave sent massive earthquakes spreading throughout the world and turned the Cascade Mountains into active volcanoes. Tsunamis ravaged the coastal areas and demolished the West Coast. No one can ever know how many people died in the week following the impact; no one cared. Everyone was busy just trying to stay alive and out of danger. The loss of agriculture from the West Coast quickly made itself felt. But even it hadn't, there was no intact transportation system left.

Dust thrown up by the impact, combined with the volcanic ash, spread through the atmosphere turning the Earth dark, cold, and in perpetual dusk. The sun appeared only as a dim disk in the sky. As food became scarce, starvation pushed people into riots governments was powerless to control. Eventually, all governments collapsed under their inability to cope with a catastrophe of such magnitude.

Lyle Gardner was a survivor. He had just entered a small town to continue his full time occupation of staying alive. Strapped around his waist was a 9 mm automatic and Bowie knife. He carried a Ruger M77, 7.62-mm rifle. He was prepared to use it as he cautiously approached a small grocery store. When he saw movement inside, his survival instinct kicked in without him being conscious of it. In the dim light, it was hard to see anything clearly from a distance, and all he could make out was a shape moving in the grocery. He moved quickly to the door and peered into the deeper darkness. His eyes widened as he saw fully stocked shelves and wondered how anyone could have missed this place. Noise quickly recalled his attention.

He moved silently between the shelves to where the noise was and wasn't surprised to see he was behind the person.
The person turned, saw him, and dropped in a dead faint. It was a woman! Lyle put the rifle down and slipped his arm under her shoulders and lifted her from the floor. He patted her cheek and she started coming around. Even in the dark, he saw the fear in her eyes when she opened them.

"It's all right," Lyle said, reassuringly. "I'm not going to hurt you." She stared at him like a trapped animal.

"My name is Lyle Gardner. What's your name?" The question, and his tone, seemed to break her tension.

"Susan," she replied. "Susan Pell." He stood and helped her to her feet.

"Sorry I frightened you." An annoyed look flashed across her face.

"You scared the shit out of me! Lyle smiled and glanced around.

"Let's eat," he said. "I'm starved."

After eating, they filled their packs with canned goods and cached the rest. They had only gone a short distance when it began to rain. It quickly turned to freezing rain and it got colder. They found shelter in a tall building. Entering, Lyle took a flashlight from his pocket, shook it vigorously, and turned the beam along the dark corridor. They went to a gray metal door. Lyle pushed it open and turned the light down the metal stairs.

"This will do," Lyle said, and started down the stairs with Susan following. Their footsteps drummed on the steps as they moved into the basement. He handed her the flashlight and removed the pack from his shoulder, took out a small camp stove and lantern that he lit. He took the flashlight back and stuck it in his coat pocket and regarded Susan for a moment.

"We'll be safe here," Lyle said. "No one can see us from the outside." She sat on a blanket with her legs pulled up, her arms around them, resting her chin on her knees. She looked at a man with black hair and beard, brown eyes, and a solid build. He saw a woman with short, light brown hair and eyes. Lyle thought the dark stains on her forehead and cheeks made her look like a farm girl. She was as tall as he was with a slim figure.

They sat close to the stove in silence warming themselves.

"I used to teach history in college before civilization got knocked apart," Lyle said, breaking the silence. "What did you do?" She sat silent for a moment.

"I was in med school. Have you any family?" The sad, painful that came to him had an immediate effect on her.

"I had a wife and son. They were visiting her mother in California at the time of the impact." She averted her eyes.

"I'm sorry. I guess I was lucky in not having anyone." Lyle looked at her and rubbed his beard.

"Would you like to team up, Susan? We can be mutually supportive." She looked back at him and got a weak smile.

"Sounds good. I'm tired of being alone and afraid all the time." He nodded and got to his feet. She looked up at him, puzzled.

"Where are you going?" He nodded toward the stairs.

"To make certain we're alone, and find someway to block the door from this side. I want to get an early start tomorrow." He took the rifle, went up the stairs, and slowly opened the door. Lyle knew he couldn't use the flashlight as he moved carefully along the confines of the dark corridor. The only sounds were the rain and his breathing, with an occasional gust of wind. At the front door, he stopped and pushed it open far enough to look out. The smell of sulphur was strong, as it usually was when it rained. He began to shiver in the cold air, but slipped outside and walked a few paces from the building. There was no sign anyone else was in this small town, so he hurried back inside. When he closed the metal door, he turned on the flashlight and saw the door had a deadbolt. He slid it in place, went downstairs, and found Susan curled up on the blanket asleep. He smiled and unrolled his sleeping bag.

Leaving the building next morning, the sky was its usual gray overcast with the sun just visible. They fastened their jackets against the cold and moved quietly through the town. They saw some buildings had burned while others had been reduced to rubble by earthquakes. Once away from the town, Lyle felt better. He felt there were too many places in a town you could be ambushed from. He knew the same rule went for the countryside, but there he had room to maneuver.

They had been walking for about two hours when Susan looked at him.

"Is all you do travel around looking for food?" He glanced at her and smiled.

"I used to." This brought a baffled expression to her.

"I don't understand." Lyle shrugged.

"When I get the rare chance to talk to people, I pick up information.
I've' heard of a place in Illinois where a group of people are trying to get organized. That's where I'm headed." She gave him a wary look.

"Are you certain it's where you want to go?" He nodded.

"I've heard about it from more than one person. I decided that's the place where civilization can restart, and I want to be a part of it." He turned a steady gaze on her.

"They'll need teachers and medical people, Susan." She got a thoughtful expression.

"Sounds interesting. And I would like to work again."

A short time later, they heard gunfire. He took Susan by the hand and took them toward a grove of trees that provided cover. He dropped his pack, unsnapped the holster, and handed her his automatic. He quickly showed her how to flip the safety off.

"If I'm not back –" She grabbed his arm and regarded him with a desperate look.

"You've got to come back. We're a team now." Lyle smiled and gave her hand a gentle squeeze.

Leaving her, he crouch walked using trees to cover his path to the shooting. Lyle noted an occasional burst of fire from an automatic weapon. Looking carefully around, he spotted a man with a rifle lying in a prone position behind a log. Shots from other locations, Lyle guessed there were at least two other men. He hid the rifle, took out his knife, and moved stealthily toward the man he could see.

The man fired twice before Lyle closed on him. He stood behind him before he realized Lyle was there. He rolled over leveling his rifle at Lyle, who used the hilt of the knife to knock him out. He moved on to the next position. He wasn't so lucky this time. The man was quickly raising his rifle before Lyle was close. Lyle moved quickly, swinging the knife in an arc and almost taking the man's head off. Lyle stared in disgust as the body stood spurting blood before collapsing. All firing ceased. Lyle guessed the third man had heard his friends stop firing, got spooked, and ran.

Lyle tried looking into the glade the men had been shooting into.

"There's not going to be anymore shooting," Lyle said, loudly.

"Who the hell are you?" asked a harsh voice. This annoyed Lyle.

"The person who saved your ass."

"Why didn't you say so," came the sarcastic reply. Lyle didn't like the man's voice or his attitude. He moved beck to where his rifle was. When he passed where the unconscious man had been, he saw someone had drug him off. He retrieved the rifle and started back to Susan.

When he came from among the trees, she flung her arms around him and embraced him tightly. It had been a long time since he had felt a woman's around him.

"We have to move on," Lyle said. "There's only trouble around here." They stepped from the trees and faced a man with an AK-47 aimed at them. He had sandy hair and cold blue eyes set on a face that expressed the brutality of Hitler's SS. Lyle didn't care for the way he looked at Susan.

"Put the rifle down," he said, in the harsh voice Lyle had heard from the glade. Lyle lowered the rifle till the butt touched the ground then dropped it. The man hadn't noticed the empty holster. Susan stood beside Lyle holding the automatic behind her.

"Why the hell did you but into my business?" he asked, in a threatening tone. "It wasn't any concern of yours."

"I still like to think I'm civilized," Lyle replied. Susan stepped away from him, bringing the automatic up and aiming it at the man's head. He was quick to note the safety was off, as he stared in surprise. He slowly lowered his weapon to the ground and noticed Lyle's knife.

"I've got to get one of those knives," he said, impressed. "I saw the results you got with it. I liked it." Susan didn't relax, never moved the weapon from the position she held it. The man looked at her and smiled.

"Guess I could use a girl friend, too."

"Who are you?" she asked.

"The name's Caine. David Caine. Your boy friend saved me from an ambush I walked into."

"Is coming after him with a gun any way to show gratitude?" she asked, coldly. Lyle gave her a look of respect and noted she never wavered in her aim. Caine shrugged.

"You can't be too careful nowadays," Caine replied. "I see you're aware of that." Lyle picked up his rifle but kept the barrel turned to the ground.

"Lower the weapon, Susan." Her finger flashed to the safety and lowered the hammer into place. The speed of her move surprised Lyle. He noted she continued to hold the weapon with both hands barrel pointed up.

"Who do I think for saving my ass?" Caine asked.

"I'm Lyle Gardner." He didn't mention Susan's name and Caine seemed somewhat hesitant.

"If it's okay, I'll pick up my weapon and be on my way," Caine said, with an evil look. Lyle nodded at the AK-47.

"Go ahead," Lyle said, relieved Caine was leaving. He didn't like David Caine one bit.

As they walked, A belated moan came from Susan.

"Damnit! Why didn't I remember?" Lyle gave her a wondering look.

"Remember what?" She gave him an angry look.

"Caine! I remembered who that bastard is." He still had no idea what she was talking about.

"Who is he?" He saw her breasts rise as she inhaled deeply.

"Before the impact, Caine had been sentenced to death," she replied, in a hard tone. "He had raped, tortured, and murdered two teenage girls. If only I had remembered when I had the gun on him…" She was angry at her memory lapse. Lyle put his hand on her shoulder.

"Let's hope we never cross paths with him again," Lyle said. "I could tell he was a son of a bitch from his eyes." He felt they had come off lucky in their encounter with Caine.

They found a farmhouse and decided to spend the night there. The air was becoming frigid and they needed a warm place to stay. The flashlight penetrated the darkness below the creaky wooden steps as they went into the basement. Turning the light, they saw the place was made of concrete blocks with no windows and old furniture piled along the walls.

After eating, they relaxed in their warm hovel. The yellow-blue flames of the stove danced with every puff of air as Susan moved beside him.

"What are you thinking about?" she asked. He glanced at her with a grim expression.

"I was wondering if the human race is going to make it. After all, an asteroid put an end to the dinosaurs, and they were a more successful species than we've been." She slipped her hand over his.

"If people are trying to get organized, I've got to believe everything will be all right." Lyle looked at her and felt a strong attraction. He got a shadow of a smile.

"You're right. We've got to have hope." She leaned over and kissed him.

"Make love to me, Lyle. I need to feel someone still cares." He pulled her into his arms and pressed his lips to hers.

Just after noon, they stood before a twisted sign that showed they were moving into what used to be Indiana. They followed Interstate 74, detouring around wrecked sections of highway. The earthquakes had churned it into dangerous piles of concrete rubble. Lyle was thinking about his feeling for Susan and recalled the faces of his wife and son. He knew they were dead and that hurt, but it was something he had to live with.

"What did Caine mean about your knife?" Susan asked, intruding on his thoughts. He looked at her with a frown.

"I had to kill a man. The first one I knocked out, the second would have killed me." A rush of anger filled him.

"And I done it for a worthless piece of shit." She regarded him with an understanding.

"You had no way of knowing, Lyle. What's it feel like to kill someone?" Lyle shook his head.

"You can't feel. It's just the way of the world today, and survival is what counts. I don't like killing, but do so when I have to." She got a sympathetic look.

"I understand." She took hold of his hand as they walked on.

"Hold up," a man called. They stopped as a young man came from behind the ruins of an overpass. Lylae didn't feel threatened and kept his rifle across his arm. At first, the man approached cautiously then stopped abruptly.

"I'll be damned!" he exclaimed, loudly. "Professor Gardner." Lyle was puzzled for a moment before he recognized his former student.

"Ron Gould." He had wavy black hair and beard, gray eyes, and a thin frame.

"Who's your companion, Professor?"

"Susan Pell."

"Where you heading?" Ron asked, glancing at Susan.

"I've heard of a place in Illinois where people are trying to get back on their feet. We're on our way to find it." Ron nodded, looking pleased.

"I'm from there," Ron said. "They sent out five scouts to try to find people and send them there."

"How many are there?" Susan asked. Ron shrugged.

"About a hundred or so. But unless we can increase our population we won't be able to survive," Ron said, grimly. "We're in a small town about fifteen miles south of Chicago. Another town, about ten miles west of us, is filled with thugs and criminals. We have plenty of food, medical supplies, and quite a few women. Those people want what we have. We've infiltrated them and know what they're planning." Lyle looked at Susan.

"Still want to go there?" She cocked an eyebrow.

"I won't lie to you," Ron said. "It's only a matter of time before they have enough people to overrun us." Susan looked from Ron to Lyle.

"Sounds like they can use all the help they can get," she said. "After facing down Caine I can face anything."

"Caine? David Caine?" Ron asked, alarmed. Susan told him of their encounter with him. When she finished, Ron shook his head with a grave look.

"From what I've heard, he won't forget you for what he perceives as a humiliation, Professor. He's in charge of the other town. He'll remember you in particular, Susan." She got an annoyed look.

"What's his problem?" she asked.

"He thinks women are only good for sex," Ron replied. "And he treats them like dirt." Her annoyance changed to a look of anger.

"I wish I had remembered those girls," she said. "And shot the son of a bitch where he stood." Ron smiled at her last words.

"We can travel together," Ron said. "Not many people left around here anymore. I guess it's because Indianapolis was gutted by fire. No food, no people." They moved off toward the northwest.

Late that afternoon, they passed the blackened skeleton of Indianapolis. It stood as a scar on the landscape consisting of tumbled concrete and rusted steel twisted against the sky. The city had literally been leveled by fire and they saw the mute testimony to the inferno that had raged.

They put quite a few miles behind them before deciding to stop at a farmhouse for the night. They settled in as Lyle got the lantern and stove lit. They ate in silence, Susan sitting between them.

"What happened to your family, Professor?" Ron asked. A sad look came to Lyle.

"They were in California on impact day." Ron glanced at Susan then back to Lyle.

"I'm sorry, Professor." Lyle shook his head.

"Don't be. There isn't enough pity to go around these days," Lyle said. Susan gave him a dubious look.

"Maybe not pity, but there has to be compassion, if the human race is to survive," she said.

"You'll find no compassion in Caine's group. That's guaranteed," Ron said, his tone hard.

"What's your group done to keep from being surprised by Caine?" Lyle asked.

"Keep watch. We keep people out about half a mile so they can warn is if he tries anything."

"What sort of defenses do you have?" Ron shrugged.

"They were planning that when I left." Lyle nodded with a thoughtful look.

"After I get a look at the terrain I'll be able to suggest a defense," Lyle said. "Teaching history gives one a pretty good military education."

"How long till we get there?" Susan asked.

"Two or three days," Ron replied. "Depending on how fast we move.

"Let's bed down so we can get an early start," Lyle said. He slipped into his sleeping bag followed by Susan. Ron watched surprised but said nothing as he got into his sleeping bag.

They were moving through woodland when they heard a man shouting profanities and a woman crying out in pain. They moved cautiously to a spot where they could see a woman on her knees, her hands tied behind her back. Standing over her was a burly man cursing and slapping her.

"That bastard!" Susan exclaimed, in a harsh whisper. Lyle knew what she was thinking, unsnapped his holster, and handed her the automatic. She was looking at it when the man hit the woman again knocking her over on her side. She lay sobbing and the sound of her pain moved Susan.

She walked boldly into the clearing holding the automatic in rigid, outstretched hands. Lyle begun to suspect that she had had firearms training. She certainly seemed professional. The man wasn't aware of Susan until she spoke.

"Leave her alone, you son of a bitch." His attention quickly became focused on the woman and he turned quickly. He stiffened when he saw the weapon in her hands and made no sudden moves.

"That's one of Caine's goons," Ron whispered. The man got an arrogant smile and kept looking behind Susan.

"You want to stand in for her, bitch?" His voice was hard as he nodded to the woman on the ground. She lay watching Susan, who didn't take her eyes from the man. Getting a smug look, he reached down and picked up a rifle and looked back at Susan.

"You don't mind, do you?" he asked. The automatic bucked in Susan's hands as she put a bullet through his head exploding the back of his skull in a spray of blood and brain. The rifle fell from his hand; he dropped to his knees and pitched face forward. Ron glanced at Lyle with wide eyes.

"She's one hell of a woman, Professor." Ron was impressed with Susan.

Susan knelt and untied the woman's hands and helped her to her feet. Lyle and Ron came up to them. Susan handed the weapon to Lyle as Ron looked at the woman rubbing her wrists. Lyle regarded Susan in amazement.

"Where the hell did you learn to shoot like that?" Lyle asked.

"My father taught me," Susan replied. "He was a Green Beret." Lyle expressed his admiration.

"He certainly taught you well." She straightened her posture and brushed at her hair.

"You also helped me, Lyle. Thanks." He got a puzzled look.

"What did I do?"

"You told me you didn't feel when you killed," Susan replied, and nodded at the body. "With a son of a bitch like that, it was easy not to feel."

Ron held the woman up with his arm around her shoulders. She had long red-brown hair matted with patches of mud. She had soft hazel eyes and seemed very thin. Lyle and Susan turned to them.

"How long has it been since you ate?" Lyle asked. She had a numb look and slowly shook her head.

"I don't remember," she replied, weakly. Lyle looked at Susan.

"Feed her," Lyle said. "Ron and I will get rid of the body. This bastard won't be raiding for Caine anymore." Susan turned a surprised look on him.

"What's that piece of shit got to do with Caine?" Susan asked.

"Ron recognized him as one of Caine's men," Lyle replied. The woman's clothes hung in shreds and Susan gave her the extra set of clothing she carried.

Taking her to a nearby pond, Susan broke the ice along the edge and helped her clean up. After eating, she told them her story.

Lisa Gordon had been staying at a trailer campground and had thought she had been careful not to be seen. The man had caught her while she slept. For the past three days she had to endure his foul language and abuse. He made no attempt to rape her, giving her the impression he was taking her to someone else. She had been told that if that person didn't want her he would keep her.

Susan did what she could for Lisa's bruises and cuts, which was little with what they had.

"You happen to know the name of that asshole?" Susan asked.

"He said his name was Fred Caine," Lisa replied.

"Jesus!" Ron exclaimed. "David Caine's brother." Susan glanced at Ron showing no concern and gave no more thought to his statement. It was the beginning of friendship between the women. Lyle had an idea he thought appropriate. He unbuckled the automatic from around his waist and strapped it on Susan. He smiled as she looked him with surprise.

"Welcome to the gun club," Lyle said. She put her hand on the butt and regarded him with a pleased look. They quickly put miles between them and the site of the killing in case anymore of Caine's men happened to be in the area.

They came to the bank of a wide muddy river with chunks of ice riding with the current. The bridges they saw were twisted and buckled and had collapsed. Lyle frowned and looked at Ron.

"How the hell do we get to the other side?" Lyle asked. Ron smiled.

"I got a boat stashed about a mile up the river, Professor."

"Well I'm glad to hear that," Lyle said, as the women smiled.

"There's a cave on the other side," Ron said. "We can spend the night there."

The boat was tied among the branches of a toppled tree. Lyle noted that if you didn't know it was there you wouldn't have seen it.

"I'll row first, Professor. You can spell me after awhile. The current here is strong and it's going to be a fight getting across. Susan and Lisa climbed in the boat followed by Ron who sat down between the oars. Lyle pushed them away from the tree and stepped in quickly feeling the pull of the current.

The ice banged against the side of the boat and Lyle saw the strain rowing was putting on Ron. Hard as he tried to hold a straight course, the current carried them downstream.

Lyle took over and knew at once he was going to have some stiff muscles. Forty-five minutes later, the boat hit the bank on the opposite side and half a mile from where they had started. Ron pulled the boat along on a rope until the ground began to tremble. It was hard to stand, but Ron quickly secured the boat on the bank. They headed for level ground, but it became impossible to stand. As they sprawled on the ground, the bank they had just came along gave way, tumbling into the river. If the quake had struck minutes earlier, they would be in the freezing water. The ground became steady again and they got to their feet and continued on.

The cave sat on the backside of a small hill by an inlet. Its mouth was covered with brush and easily concealed. Ron and Lyle hid the boat as the women gathered wood for a fire. Entering, the flashlight revealed an area covered with a tarp that would keep any light from being seen. After the hard day they had had, they ate and sacked out. Susan unbuckled her gunbelt and laid it beside her head. Lisa watched her get settled beside Lyle and took the hint. Lisa didn't wait for an invitation, just climbed into the sleeping bag with Ron. Lyle smiled when he heard no complaint.

The second day from the river, Ron told them they had only three more miles to go. Susan grabbed Lyle's arm and pointed to a group of men coming across a field toward them.

"Caine's men," Ron said, in a low voice. They took cover in the ruins of a house as the men came over a hill. All were heavily armed and not one looked friendly. Some were talking but passed too far away to hear what was being said. They passed into some trees and vanished from sight.

"Stay put," Lyle said. He kept them in place until he was certain the men had moved on. When he felt it was safe they high-tailed it for the settlement.

Seeing the settlement in the distance, they stepped up their pace until suddenly confronted by a man with a shotgun appeared in front of them.
Lyle was at first uncertain where he had come from, but realized he had been in a camouflaged hole.

He was a big man with brown eyes and light brown hair. Not someone you would want to take on without considering your own size, Lyle thought.

"Ron! Back so soon?" the man asked. Ron nodded.

"Yeah. That area around Indianapolis is pretty much uninhabited now. This is Professor Gardner, Susan Pell, and Lisa Gordon. People, this is Tom Harper." Harper gave them a nod and looked back at Ron.

"I'm glad you're back," Tom said. "We've heard Caine's going to move against us soon." Lyle turned looking over the countryside. It was open to the west and Lyle didn't think Caine would be so stupid as to attack from that direction. Lyle knew Caine possessed a cruel and cunning intelligence behind those cold, blue eyes. Lyle wanted to see the landscape around the settlement.

"What's the terrain like to the north?" Lyle asked.

"Nothing to worry about there," Tom replied. "An earthquake pushed the ground up about twenty feet for almost two miles." Lyle rubbed his beard.

"That means Caine's going to have to come from the east or south," Lyle said, glancing at Ron. "Let's go see the man in charge."

Erward Smithers was tall with black hair, olive complexion, and dark brown eyes that emanated confidence. Lyle explained why he thought Caine would attack from the south.

"He could come from the west," Edward said. "Caine doesn't give a damn about anyone but himself." Lyle nodded.

"I agree. But he isn't stupid either," Lyle said. "He'll assume the west will be well covered because that's where you expect him. He could feint there, drawing people of other parts of the defensive perimeter." Lyle felt he was pointing out the obvious. Edward rose and went to a wall map with the new geography colored in. Lyle came over beside him.

"First," Lyle began, pointing to the map. "I would place one or two people at these points south. If Caine attacks from that direction, that's where he would most likely assemble." Edward nodded.

"What about the east?" Edward asked. Lyle shook his head.

"That would be too risky," Lyle replied. "But I would still put a couple of observers out there about two miles. It's possible he could feint from that direction, too." Susan came over and stopped between Edward and Lyle and looked at the map with her hand resting on the butt of her weapon. She looked at Edward.

"We could get some four wheel drive vehicles, scout this area picking up anything that might be useful to us," she said. "Chicago should have a lot we can use." Edward stared at her in surprise, and Lyle had just gotten more respect for her.

"That never occurred to me," Edward admitted. "I'll get people on it tomorrow."

Susan and Lyle looked out the windshield of the Chevy Silverado at Chicago. The city had been wrecked. Streets were blocked with the tops of buildings lying in piles of rubble. Lyle noted they had snapped like a matchstick. There were also scars of fire, but nothing like Indianapolis. They went as far with the truck as they could salvaging from buildings that looked safe enough to go into.

In one building, their flashlights fell on portable radios and a large number of batteries. They took them back to the truck, covered them, and Lyle decided it was too late to try going further into the city. As they climbed into the cab, Susan decided to take advantage of their being alone. She slid across the seat and put her hand over his on the wheel. He looked at her with a slight smile.

"Let's make love," she said, and kissed him. They embraced and started to undress.

"Wait a minute," Lyle said, started the engine and put the heater on low. Once in each other's arms, they didn't need the heater.

Over the next two weeks, the settlement's necessities increased but the population hardly grew at all. Lyle oversaw the digging of irregularly camouflaged pits to the south where people could be concealed. To the west, he set up an integrated fire network and dynamite charges where two people stood guard.

During the same time, Susan was training women, from twelve years old, how to use firearms. Lisa became one of the best shots and Susan made her an aide, turning half the women over to her to train. The hardest thing instilling in the women was not to feel when they fired. Most were eventually convinced after Lisa told how Fred Caine had mistreated her. She paced before her group.

"You don't think of people in your sights as people," Lisa said. They are targets! Remember, those people are convicts, murders, rapists, and general low life scum." Watching a demonstration of the women's shooting, Lyle didn't think many rounds would be wasted.

Three weeks after Susan and Lyle arrived at the settlement; it was a well-organized defensive group. All people on guard and recon carried binoculars and sidearms. Lyle was confident Caine would get a stiff fight when he attacked.

He hoped that Caine hadn't learned of their preparations. Also during this time, Lyle and Susan hadn't much personal time, but now that everything was in place they could enjoy each other's company and wait for Caine to make his move.

The persistent pounding on the door pulled Lyle from sleep. He took his arm from over Susan, slipped on his robe, and went to the door as the knocking continued. He turned up the wick of the hurricane lamp and opened the door to face a grim Ron.

"Professor, you and Susan need to come to Edward's. A man from Caine's group came over. I'll see you there." The urgent tone Ron had banished sleep from Lyle's mind. He nodded and Ron left.

When Susan and Lyle came into the room, they saw a man with black hair and eyes nervously dragging on a cigarette. He was tall and tough looking. Edward turned to them with an alarmed expression. "This man has brought the worst possible news," Edward said. Ron and Lisa stepped beside Lyle as Edward looked back at the man.

"Tell them what you told me," Edward said. The man regarded the new arrivals in silence before responding.

"Caine's got an atom bomb," the man said. Susan glanced at Lyle, not certain she believed what he said.

"He's got it in a garage in town," the man continued. "Caine wanted a timer set on it but nobody there knows shit about wiring, and nobody wanted to screw around with it."

"Then its useless," Lyle said. The man regarded him with a frown.

"Like hell it is! He's doing everything he can to find someone who knows about electronics. The son of a bitch has gone crazy!"

"Finding someone who knows electronics is going to take time," Susan said.

"Maybe so," the man said. "But few of us are waiting until he does. We would like to have what you have, but Caine's only interest is killing." Edward faced Lyle with a nervous expression.

"What can we do, Gardner?" Edward asked, alarm clear in his tone.

"Gardner!" the man exclaimed, narrowing his eyes on Lyle.

"Yes. Why?"

"I don't know how, but about a week ago Caine found out you and your woman was here," the man replied. "That's when he went crazy. Caine hates the both of you with a passion."

"How do the others in your group feel about what Caine's doing?" Susan asked. The man shrugged.

"We had been willing to follow him. But most, if not all, have set out for parts unknown. They believe he's gone nuts. None of us wants to screw around with a nuke." He nervously lit another cigarette.

"Why did you come and warn us?" Ron asked. The man took a deep drag and exhaled.

"I thought you should know," the man replied. "When it comes to nukes, I don't have the balls to stick around. I thought you might like to get out of this area." Lyle had no doubt the man was telling the truth. He felt Caine hadn't the ability to instill such fear in a man.

"How many men are still with Caine?" Lyle asked. The man shrugged again.

"Damned few! Most of us have already left. When Caine wakes up in the morning, he'll be lucky to have ten men left, and they'll be the ones with shit for brains." Edward returned his worried expression back to Lyle.

"What are we going to do?" Edward asked, again. Lyle was silent, considering the situation, and quickly made a decision.

"I'm going after Caine," Lyle said. Susan cocked an eyebrow as she locked her gaze on him.

"Not without me," she said.

"I'll come along," Ron said. Lisa took hold of Ron's arm.

"So will I," Lisa said. The man stared at them like they had lost their minds and shook his head.

"You won't have to worry about anyone bothering you – if anyone's left," the man said.

"Why not?" Lyle asked.

"After Caine found out you were here, he told all of us he was going to kill you. He warned that if any of us laid a hand on you, he would kill us." Lyle stroked his beard.

"If Caine wants me that badly, I've got to take advantage of it," Lyle said.

"He wants me too, Lyle," Susan said.

134

Late morning found the four walking along the broken highway. They had worked out a plan, but Lyle stressed that plans have a way of unraveling. If theirs did, he told them to do what they felt was best. He was determined that today would see the last of Caine. All wore a grim, but determined, expression.

As they neared the town, they split up, with Lyle going ahead alone. When he saw a man at the side of the road sitting on a downed tree, his head against a rifle dozing. Lyle made enough noise to get him on his feet. He stood quickly and aimed the rifle at Lyle. Lyle stopped and regarded the man.

"My name's Gardner. Tell Caine I'm waiting for him." When the man heard the name his eyes widened, he slung his rifle and hurried off.

Half an hour later, Lyle saw five men approaching. He was apprehensive when he faced them. Caine led with a snide smile.

"Well, well. If it isn't the man who saved my ass. You know this saves me the trouble of coming after you." Caine looked around and returned his gaze to Lyle with a puzzled look.

"Didn't you bring your girl friend, Gardner?" That filled Lyle with a coldness.

"This is between you and me, Caine." Lyle pulled his knife from the sheath. Caine laid his rifle aside and looked back at Lyle with a pleased look.

"It just so happens I have one similar," Caine said, taking the knife from behind him.

Knives in hand, they began posturing, circling, looking for an opening. Caine suddenly lunged forward, but Lyle easily sidestepped his thrust and brought his knife down in an arc and missed. As they faced off, Lyle saw an expression on madness on Caine's face. His cold blue eyes projected hate. They circled again ready to use their knife to hack and kill. One of Caine's men slipped behind Lyle and hit him with his rifle. Lyle dropped to the pavement. Caine turned a wild, angry look on the man.

"You dumb son of a bitch! I told you what I would do if anyone interfered." Caine was so enraged that he literally slashed the man to pieces. Seeing what he was doing to their pal the other men fled, leaving Caine alone.

Covered with blood, Caine turned back to where Lyle still lay. He stood over him twisting his knife in his hand.

"Don't even think about it, Caine." Surprised, Caine quickly turned his eyes to Susan, who was coming up the road, the automatic held firmly in her hands. Caine smiled gleefully, smeared the blood over his chin and stepped over Lyle in her direction. She stopped a short distance from him and he pointed his knife at Lyle.

"I can carve him later, girly. I want your sweet ass first." His smile was wicked and his eyes seemed to glow at her.

"Drop the knife or I'll waste your worthless ass the same as I did your asshole brother." Her words cost Caine his smile and was replaced by a look of incredulity. Ron and Lisa came up behind Susan.

"You killed my brother," he sneered. "That's a good laugh, girly. No goddamn woman could have killed Fred. No bitch can kill me. You know why, girly? Women don't have the balls to shoot. I'm sure that goes for you too." As he spoke, his voice rose and the look of madness came to his face.

"He was bringing me to you," Lisa said. "Susan saved me by shooting the bastard." Caine began to tremble as he shook his head in denial.

"No!" Caine screamed. "Not my brother." Lisa kept a calm gaze on him as she spoke her next words.

"He told me his name was Fred Caine." Caine stared at them through a madness that was consuming him. Clutching the knife in a menacing manner, he slowly advanced on Susan.

"Don't come any closer, you son of a bitch," Susan warned, in a hard, calm tone. Caine didn't stop, just slowed a bit as he considered what he was going to do to her. He lifted the knife and prepared to lunge. The shot thundered across the quiet countryside frightening birds. Caine must have been surprised in the last seconds of his life as he realized he faced a woman who had the balls to shoot. The knife fell from his hand clattering on the road as he crumpled down. Susan lowered the weapon, flipped on the safety and holstered it. They went to Lyle and began reviving him. Other than a headache, he was all right.

When they saw the man who had hit Lyle, they were sickened. As they started back to the settlement, a feeling of relief filled them as they knew Caine's brutality would no longer be inflicted on anyone. Susan had a short period of notoriety as the one who killed Caine. But eventually it faded as everyone got on with trying to build a new life.

IN DARKNESS AROUND US

As word of the settlement spread south and west, more people made their way to the only organized community in North America. The population doubled in less than two years. The sky began to clear and the Earth warmed. Susan and Lyle became the parents of a son and daughter. The daughter they named Hope as it was the one idea they held onto.

FIEND

I've always had a soft spot for attractive, long-legged, green-eyed blondes. So when she walked into my office she held my attention. Her hair was shoulder length and shiny, soft eyes and alluring lips. She was dressed in a black and white checkered jacket over a white blouse and black skirt just high enough above her knees to put my imagination into overdrive. She was about an inch shorter than my six-two.

"Lee Arlen?" she asked, in a silky voice. I had to believe that her perfume wasn't for the standard workday.

"Yes. What can I do for you?" I had stood when she came and gestured her to a chair and got an eyefull as her skirt slid up.

"I'm Mary Beth Dray. I need a private investigator. Someone has been stalking me. Whoever it is has left clues in my home that are quite alarming." Those legs, that body, her lovely face were certainly worth protecting.

"Won't the police help, Miss Dray?" I noted the haunted look that came to her as she adjusted her purse on her lap.

"Mary Beth, please. The police told me they can do nothing unless I know who the stalker is, and I haven't any idea who it might be. Sergeant Randolph suggest I come and see you." Good old Randy! I would have to thank him for this referral.

"What sort of clues have you found?" I could tell she was uneasy and let her answer when she felt comfortable.

"A week ago, I found a noose hanging from the upstairs banister. Last night, in my bedroom, I found a bloody knife on the floor." I could see the knife had really rattled her. I leaned back, pulled a smoke from the pack and lit up.

"Can you think of anyone who might have put those things where you found them?" Again, she moved her purse nervously on her lap. She turned her eyes on me and I saw the fear in them.

"Mt father died recently, Mr. Arlen, and I inherited the estate. Have you heard of Thurston Industries?" Had I! This gorgeous woman was worth a hell of a bundle and I nodded.

"The obvious question is, who inherits if something happens to you?" She raised an eyebrow.

"My cousin, Arnold Davis. But he's too damn much of a wimp to try anything so bold.

Besides, there's no way anyone can get into the house without setting off an alarm." Her tone was filled with scorn, so I concluded it wasn't the cousin. I stubbed out the cigarette as I considered her situation.

"Has any of your household staff seen anyone loitering near your home?" She thought for a moment and shook her head.

"If they had, they would have told me. But one thing I'm certain of, Mr. Arlen."

"Lee will do. What do you know?"

"Whoever is doing it is familiar with the house and grounds." I assured her I would do what I could to protect her until we discovered who was stalking her and safely behind bars. She gave me her address and I told her I would be at her home the following morning. As I watched her walk from the office, I knew I was going provide all the protection in my power.

When I arrived at her home the next morning, I saw what she meant by no one getting in without being seen. An electronically locked gate with a TV camera and intercom. I looked ay the camera and pressed the com switch.

"Lee Arlen to see Miss Dray."

"Thank God you're here, Lee." Her voice was filled with alarm.

"I just found something I hope you can take care of." The gate opened and I drove up the drive stopping in front of a spacious two-story house. I noted security lights and motion sensors around the house. Mary Beth was standing on the porch looking pale. She started for the car before I got out. As soon as I did, she took hold of my hand and began pulling me along.

"This way, Lee." I didn't like the tone she used and knew something had upset her.

She led me into a well-equipped home office just inside the main door and pointed to the desk.

Lying on it was a severed index finger in a small pool of blood. I looked but didn't see any blood on the carpet. I was at a loss to see how the finger could have gotten on the desk without leaving a trace of blood on the carpet. I looked at her.

"When did you find this?" She folded her arms and shivered.

"A few minutes before you arrived. It wasn't there when I went for coffee. How could it have gotten here, Lee?"

I couldn't blame her for being disconcerted. Finding a severed finger on your furniture isn't an everyday occurrence.

"I wish I knew," I replied, and pointed to the carpet. "There aren't any bloodstains on the carpet. Who's been in here besides you?"

"No one." I looked back at the finger.

"Someone's been here, Mary Beth."

The police weren't able to explain the lack of a blood trail either. They took Mary Beth's statement, the finger, and left. I sat with her having coffee and thinking over the situation.

"I'm not certain you're safe her, Mary Beth. I don't much care for an intruder that evades motion sensors and household staff in broad daylight. Could it be someone on your staff?" She shook her head.

"These people have been with my family for many years," she said, confidently. "I can't believe any of them would do such a thing. Besides, I haven't noticed any of them missing a finger."

"I would feel better if you were someplace else. Whoever is doing this is a damn unstable person." She turned a hard frown on me.

"And just where would you have me go, Lee?" I thought of my apartment but didn't know she might react and kept my mouth shut.

I took the next half-hour to look over the grounds and felt satisfied with the security but not the isolation of the place. I dropped my cigarette and ground it out. As I looked around, the woods at the back of the house gave me more concern about her staying here. But how the hell could someone get on the grounds, and into the house without tripping an alarm or being seen? That was what I had to find out. I was determined to protect Mary Beth from this sick son of a bitch. I was going to make certain she got what she was paying for.

I stayed up late prowling around the house, checking windows and doors. It was almost one when I heard her scream. I raced up the stairs to her room, pushed the door open, and found her standing staring at the bed making low whimpers.

I also noticed what she didn't wear to bed. I grabbed her robe from the chair and put it around her. I tried calming her but didn't know what had set her off until I looked at the bed. I didn't blame her for freaking when I saw the severed hand, minus the index finger, lying in a pool of blood. I looked around but saw no bloodstains anywhere, not even on the sheet that had covered it.

We were sitting in the living room with Detective Don Chalmers, who was a big man with a friendly face capped by light brown hair. His gray eyes regarded us with interest. I took a drink of coffee and stubbed out my cigarette. Mary Beth nervously rubbed her forehead.

"You have no idea how that hand came to be in your bed?" Chalmers asked. She shook her head.

"It woke me when it rolled against me," Mary Beth replied, still shaken

"I had been checking the house," I said. "There's no way anyone could have gotten in without setting off the alarm." Chalmers regarded me with a frown.

"Then how did that hand get in her bed?" His tone annoyed me.

"The same damn way that finger got on her desk. I don't know how you move a piece of bleeding flesh without getting blood on something else." Chalmers looked from me to Mary Beth, nodded, and put his notebook in his pocket.

"We'll try to ID it from the fingerprints," Chalmers said, standing. "If I learn anything, Arlen, I'll let you know." He turned and walked from the room. I was now beginning to think it wasn't Mary Beth's life that was being threatened but her sanity. But who the hell was doing it and how and why was the mystery. I felt it would be better for her to get away from this house as I could see how events were starting to affect her.

The next day, I paid a visit to her attorney, Howard Capel. He was in his sixties, beefy stature, brown hair with gray showing, and serious brown eyes.

"Have a seat, Mr. Arlen. What can I do to help?" I told him what I thought was going on and asked him to convince Mary Beth to get away for awhile.

"Have you checked out her cousin?" I asked. He nodded, leaning forward and resting his arms on the desk.

"Yes, but it came to nothing." He regarded me with a puzzled look.

"Where are these severed limbs coming from? And how are they getting into the house, Mr. Arlen?" I rubbed my chin.

"Beats the hell out of me." He nodded.

"Should Mary Beth be induced to leave, where would she go?" That I had thought about.

"I would like to take her to a hotel where no one could possibly know where she is."

"What hotel?" I shrugged.

"I won't know that until I get there. When I think she's safe, I'll give you a call and let you know where we are." He leaned back with a satisfied look and nodded.

"I agree it seems unsafe for her to remain at home. I've known Mary Beth all of her life, and her safety is important to me. I'll see if I can talk her into listening to your recommendation, Mr. Arlen." He picked up the phone and began dialing.

Mary Beth faced me with her arms folded and an angry expression.

"I'm not going anywhere, Lee. I won't be spooked into running away from someone whose motives aren't even clear." I was getting irritated at her stubbornness.

"Damnit, Mary Beth, you're not safe here." I got a hard look for saying that as she dropped her arms to her sides like she had spoken the last word.

"I have always faced problems squarely, Lee, and I won't change now. If you feel that strongly about my safety then you can spend the night in my bedroom while I sleep. But I'm not leaving this house." It was a tempting invitation, and it was damn clear I had lost the argument. The phone on the stand beside Mary Beth rang and she lifted it quickly to her face.

"Hello. Yes, he's here." She handed me the phone.

"Arlen." It was Chalmers and he had very unusual news. I glanced at Mary Beth as I listened.

"Thanks, Chalmers." She saw my expression and knew something was wrong. I handed the phone back to her considering what I been told, and found it hard to believe.

She put the phone down and turned back to me as I lit a smoke. She regarded me in silence for a moment.

"What was that about, Lee?" I wasn't certain it was wise to tell her, but knew it might be the only way to get to the bottom of this mess.

"Do you know Louis Clark?" Surprise exploded on her face and her hand covered her mouth.

"Yes. He was sent to prison for embezzlement. What's he got to do with this?" I slowly rubbed my eyebrow and considered how to put it.

"The finger and hand belong to him." The shock she expressed gave me some hope she might now agree to leave for awhile.

"I thought he was still in prison." I nodded.

"He is, Mary Beth. And he still has both of his hands." I let my expression turn cold.

"Fingerprints don't lie." I thought she was going to faint when she understood the implications. I took hold of her arm and sat her down.

I sat in front of Detective Sergeant Loenard Randolph's desk drawing on a cigarette and waiting for his response to the odd facts I had just put to him. Randy was a bit overweight, bulldog face, with black hair and gray eyes. He frowned as he rubbed the back of his neck.

"The prints were a match for Clark?" I nodded.

"Yeah. But how the hell he's doing this is the mystery. The guy is in state prison, Randy." He bit on his lip and folded his hands on his paunch.

"I know the warden, Lee. I'll give him a call and see what I can find out about Clark." He picked up the phone and made the connection.

"Get me the warden at the state prison." It took a moment for the call to go through.

"Hello, Hal, it's Leonard. What can you tell me about a prisoner named Louis Clark." He listened, nodded, then looked surprised.

"Thanks, Hal." Randy slowly put the phone down, not looking at me.

"Well?" I asked, wondering what he had been told.

"Except for his first three days at the prison, Louis Clark has spent the past four years in solitary confinement." I could have fallen off the chair.

"Why?" Randy shrugged.

"Every time they bring him out, he fights the guard and gets tossed back in. Seems he likes solitude."

When I returned, Mary Beth was busy in her office.

"Got a minute?" She looked up at me.

"Certainly."

"Did Clark know this house pretty well?"

"I should think so. He lived here as father's private secretary for over a year."

"What were Clark's feelings for you, Mary Beth?" She took a deep breath and straightened her posture.

"He said he loved me and wanted to marry. But I still believe he was in love with the family fortune." I had to shake my head at that.

"That would make him a damn fool." She laughed. I then told her what Randy had learned about Clark.

"Did any of the household staff become friendly with Clark?" She considered before shaking her head.

"None of them cared for him. Where's this leading, Lee?" I shrugged.

"I'm not certain. Just doing a little fishing." I was frustrated because I couldn't understand what the hell was going on.

"How could a man in solitary confinement lose a hand and get in here without being seen?" she asked. I shook my head.

"It's like being caught between a rock and the sea."

It was around midnight, I was dozing on the sofa in the living room when I got an odd feeling that woke me. I sat up, looked around, and saw I was alone. I reached for my cigarettes on the coffee table.

"Jesus!" I jerked my hand back from the severed hand lying in a pool of blood. My call to Chalmers awoke Mary Beth and I saw her go into the living room. I put the phone down and tried to get to her before she saw the hand. I got to the living room just in time to catch her when she went into a dead faint. I put her on the sofa and called the butler and explained what had happened. I saw the look of disgust he got when looked at the coffee table and handed me the smelling salts.

Mary Beth was sitting up when the doorbell chimed. The butler let Chalmers and his people in. They came into the living room and Chalmers lifted the towel I had put over the hand, then looked at me.

"What the hell is going on, Arlen?" I knew he was as perplexed as I was. Before I could answer, the doorbell chimed again.
Howard Capel came rushing into the room, his eyes falling on the towel. He stopped by it, lifted the towel, and looked at Chalmers.

"Get this damned thing out of here," Capel said, and turned to Mary Beth.

"I heard the call on the scanner," Capel said. "Are you all right, Mary Beth?" She looked up at him and nodded.

"I'm fine Howard." He took hold of her arms and got a stern expression.

144

"Now listen to me, Mary Beth. I've got a comfortable cabin about twenty-five miles from here. I want Arlen to take you there." He let go of her arms, reached in his pocket, and produced a key ring and map that he handed me.

"Take her there, Arlen. And watch out for her until we can get to the bottom of this."

I stopped the car in front of the cabin leaving the lights on the front porch. I unlocked the glove compartment and took out my 9-mm automatic and a clip of ammo. I shoved the clip in the butt and pulled the slide back and let it pop back into place. I didn't know what we were dealing with and the weapon gave some sense of comfort. Mary Beth watched with wide eyes. I took the keys from my jacket pocket and replaced them with gun.

"Wait here," I said, got out and hurried to the door. I used the wrong key, but quickly got the door open. I turned on the lights and went back for Mary Beth.

As she sat down, I poured her a shot of brandy.

"Here," I said, handing her the glass. "This will warm you up. You need to sleep, you're exhausted." She almost had the glass to her lips when her eyes went wide and the glass fell from her hand. I turned to see what she was looking at. It wasn't possible! A human head lay in front of the fireplace.

"That's Louis!" she screamed. Whatever was doing this knew how to find Mary Beth.

"Son of a bitch!" I grabbed her hand.

"Come on. We're getting the hell out of here."

When we got to my apartment, Mary Beth was drained physically and needed sleep.

"You take the bed, Mary Beth. I'll sleep here on the couch." She turned a fearful look to me.

"No, Lee. I don't want to be alone." I nodded and gave her arm a gentle squeeze.

"All right. Just get some sleep." She fell asleep almost as soon as her head touched the pillow on the couch. I sat for the next few hours trying to make sense out of what had been happening. There wasn't much to piece together and I didn't like that. I knew that somehow Louis Clark was behind it. But I didn't know how.

That's when I decided to see a friend at the university. Maybe he could give me some answers.

It was almost ten when we saw Grant Fielding. He was stocky with red hair and light green eyes. He was a professor of eastern religions and that's where I believed the answer lay. I just sat quiet and let Mary Beth relate what had happened.

"That's amazing." Grant's comment was certainly an understatement as far as I was concerned.

"Do any of those eastern religions claim to be able to do anything like she described?" I asked. Grant got that studious look that must have annoyed the hell out of his students.

"Have you heard of astral projection, Lee?" he asked.

"Yeah, but I don't believe it." He cocked an eyebrow.

"Don't be so quick to write it off. It's pretty much accepted as a power of the mind." Mary Beth leaned forward with a tired look.

"Where did those human parts come from?" she asked, her tone desperate. Grant leaned back and folded his hands on the desk.

"They could have been created by someone who was able to concentrate intensely," he replied. "I've heard from reliable people of one Indian Shaman who publicly produced physical objects by thought alone." He had just verified what I had only suspected.

"Could someone who's spent a number of years in solitary confinement be able to produce similar results?" I asked. Grant nodded.

"Quite possible. That would be the ideal environment for training one's mind." Mary Beth was staring at me knowing whom I was thinking about.

"How can he be stopped, Grant?"

"That's easy," he said, spreading his hands. "Put him with other prisoners. There he won't be able to achieve total concentration due to the distractions."

"Miss Dray, Lee, have a seat," Randy said. I told him what happened the previous night and what Grant had told me. Randy listened with a neutral expression.

"And you would like me to call Hal and have Clark removed from solitary?" I quickly shook my head.

"Not until I have a talk with Clark." Mary Beth's hand gripped my arm.

"No, Lee. If he can do what we think he can, you would be in danger." Randy nodded.

"I agree," Randy said.

"Someone's got to stop him. I might be able to get him to admit what he's been doing. I want to be wired when I talk to Clark so we'll have evidence rather than just guessing."

I sat in the warden's office waiting for them to bring Louis Clark in. The guard opened the door and a small, pale man with blue eyes and sandy hair stepped past him and locked his eyes on me. I nodded and the guard stepped out and closed the door. Clark got a snide smile, strutted to the desk and sat down. I took an instant dislike for him.

"I'm Lee Arlen. I was hired to protect Mary Beth Dray." He got a cocky look.

"What's that got to do with me?" he asked, in a bored tone. I came around the desk, folded my arms, and leaned against it.

"I know what you've been doing, Clark." The only reaction from him was a smirky smile. I had an urge to knock that smile off his face.

"I also know how you're able to do it and intend putting an end to it." He pulled himself up in the chair, never taking his eyes from me.

"You can't prove a thing, Arlen." I nodded.

"I know. But I can take Miss Dray someplace where she'll be safe." The more I watched his expression, the harder it became to control my anger.

"You didn't learn a fucking thing last night, did you, Arlen?" I was puzzled by his statement.

"What do you mean?" He leaned forward with his shitty-ass grin.

"Mary Beth can't hide from me. I thought that would have been clear at the cabin last night." He stood and gave me a hard look.

"Anywhere you take her, Arlen, I'll find her." I dropped my arms to my side and stood erect.

"Why are you doing this to her?" An expression of rage exploded on his face.

"Revenge! She refused to marry me and her old man trumped up charges that got me sent here to keep me away from her." His expression didn't change as he shook his head.

"I'll go on haunting Mary Beth. Her suicide will be my revenge and nobody will be able to prove I had anything to do with it."

The warden sat listening to the recording with a pained expression. He looked at me across the desk where his hands were folded.

"I didn't believe your story, Mr. Arlen. Now I see Clark is a threat to Miss Day. I'll have it taken care of." His phone rang.

"Yes?" He listened and looked at me.

"He's still here." The warden got a shocked expression.

"Miss Dray has been stabbed, Mr. Arlen. Leonard wants you to come to the All Saints Hospital as soon as possible. He'll meet you there." Clark's face was looming in my mind.

"That son of a bitch."

I walked into the waiting room and saw Randy.

"What happened?" I asked

"I took her back to your apartment. Half an hour later, she called me and said she had been hurt. I took a couple of officers and we went to your place. We had to break in, and found her unconscious. She had a knife wound in her back. Its location ruled out any suicide attempt." It was hard to control the anger I felt for Clark, but knew there wasn't anything I could do about it.

"So Clark couldn't wait for her to act on her own." Randy got a baffled look.

"We can't consider Clark a suspect, Lee. He's in prison, for Christ sakes." The doctor came in and Randy and I turned to him.

"She'll recover. Now she needs to rest," the doctor said. That's when I got the idea.

I went back to Grant, told him what had happened, and explained what I wanted to try. He gave me a hesitant look.

"I don't know, Lee, that's risky." I leaned forward and let my determination come through in my tone.

"Do you know someone who can help, Grant?" He frowned and nodded.

"Dr. Raner might. I'll call him." Grant talked for a couple of minutes then put the phone down. His expression was uncertain as he regarded me.

"He'll talk to you, Lee. Are you certain you want to try this?"

"It's the only way I can protect Mary Beth. Let's go."

After the introduction, Raner led us to his study.

"Have a seat," Raner said, and sat down across from Grant and me.

"What's this about, Mr. Arlen?" I told him what had happened to Mary Beth and who had caused it. I told him what I had in mind. He cupped his chin and sat quiet for a moment before looking back at me.

"Under the circumstances, I think your task can be done with minimal risk, Mr. Arlen." I made a quick call to Randy and got my plan in motion.

Mary Beth was pale but resting as I waited in her room. I began to sense the same thing I had the night the second hand appeared. I moved to the darkest corner of the dimly lit room and watched a milky shape begin to form beside her bed. It was a couple of minutes before I recognized it as Clark and saw the knife forming in his hand. Before it was complete, I slammed against him startling him. He dropped the knife and it vanished before hitting the floor. He wasn't aware of my astral projection as I bumped him again. He was scared shitless not having any idea what was going on. I saw the desperate expression he now wore and formed into a ghost-like shape with an aura and slowly moved toward him. When he saw me, he covered his face with his hands, cried out in terror and was gone.

Next afternoon, Randy and I paid Mary Beth a visit. She was awake and smiled.

"Hi," she said, softly.

"How are you feeling?" I asked.

"Pretty good, considering."

"You don't have to worry about Clark anymore, Miss Dray," Randy said. "Lee took care of him last night." A startled look came to her.

"How did he do that, Sergeant?" Randy looked at me and shook his head.

"Lee had himself hypnotized and used his astral projection to protect you." She glanced at me with a dubious look then back to Randy.

"But I thought Clark wouldn't be a threat once he was out of solitary confinement?" She looked back at me.

"And you don't believe in astral projection, Lee."

"I asked the warden to leave Clark in solitary," Randy said. "Lee wanted to make certain he wouldn't get the chance to try to kill you again." I saw a twinkle in Mary Beth's eyes as she looked at me.

"I had to do something," I said. "It was the only thing I could think of."

"The warden called me earlier," Randy said. "He told me Clark has lost his mind and was being transferred to the state mental hospital." I smiled as I looked at her.

"He was afraid of ghosts," I said. She got a pleased smile.

"That was going above the call of duty, Lee," she said.

"I only done what you paid me for."

ALIEN PLANET

The cloud had been traveling through the endless reaches of space for uncounted millennia. It had passed infinite numbers of stars, galaxies, and solar systems. This was its first time going through a solar system. It was passing a blue planet with milky clouds drifting in its atmosphere.

As it passed Earth, the shuttle Atlantis was in low Earth orbit. The timing was perfect for Atlantis and the cloud to come together. The crew of Atlantis was sleeping and unaware that anything out of the ordinary was befalling them. Mission Control had not discovered the cloud. It wasn't large but it enveloped the Atlantis. The cloud sensed stirrings and its energy was attracted to the minds of the crew. Their minds, in turn, absorbed the energy from the cloud. Atlantis passed through the cloud and continued in its orbit. The cloud moved away from Earth continuing its eternal trek through space.

Ashley Ames was the first to awaken. Opening her eyes, the idea was fresh in her mind. They had reached their destination, and the thought excited her. One by one, the other five crew awoke with the same strong belief. They knew they had reached across light years and were now orbiting a planet in another solar system. They began their normal routine when the radio unexpectedly crackled into life.

"Atlantis, this is Houston. Do you copy?" They glanced at each other in shock. This was impossible! Houston was on Earth – light years away.

Martin Crick, mission commander, pulled his headset over his brown hair; his gray eyes nervously flitted to each of the crew.

"Who are you?" Crick asked, into the mike. The first thought of the ground tech's was, is this a joke?

"This is Mission Control, Atlantis," he replied.

"That's absurd! Mission Control is on Earth, light years from this planet," Crick said, bewildered. The ground tech covered his mike and motion for the nearest person. When she came over, she saw his odd expression,

"Jean, get somebody in here right away. I think we have a problem with Atlantis' crew." She quickly walked off thinking of whom she should call first.

"Why do they want us to believe they're Mission Control?" Ashley asked. Crick regarded her with a puzzled look.

"I don't know," Crick replied. Gary Long, the pilot, adjusted his headset over his sandy hair, his brown eyes on Crick.

"They're aliens," Gary said. "They must be curious and want to have a look at the ship."

"What are we going to do?" Jonda Perry asked. She was adjusting the headset over dark blonde hair, her blue eyes expressing the trace of fear she felt. Jim Scott looked at his crewmates.

"All we can do is wait and see what they try," Jim said.

"He's right," Edward Longway agreed. "We're going to have to wait until they make a move, then consider our options."

"How do they know about Mission Control?" Jonda asked. "And the name of our ship?"

"I would guess they're using telepathy," Gary said. "That's the only way they can know what we know." Again the radio crackled in their ears.

"Atlantis, this is Houston. What the hell are you trying to pull?" an authoritative voice asked. "This is Charles Slate. Do you recognize my voice?" Crick glanced at the crew before answering.

"You sound like Slate," Crick replied, slowly. "But he's on Earth, not this planet."

"Listen, whoever you are," Jim interrupted. "We know who we are and where we are. But we don't know who you are."

Slate leaned back in the chair puzzled by what he had just heard. He was stocky with gray eyes and graying hair. He clamped his hand over the mike.

"My God! What's happened to them?" Slate asked, looking at Jean. "Call everybody in, Jean. We have a crisis with Atlantis." She nervously brushed black hair from her forehead and regarded him with bewildered blue eyes.

"Do they believe what they're saying, Mr. Slate?" she asked. He nodded.

"They sound too damn serious to be joking," he replied, his brow furrowing in bafflement. "But what's causing them to hallucinate?"

The Atlantis now refused to acknowledge any communication from Mission Control.

The room was quiet, cold coffee sat in individualized mugs on the long table, and the air smelled of tobacco smoke the air conditioner hadn't yet purged. The people sitting around the table knew they had less than seventy-two hours before Atlantis was due to return. Theo Harriman, a heavily built man with gray hair and sharp brown eyes, looked to Slate for answers to the problem they faced. Answers Slate didn't have.

"Did anything show up on the boards that might explain what's happened, Charles?" Theo asked.

"Nothing we've been able to find," Slate replied. "They were normal when they went into sleep mode, but they woke up on their own." Harriman got an annoyed look.

"Then something affected them while they slept. What are the possibilities?" Harriman said. The room flooded with silence again.

"Damnit, I want answers from you people," Harriman demanded, thumping the table with his palm.

"It does resemble Earth somewhat," Ashley said, to no one in particular. She was staring down at a planet whose inhabitants posed an unknown danger to her and the rest of the crew. Jim floated over beside her and looked down.

"So it does," he said, dryly. "But you can tell the difference in the shape of the land masses. You can plainly see they're not the same." It became as quiet in the shuttle as in the room below. The crew thought of their plight as they ate, feeling they had awoke in a nightmare.

"Why would they want the ship?" Jonda asked, breaking the silence.

"That's hard to say," Crick replied. "We're dealing with an alien race that seems to be able to probe our minds. There really isn't anyway we can guess their motives." The radio suddenly had the voice that sounded like Slate back on it.

"Atlantis, this is Mission Control. We don't know what's happened to you, but you're scheduled to return in sixty-two hours. We have to have your cooperation for a safe landing."

"Damn you!" Edward exploded, grabbing his headset. "Quit trying to trick us with your telepathy. We are not going to land this ship for you."

"Goddamnit, Atlantis, we're not trying to trick you," Slate retorted, losing his temper. "What we want to do is get you down in one piece." None of the crew responded to the outburst.

Slate angrily pulled off the headset and turned to Harriman, who began to pace with his hands clasped behind his back. There seemed only one solution to the problem that Harriman could see. He quickly made up his mind.

"I want Discovery ready for launch in thirty-six hours," Harriman said, looking over his shoulder. "Can it be done, Charles?" Slate nodded.

"Under the circumstances, we'll get it done." Slate turned to the people in Mission Control and saw all eyes were on him.

"All right, people, let's get the new show on the pad," Slate said. They moved swiftly to the daunting task before them.

"What can we do?" Ashley asked, a nervous tremor in her tone. Before Crick could answer, Gary grabbed his head with both hands and cried out in pain. He was then floating, unconscious. Edward pushed off the bulkhead and floated over to him. He pressed his fingers against Gary's throat and felt a slow, steady pulse.

"Help me put him in his sack, Jim." As they took Gary away, Jonda felt a surge of fear.

"What happened to Gary?" Jonda asked, a trace of hysteria in her voice. Showing fear was something she didn't want the others to see.

"I'm not certain," Crick replied. "Anyone feeling different?" All shook their heads. Now they had the mystery of what had happened to Gary on their hands.

The reports Slate and Harriman were getting made them confident Discovery would be able to launch in twelve hours. The weather remained favorable and no problem seemed to hinder the preparations.

"What about the emergency crew?" Harriman asked.

"They're all veterans, except the doctor," Slate replied. "But we haven't considered how we're going to get onboard Atlantis."

"What about the docking tube?" Harriman asked. Slate got a hesitant look.

"It's never been tested in space. We can't be certain they won't lock us out or even fight when we get onboard." Harriman got an annoyed look.

"Stop being so damn pessimistic, Slate." The intercom sounded. "Slate."

"You better get down here, Mr. Slate. We're getting a transmissions from Atlantis."

When Gary regained consciousness, he saw the others were forward, leaving him alone. He slipped out of his sack and floated to the nearest headset. He had to contact Mission Control

Slate and Harriman wasted no time getting to the communications console. Slate grabbed a headset and slipped it on.

"Slate here."

"This is Long. I don't know what's happened. The others –"

"How were you able to overcome it, Gary?" Slate asked.

"I had a sharp pain shoot through my head that knocked me cold. Now I'm over whatever happened."

"Listen, Gary, we're going to send up Discovery," Slate said. "Can you open the cargo bay hatch so emergency personnel can come onboard?"

"Sure." Slate told him Discovery's ETA, and until then Gary was going to have to convince the crew that he was still believing what they did.

Ashley felt Gary was different now, as they ate in silence.

"Are you certain you're okay, Gary?" she asked, giving him an odd look. He nodded.

"I'm still not feeling like my old self. The pain that hit me was like nothing I've experienced."

"Probably those goddamn aliens trying a mind probe," Crick remarked.

"The only thing I was aware of was that god awful pain," Gary said.

"I don't think they can touch us," Edward said, confidently. "Or else they would have tried something by now."

"I agree," Jonda said. "The only way they can get us is by tricking us into a landing." Gary nodded.

"That makes sense," Gary said.

Discovery had less than an hour to launch and everything was on schedule.

"I'm glad we don't have to try that damned docking tube," Slate said.

"Let's hope everything goes smoothly when they get to Atlantis," Harrison said. Everything was ready as they waited for the mission to get underway. Mission Control people kept monitoring Discovery, making certain everything remained green for launch. Then Discovery lifted from the launch pad and knifed a flaming path through the clear sky. It appeared like an angry comet hungry to get back into space. In orbit, it took critical maneuvering to achieve the correct distance behind Atlantis.

Gary moved around as though going through his routine of checking instruments. Glancing out, he saw four space suited figures moving toward Atlantis and quickly flipped the cargo bay hatch to automatic. As a diversion, Gary drew the attention of the others to the blip on the radar that appeared to be following them.

"What the hell could that be?" Edward asked.

"Looks like a large satellite," Gary replied. Jonda felt a growing apprehension and struggled not to let it show.

All eyes suddenly turned to the airlock as it began to cycle. They became paralyzed with fear at the thought of a first encounter with aliens. It was an idea that had been in the back of their minds since they had entered the space program. But even in their wildest dreams, they had never considered that aliens would board their ship. It was incomprehensible.

Gary moved back to the airlock as the space suited figures came through. They moved to where they could see the crew, who stared in terror. The thought of what these aliens might do to her was more than Jonda could stand. Fear overwhelmed her and she fainted.

Before any of them could recover from their paralysis, the loud venting of compressed air sounded on the flight deck stinging them with tranquilizing darts.

Gary noted Ashley glaring at him as she sank into unconsciousness. He knew what she was thinking in her last seconds of consciousness. He was controlled by the aliens and had betrayed them.

Three days later, the crew from Atlantis were recovering from the effects of the cosmic cloud, but had no memory of what had occurred. Gary walked into the hospital room where Ashley and Jonda were.

"How are you two feeling today?" he asked. Jonda was the worst because of the extreme fear she had experienced. Both women were recovering.

"We're fine," Jonda replied. "Did that really happen to us?" He nodded.

"Yeah. The pain I felt snapped me out of it. I'm the only one who remembers what happened." Ashley regarded him sullenly and he smiled at her. Slate and Harriman came into the room.

"You two girls look beautiful today," Slate said.

"Have you been able to determine what happened to us?" Ashley asked. Slate shrugged.

"We'll never know for sure," Harriman said, and looked at Gary.

"We were damned lucky to have Gary there," he continued. "Now the doctors want to put him in a test tube." He clasped Gary's shoulder.

"They want to see you, Gary. They want to see you, Gary. They hope to find out why you were able to shake off the hallucination."

"Thanks to you, the crew and Atlantis are safely back on Earth," Slate said. The praise embarrassed Gary in front of the women.

"I better go to the medics," Gary said. "I don't know what they expect to find. I lived through it and haven't any idea what happened." He turned and started from the room.

"Gary," Ashley said.

"Yeah?" He turned back to her.

"How about dinner when I get out of here?" Gary smiled and nodded.

"It's a date." He left the room as Jonda looked at Ashley and smiled.

The cloud moved away from the Earth on its endless path through the universe. But now it was wanting company again.

A STILL, SMALL VOICE

"It's for your own good, dear," she said, bringing the hard leather strap down with a wishing sound. Edward Leash sat stiffly up in bed drenched with sweat and feeling the pain his nightmare always brought to him. He could remember nothing of the dream, but still felt the pain. Pain caused by what? Edward was thirty-three years old with dark brown hair, hazel eyes and was on the thin side. His nightmare was a recurring one, but random. Why? Edward didn't know. He is aware that it comes when he doesn't feel right before going to bed. It was as if something had happened he should know but couldn't recall. There's nothing to summon from his memory. He doesn't recollect doing anything. How could he? He hadn't left the apartment since he came home from work.

Edward Leash is a nondescript anonymity; someone who doesn't stand out in a crowd. He's still a virgin, although he thinks about women he has never been bold enough to ask one out. Betty, the receptionist at the warehouse where he works, likes him. She's cute with her short brown hair and blue eyes. He likes her, but can't bring himself to talk to her. That was too difficult for him.

He now sits in the semidarkness of his apartment unable to stop sweating. He uses the sheet to mop away the sweat running down his face. It's after four A.M. and he lies back down, closes his eyes, and tries to go back to sleep.

"It's happened again," a voice said. He opened his eyes, knowing he had plainly heard the voice. Edward sat up and looked around his one room apartment. There was no one else in the room. He pushed the sheet from him and got out of bed. He went to the open window and stuck his head out. No one was on the shadowed street below. The night air was hot and muggy, a typical summer night. Edward was puzzled at having heard the voice. It had to have come from someone, but whom?

There was no one around, so who was it who had spoken to him? He suddenly recalled that he had heard that voice before. Every night he had the dream and awoke in fear and pain. Whose voice was it?

Edward didn't know. On thinking about it, he felt it was the same voice that always said the same thing.

Edward had to go through the office of the warehouse to get to the time clock.

"Good morning, Edward," Betty said, smiling at him.

"Uh, morning, Betty," he said, quickening his pace. In the warehouse, Edward found a sense of order, unlike his life. Nothing was out of place here. With that thought came the voice.

"It happened again, Edward." He looked around and saw no one. But he had heard the voice! There had to be someone here. Someone who had been in his apartment hours earlier. But there was no one to be seen.

He sat down at his desk and scanned the lading orders to see what would be coming in. Edward had to find space for the incoming material and knew what space was available to put it. He walked through the warehouse checking to make sure the space was available.

He worked through the day driving the lift truck. He placed skids, burdened with cartons, in the spaces he had picked for them. It was time to go home, the day's work done. A coworker named Al came over to him.

"How about coming by the bowling alley later for a beer, Eddy?" This alarmed Edward. He wanted no friends that would cause complications in his life; lead to disorder.

"I'll try," Edward replied, coolly, knowing he was lying. He had told the same lie many times. Al knew Edward would not be coming by the bowling alley.

After finishing the TV dinner, Edward picked up the book he was reading. There was no TV in the room as Edward didn't care to hear about the troubles of the world or entertainment. He became engrossed in reading.

I had to go out I was compelled to do so. There was something I had to do. What? I don't yet know. But I had to do it. I prowled the dimly lit street alone when I hear footsteps. I slipped into a doorway and waited. She staggered past, drunk, and didn't see me.
I became incensed, unable to control my rage. Nobody should allow themselves to get into such a condition. Now I knew what I had to do.

I came up behind her as she stopped and turned. When she faced me she smiled. My hands clasped her throat and pressed on the soft flesh.
Her eyes bulged in fear, her tongue flopped out over her lower lip. I squeezed more tightly. I was here to teach a lesson about being a drunk.

"It's for your own good, dear," she said, raising her hand with the strap. Edward jerked up in bed, his back paining. It had been the nightmare! He couldn't remember it but knew it had been the same dream. It always was. Then he heard the voice.
"It happened again, Edward."

He walked through the office to the time clock. Betty greeted him in her soft voice and sexy smile. As usual, this made him quicken his pace. Back in the warehouse, he was alone again. He sat down at the desk and began his daily routine picking up the morning's orders.
"Why do you do it?" someone asked. Edward looked around and saw he was alone.
"This is my job," he replied.
"Not the job, Edward. Those other things you like doing so much."
"What other things?" Edward asked, not understanding what the voice meant.
"You know, Edward. The awful things you do," the voice said, sounding like a fading echo.
He forced the words of the voice from his mind because he didn't know what it was talking about. Edward concentrated on his work. Why was the voice talking to him? He pushed the question aside that had intruded into his orderly life. He didn't want to hear anything that would disrupt his life.

At his apartment, Edward wasn't very hungry. He had a sandwich and pretzels that he washed down with a glass of milk. He would finish the book tonight. He got comfortable and began to read. The words on the page began to blur and quickly became black squares on a white background.

I saw her get out of the cab and pay the driver. She quickly crossed the street as the cab moved away. She was very lovely. She had long, silky blonde hair that seemed to shine under the streetlight.

Her figure was perfect. She was so captivating I had to stare. I felt a rage coming over me. No woman should be that lovely, that perfect. Without makeup she couldn't be so captivating.
I went quickly toward her as she slipped her key into the lock. When she opened the door, I moved fast.

My left arm went tightly around her waist. My other hand clamped over her mouth. I lifted her off her feet and we went inside together. I shut the door with my foot and put her down. She tried turned her head and I looked at those fearful brown eyes. They were alluring. My rage grew knowing no woman should have such eyes. Before she could say a word, I smashed my fist against her throat. She gasped for breath and began turning blue. I caught her before she fell and laid her on the sofa. This would teach her not to be so beautiful. I had showed her how wrong that was.

"It's for your own good, dear," she said, the strap coming down hard. Edward was sitting up in bed soaked with sweat. He heard the voice.

"Before she could scream, Edward," the voice said, reproachfully.

"You're not supposed to say that." Edward spoke aloud to the dark room, bewildered at the words he had heard. He didn't know what the voice meant, but it frightened him. The voice was trying to tell him something. What? It was something he didn't want to know. He was certain of that. But it was something he should know. He quickly rejected that idea. It would bring disorder to his neat life. This Edward would not allow. People cause disruption, and he would allow no part of that. The voice was bringing disorder to his mind. He would simply refuse to listen to it anymore. Edward would not listen.

It had worked! Edward hadn't heard the voice all day. He had regained an ordered mind. Now it was quitting time on Friday. He punched his time card, replaced it beside the time clock, and walked through the office.

"Have a nice weekend, Edward," Betty said, smiling.

"You too, Betty," he said, scurrying for the door.

He stopped by the bank and cashed his check; the same bank he always stopped at. He bought groceries for the week at the market where he always shopped. At the apartment, he put the groceries away and fixed a TV dinner.
After eating, he picked up the book he had been looking forward to reading for a long time. He settled in for an enjoyable evening.

I saw her walking by herself. She had short black hair, and I was very much attracted to her. She couldn't be much older than fifteen. That didn't matter to me as my mind filled with uncontrollable rage. No girl should be so pretty at Fifteen! I followed her, staying far enough behind so she couldn't hear me. She started up the walk to a two-story house in a residential area. I made my move.

"It's for your own good, dear," Edward's mother said, bringing the strap down. The pain tore through his back. He was sitting up sweating.

"She's dead! That bitch mother is dead," Edward said, as if to reassure himself. That must have been who the still, small voice was. That bitch!

"No, Edward. I'm not her voice."

"Who are you? Tell me."

"Look beside you, Edward." He didn't want to look, and stubbornly kept his face in the opposite direction. Whatever it was would bring disorder. Edward was certain of this. He wouldn't look.

"You must look, Edward," the voice sternly insisted. "After all, you brought her home. And it's the other thing you do so well, and enjoy so much." Edward swallowed hard, his throat dry, and his insecurity stirring. Slowly, reluctantly, he turned his head. In the bed beside him was a very pretty teenage girl sleeping. How did she get here?

"You brought her here, Edward. Only she isn't sleeping, she's dead. You murdered her."

"No, no, no!" I could never do anything like that. I would never harm anyone. Never." He loudly denied his guilt

"Who are you to tell me I've done such a wicked thing?"

"I am you, Edward. You have killed many times."

"No! I couldn't..." He couldn't finish the sentence. He closed his eyes and put his hands over his face. That would make it go away. But faces began appearing in his mind. Faces of people he didn't know. He began to sweat again as he became frightened. He began to hear those peoples' voices, which were pointing at him, accusing him of their murders.

I looked down at her lying on the bed. She was such a pretty girl. I had brought her here. I ran my fingers through her soft black hair. He had killed her! The son of a bitch killed this pretty, young woman instead of making love to her. I squeezed hard on the handle of the butcher knife. My rage grew at what that man had done. I was here to teach him a lesson. I looked long and hard at his face.

It was the face of a pathetic murderer. A person I could feel no pity for. A vile monster who couldn't be left alive any longer. My thirst for revenge grew as I looked into his troubled eyes. He had to die! He was evil. I took the knife to his face and I slashed time and again. As I brought the knife down hard, I could feel his pain and fear. No matter. He had to die! I took the utmost pleasure in shoving the knife into his dark heart.

Two detectives stood looking around as the forensics people went over Edward's apartment. The bodies had been taken away. They had found Edward's body lying in front of his mirror. The girl's body in the bed, fully clothed.

"What's this look like to you, Fred?" the detective asked.

"My first assessment would be a murder suicide. But the girl wasn't sexually molested," Fred replied.

"It doesn't make any sense," the other detective said.

"I've never heard of a case of a suicide mutilating himself," Fred said.

"How do we carry this?"

"A double homicide," Fred replied. "That damned serial killer must have done this. It fits his MO. The insane bastard has struck again."

UNKNOWN

The ship emerged from the wormhole successfully. Once through it hit something it had been unable to avoid. The bridge crew was knocked off their feet by the impact. The main engine automatically shut down and the ship began to drift.

"Damage report," the captain asked, into the intercom after regaining her feet. Each deck reported quickly. No major damage, but some minor injuries among the crew. It had been a glancing collision. The Olympus was a lucky ship.

"How far to the nearest base?" the captain asked.

"That would be Altair Four, Captain," replied the science officer. "But there's a Class G star about five hours away at sublight."

"Engineering."

"Yes, Captain?"

"Can we make sublight?"

"Yes, Captain."

"Good. We're to make for a G Class star and hope it has a planet around it. Let me know when you finish the engine inspection."

"I'm on it now, Captain."

"The fourth planet from the star is now a confirmed M Class, Captain," the science officer said, looking away from the instrument console.

"We'll go in orbit around it," the captain said.

The Olympus limped into orbit using its sublight thrusters. Captain Anita Scholl paced the bridge waiting for the report from engineering. She was an attractive woman with a square face, light brown hair, and green eyes. Captain Scholl, at thirty-five, was the youngest woman to command a star cruiser. Her command channel sounded.

"Captain."

"The engine's containment chamber has a micro crack, Captain, and there's no way we can repair it."

"All right, Harry. I'm calling a department heads meeting in the ready room, so come on up."

"On my way, Captain."

Anita stood at the head of the readyroom conference table. Seated was Commander Mark Anson, exec. A solid built man with black hair and mustache above which set piercing gray eyes. Next to him was Heather Lockhart, chief medical officer.

She had long copper hair and brown eyes. On the opposite side sat Melissa Bennet, science officer who had raven hair and brown eyes. Next was Crystal Groves, chief of security, with short blonde hair and blue eyes. At the far end of the table sat Harry Turner, chief engineer, with sandy hair and brown eyes. Anita sat down and leaned forward putting her elbows on the table and locking her fingers together resting her chin on them. She looked at her officers, who sat quiet.

"Recommendations?" Anita asked.

"The only feasible option we have is to send one of the shuttles back through the wormhole to Altair Four, Captain," Harry said. "We don't dare risk using the sublight thrusters more than we already have. The power drain is only aggravating the micro crack."

"I agree," Mel said. "There's nothing we can do to repair the engine. We need a repair ship for that." Anita nodded.

"How long will it take a shuttle to reach Altair Four from the wormhole, Harry?" Anita asked.

"Traveling at sublight," he said, working the computer in the tabletop. "Twenty-eight days, Captain. A repair ship can be here in a month."

"Captain, I recommend we use a shuttle to explore this planet," Mel said. Anita considered exploring would be a lot better for morale then just sitting in orbit.

"Okay, Harry, prepare a shuttle for the trip back through the wormhole, and another for planetfall."

"I'll take a security team for a spot check, Captain," Crystal said.

"Not until after we have a full sensor scan of the planet," Anita said. "Let's get moving."

Anita stood behind Mel letting her eyes wander over the sensor console.

"Anything down there, Mel?"

"No indication of intelligent life or civilization, Captain." Anita caught the inflection in her tone.

"What, Mel?"

"There's something I can't clearly define. It's right on the edge of the bioscan. Almost as if…"

"As if what, Mel?" Mel looked over her shoulder at Anita with an uneasy look.

"As if it's becoming alive, Captain." Anita considered what she had been told and turned to Crystal.

"Do you anticipate any security problem on the planet, Crystal?" Anita asked. Crystal shook her head.

"Not at present, Captain."

"Then I'll accompany the security. Mark, you have the bridge. Keep an open channel while we're down there."

The security team fanned out from the shuttle. After a few minutes, they reported all clear. It had been over a year since the three women had set foot on an Earth-like planet. It was invigorating to breathe fresh air and smell the strange scents of alien wildflowers. The sky was a lighter blue the Earth and the gravity closely matched. A planet where life had evolved on a small scale.

"Captain, the bioscan is only showing animal life," Mel said, turning the instrument in an arc. "There it is again>"

"What, Mel?" Anita asked, alarmed. Mel glanced at her.

"I don't know, Captain. One scan, there seems to be something alive. The next scan nothing." Anita turned to Crystal.

"Alert your people, Crystal. I don't want anyone out there alone."

"Yes, Captain," she said, lifting her communicator. "Alert! Everybody on your toes. Form in twos, report anything unusual." The acknowledgements came in quickly.

"Was that last reading you had the same as you picked up from the bridge?" Anita asked. Mel made a check of the instrument.

"Yes, Captain. The bioscan now shows normal."

"Can you trace that pulse, Mel?"

"Only if it lasts longer than it has, Captain."

"Let's try to find it," Anita said. They moved off in the direction the bioscan had indicated the life pulse had come from.

They came to a thick woodland and stood looking into it. Crystal glanced at Anita.

"We can't go stumbling around in there, Captain," Crystal said. "It would be too easy to get lost." Anita looked at Mel.

"Well?" Anita asked. Mel nodded.

"Whatever it is, it's in this forest," Mel said.

"What sort of reading do you have now?"

"Normal, Captain. There it is again! Now it's gone," Mel replied, moving the instrument back and forth, shaking her head in puzzlement.

"What kind of reading did you get?"

"The same as the previous pulses, Captain. It's as if something comes to life and just as quickly dies." Anita frowned and thought, clasping her hands behind her. She glanced at each of her officers.

"We're going to have to find out what's in this forest. But I'm not going to risk lives to do so." The women nodded.

"Call in your security team, Crystal."

Anita had her officers assembled in the readyroom.

"The shuttle left for Altair, Captain," Harry reported.

"Have you been able to determine what we collided with, Harry?" He shook his head.

"Whatever it was, Captain, it left no residual trace on the hull." Anita nodded.

"Then our priority will be to discover what that life pulse on the planet is. Recommendations?"

"I could go into the forest, Captain. I can use the bioscan –"

"No, Mel. I'll not risk anyone until we know more," Anita said. "Even if you kept in communication it would take time for the security people to reach you if something happened."

"The captain's right," Heather said. "This is an unknown life form. We don't know if it poses a threat or not."

"I can rig an energy analyzer into the bridge's bioscanner," Harry said. "We can get some idea of what kind of life is down there."

"Give the computer those three readings of that pulse, Mel," Anita said. "If it can't give us an answer then Harry can proceed with his idea." Mel looked at the monitor and looked at Anita.

"The readings were too brief to be of any use to the computer, Captain. It couldn't identify them." Anita looked at the engineer.

"Install the energy analyzer, Harry."

"I'll get on it right away, Captain."

Mel and Harry stood watching the bioscan monitor as the it picked up the pulse again. This time it was stronger as it suddenly appeared on the monitor, and then was gone. Heather looked at Anita.

"I've never heard of anything with such a short life span, Captain" Heather said. "Let alone one large enough to be detected from a bioscan on the bridge."

"Well, Harry?" Anita asked.

"It's definitely biological, Captain. I don't understand why it lives so briefly, but the type of energy it generates is electrochemical. Almost the same reading we produce on the bioscan."

"We're getting little information about this thing," Anita said. "And none informative." She began considering a course of action.

"Could whatever it is be shielding itself, Harry?" He shook his head.

"If that were the case, Captain, we would be reading another energy source. It's like Mel said. It comes to life but doesn't have the energy to maintain itself for more than a few seconds."

"There's one more thing, Captain," Mel said. "The readings have all been from something stationary. There's been no movement between the pulses."

Anita was in her quarters trying to figure out what to do about the almost alive unknown on the planet. Her main priorities were to discover the source of those pulses and not to risk anyone doing so. She knew they would probably have to go into that forest to discover what it was. Her door signal sounded.

"Enter." Mark and Heather came in and faced Anita.

"What is it?"

"Captain, we want permission to go down to the planet," Mark said. "See if we can't get a better reading on what ever it is."

"It only lives for seconds," Heather said. "And it's stationary. I don't think it can pose much of a danger, Captain."

"I wouldn't be so quick to assume that," Anita said. But she was considering something she didn't know. They were willing to take the risk to get more data.

"All right," Anita said. "Take Campbell along as backup and keep your communications open." Anita regarded them for a moment.

"I'm allowing this because we need to know more about this unknown life form. I hope you can find something useful."

"Yes, Captain," Mark said. Anita frowned.

"I'll feel a lot better when you're safely back onboard the Olympus," Anita said.

Heather, Mark, and Jack Campbell, from security, walked slowly toward the forest. It was late afternoon and little daylight made it down through the tall bushy-topped trees. They had left the shuttle's comlink open to it would be easy for them to find their way back.

Each wore a sidearm as the captain had insisted. Mark walked beside Heather who was moving the bioscanner back and fourth.

"There," she said, pointing.

"How far?" Mark asked.

"It didn't last long enough to get a lock on it," Heather replied. They moved among the trees and into a shade where one couldn't see too far ahead.

"Getting anything, Heather?"

"Only animal life, Mark." They had walked half a mile into the forest and had gotten no further indication of the pulse.

"Whatever it is, Mark, will have to be located from the bridge," Heather said. "We could walk around in here for days without finding anything. The time of those pulses are just too short to pinpoint."

"Captain," Mark said, into his communicator.

"Yes, Mark? Have you found anything?" He related what Heather had said about locating the pulse.

"All right, Mark. Return to the ship." As they turned back to the ship, Heather gasped loudly.

"What is it?" Mark asked quickly. Campbell's hand went to his sidearm and he began turning slowly, alert for anything.

"I don't know," Heater replied. "But it was an extremely strong pulse. Nothing like the one's we've been looking for."

"None of you saw anything?" Anita asked.

"Did Mel get it on the bridge bioscan?" Mark asked.

"Yes. I'm getting really nervous about these pulses," Anita said. "I'm issuing a standing order that anyone going down to the planet wear sidearms."

Mel stepped beside Anita and she looked from the command seat.

"Find something?" Anita asked.

"That strong signal is the same frequency as the weaker ones, Captain. "But it's been amplified. Since that strong pulse, there have been no more of the weaker ones."

"Meaning what, Mel?"

"I have to assume the stronger pulse came from the same source as the earlier ones. Almost like it's evolved!" Anita frowned, not liking what she heard.

"We've got to locate the source of those pulses," Anita said. "And what they are. Mel, get with Harry and see what you two can come up with."

"Yes, Captain." Mel hurried from the bridge.

The Olympus had been in orbit for over twenty-four hours and the planet had become dynamic. The elusive pulses were now showing at regular intervals and moving. This development had saved Mel and Harry a lot of needless work. Now they could easily track the pulses on the bioscan, and they remained close to the forest.

"Now that we can follow them, Captain, what are we going to do about them?" Crystal asked. Anita stood with her arms folded considering what to do now. Her priorities hadn't changed.

"I'm going to send Mel and a security team down," Anita replied. "I hope she can learn something about these elusive ghosts. But I don't want anyone taking any needless risk. I want you to make that clear to your people, Crystal."

"Yes, Captain."

In the inky forest, the bioscan Mel carried was pulsing red at intervals of fifteen seconds. Each pulse thought came from a different direction. That made locating its source impossible. Each pulse was strong, but just far enough away so that no one could see anything in the deep shadows of the forest. After an hour's fruitless search, they returned to the shuttle.

Back on the bridge, Mel explained what she thought was going on.

"I don't think this – whatever it is – is trying to elude us, Captain. The pulse locations were much too random."

"What do you suggest, Mel?" Anita asked.

"I want to do a three orbit planetary scan. I especially want to check the other forests on the planet."

"You think there may be more of these things in those forests?"

"It's possible, Captain. I want a thorough check just to be certain. I can't believe one of these things exists in only one forest."

"All right, Mel. Let me know the results when you finish," Anita said.

For the next three orbits, Mel turned the bioscan on the different forests and recorded her findings. Scanning in both daylight and darkness had been a daunting task. Mel headed for Anita's quarters.

"Enter."

"Captain, I've got some data bit no definitive answer."

"What's the data, Mel?"

"I've determined these things are active in all the forests, and that they're more active at night than daytime."

"They're the same on all three continents?" Anita asked.

"Yes, Captain. There was no variation. I could almost believe it's some natural phenomena, but I wouldn't be able to explain the life signs."

"But they are definite life readings."

"Yes, Captain. The bioscan says they're life forms but can't tell us of what." Anita nodded.

"You look tired, Mel. Get some rest. We'll figure something out later."

"So what can we assume about these life forms?" Anita asked, sitting at the head of the readyroom table.

"They seem to have no hostile intensions, Captain," Heather said.

"Maybe so," Mark said. "But we've yet to see one."

"What I don't understand is how these things came into existence so suddenly," Mel said. "And proliferated so quickly."

"You're certain they only inhabit the forest regions, Mel?" Mark asked.

"Yes. When I scanned the open areas, I could find no trace of them."

"Could they be subterranean?" Harry asked.

"No," Mel replied. "Their signals are too strong."

"I want to give the crew some leave time on the planet while we wait for the repair ship," Anita said. "Let ten of the crew go down for five hour intervals. But warn them to stay away from the forests."

"What about my people, Captain?" Crystal asked.

"I want two of your people to accompany each group. And make certain everyone wears a sidearm."

"Very well, Captain," Crystal said.

"Captain to the bridge," Mark said, over the ship's PA system. Anita was on her way from her quarters when she heard the call. She stepped to the intercom in the bulkhead, pressed the switch and spoke.

"What is it, Mark?"

"We have a missing crewman on the surface, Captain."

"I'm on my way." As Anita stepped in the bridge, Mark vacated the command seat.

"What happened?" Anita asked.

"That's the mystery, Captain," Mark replied. "Nobody saw Henson go anywhere. They only missed him when they assembled at the shuttle to return."

"Have they searched for him?"

"Yes, Captain," Mark replied. "They've found no trace of him."

"Cancel planetfall," Anita said. "I want Crystal and a security team standing by in the shuttle bay. I'm going down and see if there isn't some simple explanation to this whole damn thing."

"This is the same spot the shuttle landed earlier?" Anita asked.

"Within inches, Captain," the pilot replied. Anita turned to Crystal.

"How far is the nearest forest?"

"About half a mile, Captain."

"Captain," Mark said, from the communicator.

"Yes, Mark?"

"I've talked to the people who went down with Henson."

"And?"

"No one recalls seeing him get off the shuttle." This was not the kind of news she needed or wanted. Anita already had enough mystery on her hands.

"Does anyone remember anything unusual on the shuttle?" Anita asked.

"No, Captain," Mark replied. "Five of the crew, and the security people, remember seeing him get on the shuttle, but nobody saw him on the planet." Anita considered this. It would have been impossible for Henson to have gotten off the shuttle without being seen, and he certainly didn't get off during the descent.

In the readyroom, Anita was impatient for an answer to the mystery.

"People, we have got to get to the bottom of this, and determine what happened to Henson." Everyone remained silent and Anita exploded.

"I'm not hearing any recommendations." Still no one said anything.

"Goddamnit! I want a course of action."

"Captain," Mel said, hesitantly. "I've been studying what's been found so far."

"And?" Anita asked, sharply.

"I would like to take a shuttle down near a forest on the nightside," Mel replied. "I prefer not to say anymore until I know if I'm right or wrong." Anita regarded her for a minute knowing she trusted Mel's judgment.

"You want to expose yourself to an unknown risk, Mel?"

"Yes, Captain. I would also like Mark to accompany me to confirm what I suspect, and I need a pilot." The last words got a laugh from around the table, and even Anita smiled. Mark didn't laugh.

"Well, Mark?" Anita asked, looking at him. He glanced at Mel. He had respect for her as a person and officer. If she thought she was close to a solution of the mystery, he couldn't refuse to go.

"I'll go, Captain. I want to get this cleared up too."

Mark set the shuttle down with a bone-jarring impact. He hadn't made a night landing since his training days. He breathed a sigh of relief as he turned his seat to face Mel.

"What have you got on your mind, Mel?"

"I believe these pulses are biomechanical devices," she replied. "Stay with me on this." Mark nodded.

"Something triggers them to greater activity after dark," Mel continued. "It took me awhile to put it together so that it made sense."

"What do you mean, Mel?"

"I think someone put dream machines down here, Mark."

"What?"

"It's the only thing that makes sense. The random pulses, the biological readings, the high nighttime activity, and the disappearance of Henson." He gave her an incredulous look.

"What would a dream machine have to do with Henson's disappearance?"

"Everything! Don't you see, Mark? That's how he got off the shuttle; he fell asleep. Being close to the surface, his brain waves activated one of the machines."

"Then what?"

"Henson was physically transported off the shuttle," Mel replied, with conviction. Mark shook his head.

"Come on, Mel. Do you believe what you're saying?" She nodded.

"That's why we're here, Mark. To prove or disprove it. We're near a forest, it's night, and we came here to sleep."

Anita was pacing on the bridge thinking she should never have let them go. She felt even worse at agreeing to Mel's request for a five-hour communication blackout.

"Captain." She stepped to the command seat and activated the intercom.

"Yes, Harry?"

"Can you come to engineering, Captain? I think I might have something for you."

"I'll be right there."

When she arrived in engineering, Harry took her aside.

"I think I know what Mel might have been considering, Captain. I didn't want to say anything over an open channel."

"Well tell me."

"I think there are biomachines on the planet, but I don't know what kind. I considered the fact that it wasn't long after we came into orbit that they became active. I concluded the only thing that could have activated them was our minds." Anita smiled.

"Harry, you're making the first sense I've heard since we got here. You think Mel thought the same thing?"

"Yes, Captain. To prove it, she had to go down to the planet." Anita nodded.

"Keep on it, Harry. See if you can determine what those machines are for."

Mel and Mark had fallen asleep. Now they were standing amid the ruins of a vast alien city. The tall towers had collapsed into the wide streets as time had taken its toll on the structures. It was a very ancient city. They began making their way through the ruins.

"Commander," someone shouted. They turned to see Henson hurrying toward them.

"Am I glad to see you two," he said, relieved. "How did you get here?"

"The same way you did," Mel replied. "We fell asleep."

"Can we get back?" Henson asked.

"There's only one way back," Mel said.

"How?" Mark asked. She smiled.

"We've got to go to sleep."

"Captain, sensors show the shuttle has lifted off from the planet," a crewman said, watching his monitor.

"Open a channel."

"Channel open, Captain."

"Mark, Mel, are you all right?"

"We're fine, Captain. We found Henson," Mark replied.

"Henson? In the dark?"

"I'll explain as soon as we're back onboard, Captain," Mel said.

They were seated in the readyroom. Mel stood beside Anita.

"I have to begin by telling you there's a lot I don't understand," Mel said. "Much I can guess. I'll present what I believe to factual so far as I've been able to determine." All eyes were on her waiting to hear the answer to the mystery of the planet.

"There are dream machines on the planet," Mel said. "That's the only definition adequate to explain them." All the faces were attentive.

"But they are infinitely more than that simple definition. They must have been inactive for ages. Then we came into orbit. Those first pulses were what detected our brain waves and that activated the machines."

"That's why the pulses appeared on all the continents and were the same frequency?" Harry asked.

"That's right," Mark replied. "The people that built them used this planet as a park or recreational area."

"Mark and me were physically transported to their home world after falling asleep," Mel said. "We were actually among the ruins of their civilization."

"It appeared they had no place on their planet that was free of civilization," Mark said.

"So they built their machines on the planet," Mel added. Everyone was looking at her with the same question in mind. Mel smiled as she shook her head.

"Don't ask me how they function," Mel said. "They're a totally alien technology."

"Henson fell asleep on the shuttle," Mark said. "The machine sensed this and sent him to the home world. When we fell asleep on that world, we were transported back to the shuttle."

"That's why the pulses were so active at night," Mel said. "The reason the pulses were random was that they were searching for sleeping minds."

"Is it safe for the crew to get some R&R on the planet, Mel?" Anita asked.

"As long as they don't go to sleep, Captain.

When the repair ship had finished work on the Olympus, Anita's crew was invigorated from their extended planetfall. Now they were ready to resume their tour of duty.

"Harry, take her up to standard speed slowly," Anita said. "Let's see if there's something more understandable out here than dream machines."

FUGITIVE

The small patrol ship had arrived at Varian Four. Marshal Les Alden showed the clerk at the immigration desk his identity card. The clerk looked up from the card.

"Well, Marshal, what brings you to Varian Four?" Les took out a small device and produced a hologram.

"Have you seen this man?" The clerk looked at the hologram for a moment and slowly nodded.

"Yeah, I think he came through here about a week ago. I can't recall his name." Les nodded.

"It would have been an alias. Thanks." Les started away from the desk.

"Marshal, if you're here after this man you better check in with Chief Corey. She's the law around here."

"She?" The clerk smiled.

"Don't let a pretty face fool you. Chief Corey is one tough woman."

"How do I get to her office?"

Les followed the clerk's directions and now stood looking at a door with Angelina Corey on it. He went in. Behind a desk sat a big built man with light brown hair and blue eyes. He wore a dark blue uniform with a gold badge on the left breast pocket. He looked up.

"Can I help you?" he asked, remaining seated. He was quickly on his feet when Les introduced himself.

"I'm Federal Marshal Les Alden. I'm here to see Chief Corey." The deputy bent and pressed the intercom switch and spoke quickly. Les heard her voice reply.

"Show him in. The man went to a wood paneled door and looked over his shoulder at Les.

"This way, Marshal."

As Les went into the office, she stood and extended her hand.

"I'm Angelina, Corey. Call me Angel. Everyone does. Although I doubt I'll ever be one."

"I'm Les Alsen. Les will do," he said, shaking her hand. She had chestnut hair styled into a wave on the right side of her head.

Gray eyes, softly curving nose, and full red lips. The clerk was right; she was very pretty.

"How can I help you, Les?" He showed her the hologram.

"This is Jovan Garnet. I've been after him for over a year. As far as I know, he's committed nine murders on as many worlds." She looked from the hologram to Les.

"Sounds like a ruthless son of a bitch."

"He is, Angel. He's wounded me three times." She gave him a quick once over.

"Then why aren't you wearing a sidearm?"

"Regulations, Angel. I have to get local permission to be armed. Some planets have strict bans on arms."

"Well you just got permission to wear your sidearm, Les. I take it this Jovan Garnet is here?" he shut down the hologram and returned it to his pocket.

"That he is, Angel. The immigration clerk identified the hologram and said he arrived about a week ago."

"You got a place to stay, Les?"

"No. I came directly here from immigration."

"Across the street is the Crawford Inn. They have decent rooms and a good restaurant. You get settled in and I'll see what records I can get on Garnet from the computer. I'll meet you in the restaurant about seven for dinner. It's where I usually eat."

"Okay, Angel, see you around seven."

Les went back to his ship. He unlocked the compartment where he kept his pulser, took it out, and pulled it snugly around his waist. It made him feel better. He picked up his light luggage and headed back out of the ship. As he went through immigration, the clerk grinned and pointed to the pulser.

"Looks like you and Chief Corey hit it off, Marshal."

"Yeah. We got a lot in common. Law enforcement."

The desk clerk at the Crawford Inn got a nervous look when Les walked in. He stared at Les' pulser.

"Don't worry," Les assured him. "I only shot bad people." He took the elevator up to the fifth floor and entered his room.
Algen was right, these were nice accommodations. He put his clothing away, except for a change.

By the time he had shored, shaved, and dressed, it was almost seven. He strapped on his pulser and went down to the restaurant. He ordered a drink. A few minutes later, Angel came in and he started to stand but she motioned him not to. As she sat down the waiter brought her a drink. Les looked surprised. She smiled.

"I told you I eat here most of the time. They know what I want."

"Were you able to find out anything about Garnet?"

"He came through immigration eight days ago," Angel replied. "Using the alias Arthur Green. He was checked, as was his luggage, and he was unarmed." Les frowned.

"That don't sound like Garnet. Since I've been on his case, I've never known him to be unarmed."

"He's armed now, Les. The record showed an Arthur Green purchasing a pulse rifle and chemicals. Have you any idea why he came here?"

"Not a clue, Angel."

"After we eat I'll take you to the morgue. A man was murdered three days ago. Maybe you can ID him or, at least, tell me if Garnet left his signature on the crime."

The coroner's assistant pulled out the drawer and opened the bodybag.

"Christ!" Les exclaimed.

"You know him?" Angel asked.

"Yeah. His name was Martin Fowler. He was the one who put me on Garnet's trail a couple of weeks ago." Les looked at the assistant.

"How did he die?" Les asked.

"Can't figure that out," the assistant replied. "His insides are a mass of jelly." Les looked at Angel.

"Now we know why Garnet came here," Angel said. "Revenge. We have to find Garnet, Les." He looked at her with a frown.

"You know, Angel, there's one regulation I can't quite come to terms with."

"What one is that?" He put his hand on the butt of the pulser.

"The one that says I can't shoot the bastard unless an innocent life is endangered. And right now I sure as hell feel endangered."

"I'll put extra security people at Immigration," Angel said. "In case he tries to leave." Les shook his head.

"He won't leave through immigration," Les said. "Too risky. He's got another way to get off the planet."

Les paused and rubbed his chin.

"If he knew I was here, Angel, he might not be in such a hurry to leave."

"Why not?"

"I told you he's wounded me three times. But he hasn't been able to kill me. I've heard he wants me dead in the worst way. He knows it's the only way to get me off his back."

"You mean to use yourself as bait?" Angel asked, surprised.

"Precisely. It just may be our only chance to nab the son of a bitch."

The next morning, the city was aware of the arrival of Les. He had come looking for a fugitive. Who he was after wasn't mentioned in the computer press. Les was impressed at how quickly Angel had gotten his presence so widely circulated. She was all business. As he was going across the lobby, the desk clerk called to him.

"Marshal." Les went to the desk.

"There's a message for you, Marshal. The clerk handed him an envelope. Les opened it, took out the one page and read it.

'I know you're here after me you bastard. Figure out how I'm getting out of the city. The come after me, if you've got the balls. I want to get our score settled for good.' It was signed Garnet.

Angel put the note down and regarded Les with a dour look.

"He does seem to want you dead, Les."

"How can he get out of the city, Angel?" She considered the question for a moment.

"Through the underground access tunnels. They're how the city is maintained. But there are at least a dozen exits, Les. And nothing outside but jungle, and no one knows much about what's in that jungle."

"He'll make it obvious which exit he uses. He wouldn't want me to make a mistake and miss him."

"I'm going to have to go with you, Les. You can extradite Garnet, but he's committed a murder in my jurisdiction."

"I wouldn't know where to start without you, Angel. And I appreciate the company." Angel smiled.

"Then let's go, Les."

It was the ninth exit they came to that showed the way Garnet had left the city. Les knew someone would be out there to pick him up. Back in Angel's office, she was turning things over to her deputy. They got the equipment and food they would need. Deputy Thomas drove them back to the exit.

"Keep the air scan on us, Sol," Angel said. "It's the only way we dare communicate."

"It's certain Garnet will be monitoring the channels," Les added. They settled the packs on their backs, slung their rifles, and moved out into the jungle.

It was filled with unusual sounds and scents. They hadn't gone far when Angel took the rifle from her shoulder and armed it.

"What's that for?" Les asked. She looked around the jungle.

"Because I haven't any idea of what sort of animals inhabit this jungle." Les quickly followed suit.

A short time later, a question occurred to Angel.

"How can you be sure Garnet came this way, Les?" He pointed to a small branch that had been deliberately broken and left hanging.

"He doesn't want me getting lost." Angel regarded him knowing she would have missed that clue. Les knows his msn, she thought. She respected that in a law enforcement officer.

"Garnet wants me too badly to miss any chance to get me, Angel." Her eyes widened.

"We're dealing with a psychopath?"

"A damned dangerous psychopath. But I have no intension of being wounded again or ending up dead. You heard how Fowler died. Garnet gets his greatest enjoyment from the suffering of his victims. He's not kind enough to offer you a quick death, Angel." She slowly shook her head.

"He must have something special in mind for you." He grabbed her arm and pulled her roughly back. He knelt and began examining the ground. He found a trip wire and pulled it. A small metal dart flew past and lodged in a tree. Its height above the ground would have put it into one's calf. Angel pulled the dart from the tree and sniffed the tip.

"Amphorine. It causes a slow, painful death, Les. It's a poison found in the sap of certain trees here."

"He's sending a clear message, Angel. He made this trip wire obvious. We're going to have to be cautious because he won't leave anymore traps this obvious."

They moved on through the jungle accompanied by the roar of large beasts. This made it difficult for Les.
He had not only Garnet's traps to consider but the animals as well. Something flashed past him and he heard Angel's rifle fire. The animal fell from the tree with a heavy thud. It was scaled and dark green and bigger than Les. Its body looked humanoid but instead of arms and legs it had tentacles.

"Thanks, Angel. What the hell is that thing?" She shrugged.

"Anything you want to call it. I've never seen one before." Les was now quite wary.

They had traveled for over two hours, and there hadn't been a second boobytrap. But there just enough evidence to keep Les on Garnet's trail. He slowed their pace.

"What is it, Les?" She could see he was tense.

"He hasn't set anymore traps, Angel. He's up to something." They heard the rifle fire and the branch above Les' head was vaporized. Angel and Les dropped to the ground.

"I could just as easily have killed you, Alden, but I'm a sportsman at heart."

"What do you want, Garnet?"

"Only your life, Marshal. I'm going to make your death a very interesting game. I'm going to enjoy myself, Alden. But you had better sharpen your wits. You're making it too easy for me."

"I'll go around," Angel said.

"No. He'll be gone by the time you get there. Besides, you don't know what you might run into, Angel. He's sure right about one thing."

"What's that?"

"I better get my wits about me. All that time and no boobytraps should have given plenty of warning. Maybe I'm getting too old for this."

"Don't be too hard on yourself, Les. It happens to the best of us."

"What pisses me off the most is that I've been after Garnet for over a year, and he can still surprise me."

"You know how unpredictable psychopaths can be."

"I seem to forget that, Angel. We can get up now."

The rest of the day, they followed Garnet's trail through the jungle. Les was more fully alert now, and when they came across the next boobytrap, it wasn't easily seen.

Luckily this poison dart stuck in Les' pack.

"I'm going to have to keep a much sharper watch for these things, Angel."

"That will slow us down," Angel said. "Maybe that's what he wants, Les. He could backtrack and take us from behind." Les shook his head.

"I doubt that. He doesn't know this jungle and he's got a rendezvous to keep."

Late in the day they came across a cave by a small stream and decided to spend the night there. They laid out their sleeping bags and turned on the electric lantern. They ate from cans and then relaxed.

"How long have you been a marshal, Les?"

"Almost five years."

"My father and grandfather were both in law enforcement. I think my father was disappointed when his only child was a girl." Les smiled.

"What does he think now?"

"I've made him proud of me," Angel replied, with a contented look.

"I've got two brothers and both imagined they were safe in labs. They both have wives and kids. I wanted adventure so I applied to be a federal marshal. And here the hell I am spending over a year of my life chasing a damn psychopath."

"How long has it been since you've been with a woman?"

"Huh?"

"How long has it been since you got laid?" He shrugged.

"Hell, I don't remember. It seems I never have the time, Angel."

"It's the same with me. But we've got time now." Les could see she was serious.

"You're the chief here, Angel. And I am under local jurisdiction."

Next morning, they couldn't find a trace of Garnet's trail. He had stopped being obvious, and this alerted Les.

"Garnet is now extremely dangerous, Angel. We're going to have to be especially alert now." Angel turned, looking into the jungle. She, too, now felt the tension. As they moved on, Les kept looking ahead for any indication that Garnet had come this way. He found one footprint, then pointed his rifle at a clump of trees.

"something's in there, Angel," he said, in a low voice. They heard a grunt and growl.

A large black, four-footed animal came into the open. They stood still but kept their rifles ready for use. The beast's yellow eyes stared at them. It had very nasty looking fangs and hook like claws on its front paws. It turned away into the jungle paying them no more attention.

"I'm glad it was only an animal," Les said, breathing again. Angel picked up on his meaning. If it had been Garnet, they would both have been wounded and left to die. It was beginning to get hairy chasing Garnet.

About an hour later, they stopped to eat. As Les stuck his fork in the can, he noticed something shiny in the brush. He set his can down, went to it, pushed the brush aside and took a look.

"We're on the right path, Angel," he said, pointing to the silver canister.

"What is it?"

"A small, homemade fragmentation bomb. Big enough to put a lot of holes in you, but not big enough to kill you. I've got to find the trip wire." He carefully examined the bomb and found the wire stretching across the trail. It had been luck that they had stopped when they did. It was fiendishly camouflaged and Les knew he wouldn't have seen it.

"Let's see if we can fool Garnet," he said, pulling his pulser from the holster and setting it.

"Let's get to cover, Angel." They both got behind trees and Les fired. The bomb exploded with a loud roar and formed a column of rising white smoke.

"You think Garnet was close enough to have heard the explosion, Les?"

"Bet on it. He likes to see how his little tricks work."

On they went through thick, tangled jungle. Twice during the afternoon they had to avoid very large animals. Les thinking about how Garnet planned on getting off the planet. No ship could land in this jungle.

"Is there anyplace a ship could land, Angel?" She thought for a moment.

"There's open savanna another couple of miles ahead. You think that's where Garnet is headed?"

"It has to be."

"Can we catch up with him in time to stop him?"

"I hope so, Angel. I'm getting tired of chasing the bastard."

"We're going to have to move faster." Les nodded as he regarded her.

"Faster, yes, but cautiously. He's probably got more surprises in store for us."

That night, they took shelter among some boulders on a rocky outcrop.

"Think we'll get him tomorrow, Les?"

"That or he'll get us." She gave him a shocked look.

"You believe that's possible?" He looked at her with a grim frown.

"Angel, Garnet has all sorts of deadly tricks up his sleeve. Damn right there's' a possibility of us walking into one of those tricks."

"Then we better take advantage of tonight," she said, putting her hand over his.

Next morning, the jungle began to thin out. They cautiously approached an open area. Les looked around carefully but saw nothing out of place. As they passed a tree at the edge of the clearing, they heard a rifle fire There was an explosion that knocked Les unconscious.

When he came to, Angel was gone. Her rifle and sidearm were beside her pack. Garnet had taken her! As he got his head straight, it became obvious what had happened. Garnet had put a bomb in a tree above them and had detonated it with rifle fire. Now Les had to think of a way to get Angel back safely. That would not prove easy, he knew, but he had become very fond of her.

He set out south away from the trail they had been following. Now he was in open country and might be able to get around and ahead of Garnet. He had gone about half a mile when he began to arc back to the north. He tried to think of a plan, but knew he would have to react as events unfolded.

It was just after sunset when Les headed toward some rocky hills that he saw the glow from a lantern. He had caught up with them. He saw Angel sitting with her hands tied behind her. He heard Garnet but couldn't see him.

"Doesn't look like the marshal's coming after you. I know my bomb didn't kill him, it wasn't that powerful." Angel just glared at him in silence.

"Maybe one of those animals had him for lunch. That's something to think about. Marshal Alden ending up as a meal for a jungle beast.

I like that." Garnet was keeping out of sight. He left Angel in the open so Les could see her.

What to do? Les couldn't climb around because of the loose rocks, and he sure as hell wasn't going to just walk in there. It seemed Garnet had all the advantages, except the darkness. It would take time, but if Les could work his way around to where he was above Angel, then he might have a chance to get Garnet.

Les had gone about a quarter of a mile when he went over to the far side of the hill and back toward Angel. When he saw the glow, he began climbing carefully to keep as quiet as possible. Finally he could look over the crest. There sat Garnet in the open with the hill at his back. Les took a chance and leaned over slowly until he could see Angel

"Shit!" he exclaimed, in a whisper. Garnet had strapped a bomb to her back and it had to be the detonator he held. Les faced a dilemma. He couldn't risk stunning Garnet because he most likely had the detonator rigged so that if his finger came off the trigger it would detonate the bomb. The only thing he had accomplished was to learn that Garnet still had the advantage. For the time being, all Les could do was wait for daylight and hope some opportunity would present itself.

With daylight, nothing had changed. Garnet got up and began to pace. Les figured this must be his pickup day. He had to do something because Garnet would kill Angel as soon as he saw the ship.

"Garnet." Garnet started, then smiled.

"Well, well. The marshal's made it after all. But that's a disappointment. I had hoped one of those beasts had made a meal of you."

"Let the woman go. It's me you want."

"Ah! There's the rub, Marshal. As long as I have her I have your undivided attention."

"I can drop you right now, Garnet." Garnet smiled and held up his hand with the detonator.

"I don't think so, Marshal. You've probably been here long enough to figure out the situation."

"Goddamnit, Garnet! What do you want?"

"You dead. That's all that comes to mind." Les had to get the detonator before Garnet could take his thumb off the trigger. It was a wild card, but it was the only thing he could think of.

"Come on, Marshal, make conversation." Les laid his pulser he could quickly pick it up. He got the rifle pressed against his shoulder and aimed at the detonator.

The sound of the police aircraft distracted Garnet as Les fire. The pulse charge vaporized the detonator along with Garnet's hand. Les didn't give him anytime to feel pain. He stood with the pulser and fired. Garnet was hit with a stun charge and dropped to the ground. Les went over the crest and down to Angel.

"That was fancy shooting, Les." He began disarming the bomb and then removed it from her. When he had it safely put aside, he untied her hands.

"What just happened, Angel, was an act of desperation." She looked at him and smiled.

"Well if I'm ever in another situation like this, I hope you'll be around and desperate."

The two officers from the aircraft gave first aid to Garnet. He was still out when they put him in the craft. It was crowded but they managed in the flight back to the city. Les was feeling relief that he had saved Angel, and that he would no longer be chasing Garnet all across the galaxy.

Les walked into Angel's office and sat down.

"I have the extradition papers all cleared, Les."

"Thanks, Angel What about that ship that was coming for Garnet?"

"We got it in orbit. Three other wanted felons are now in custody."

"After I take Garnet back, I'm resigning." Her eyes widened. He came around the desk and leaned against it. She looked up at him.

"You're a law enforcement man. What the hell would you do?"

"Oh, I don't know. Could you use another deputy?" He bent down and kissed her.

THE LOST SEED

I really don't know why I'm writing this personal history. There are after all only two human beings alive that I know of. Phil and myself. I guess maybe I'm doing it so I can finally get it clear in my mind that the human race done a goddamn bang-up job on their own extinction. And probably well deserved. But I might as well start at the beginning. My new beginning and the sudden demise of the rest of humanity.

It was about six or seven years ago, I'm not sure because I didn't bother to keep track. I didn't see any need to. I had been put in an isolation ward in a hick hospital in Southern California. Hell! I don't even remember the name of the town. Come to think of it, I never bothered to find out. I was under heavy sedation because I had been in a delirium, raving like a lunatic. I had picked up a dose of bubonic plague while hiking in the Rockies.

Anyway, when I finally came around I was alone. Not just in the isolation ward but the whole damn hospital. I rang for the nurse but all I got was silence. Gradually, I was able to get out of bed moving slowly, using the wall for support, to the door. I opened it and looked up and down the corridor. The place was empty. Everybody was gone except me. What the hell? That was the story of my life, I thought. Always forgotten or pushed aside. That's right! I was beginning to feel sorry for myself. It was something I had learned quite early in life. That was how my marriage had ended; with me being rudely pushed out of the way. My wife had divorced me without so much as a fuck you, jerk.

So I was left with my clothes and one hundred and three dollars, not counting change. I was to subsequently learn the money quite worthless. I could now have anything I wanted without money, credit card, or any goddamn hassle from salesmen. But at that time, I didn't know that. All I knew was that I was alive and relatively healthy.

I dressed slowly and began thinking about something to eat. I didn't know how long I had out, but my stomach was saying at least twenty-four hours.

I didn't think too much about the people being gone. I just figured the local nuke had fucked up and scared everybody off. That wasn't exactly late breaking news in those days.

The lights were on and a clock on the wall showed one-thirty. Since I could see daylight I knew it was the P.M.

The lights in the ceiling reflected off the cream yellow walls. As I went along the corridor I saw all kinds of stuff scattered across the floor. There were medical instruments; hypos mixed with sheets and towels. Medicine odors were strong in the area around the desk where a pill cart had overturned making a colorful kaleidoscope radiating across the blue-green tiles.

I found the coffee shop and fixed myself a meal from vending machines and heating it in a microwave. Not knowing the situation, I got change for dollar bills and paid the goddamn machines for my coffee and sandwich. I sat and ate in a fluorescent silence, disturbed only by the low humming of the vending machines as they cut on and off. After eating, I relaxed with a smoke. I was feeling like I could face the world, and whatever the hell it was that had gone wrong in my small part of it.

I left the hospital and wandered into the downtown area. The sky was a gray-white overcast with a stiff ocean breeze that meant rain soon. The town, too, deserted, as empty as the hospital had been. There was a difference: bodies lying to the sidewalks and others in cars that had hit the fronts of buildings and into each other.

I don't know why, but the bodies made no impression on me. I didn't associate them with a wild nuke plant. Hell, I didn't associate them with anything. To me, they were just bodies. The lights in stores and streetlights were blazing away. I saw doors standing open, and tried a few closed ones only to find them unlocked. It was as if the people had fled in panic without bothering to put anything in order. But what were they running from?

I was getting curious as to what had happened. It never crossed my mind that the nuke plant, clearly visible, was spitting out deadly radiation. I only thought that if left unmanned it would become unstable. But that was only what I had heard. That I could be getting a deadly dose never occurred to me. I had never been interested in science.

So I began to think, if you want information you get a newspaper. I walked through the town until I came to a newsstand.

I had no idea how old the paper was, but judging by what my stomach had told me, no more than two days old. Not knowing didn't bother me.

I had quit wearing a watch when I decided time wasn't important in my life anymore. But the paper had the damnedest story I ever read.

Scientists had been screwing around with something called recombinant DNA. The lab had blown up.

Once free, those little bugs had rapidly spread over the country killing people by the millions. Let me clarify. Those bugs that got lose, I know nothing about except for two things. One, they didn't' live very long or I would have died before I left the hospital. Two, they had no effect on animals, birds, or insects as far as I know. They only affected people and killed them very quickly. The short life span of those bugs has led me to believe that it must have been a military lab that had been blasted away. I mean, if they would make a neutron bomb that would only kill living thins and only slightly damage buildings, why not just eliminate the bomb? Make little bugs that would only kill people. But to recall the world the way it was then, that doesn't surprise me. But I'm getting away from my story.

While the bugs were creating a catastrophe here, the Europeans were trying their damn best to prevent the bugs from spreading over there. They were so desperate they were shooting down aircraft flying in from North America. Apparently that had little, if any, effect at all. I found a one-page paper with a later date that said Europe was being wiped out. I used to wonder who got out that last newspaper.

After I got over what little shock I felt, I began to think I might not be the only one still alive. After all, I had lucked out. So why not others? I got myself a small RV, stocked it, and began my six long years, (or has it been seven?) of searching from the West Coast to the East Coast. I went from Florida up to Canada. I crossed Canada and went down into Mexico.

By taking a different route each time, I covered one hell of a lot of territory in those years. But there wasn't much of anything else I could do. All I ever saw was empty cities and decaying farms. I never had to worry about clothing, canned food, or parts for my RV. Although I've had to replace it twice when it developed mechanical problems I couldn't cope with.

Surprisingly, nature was quick to take back what humanity had taken from her. The whole damn country was spooky.

No jets roaring across the skies, no cars or trucks on the highways, and only static on the radio. Those first six months still have an eerie air of unreality about them.

IN DARKNESS AROUND US

I was making my way back west on State Route 281 through Nebraska. That, as it turned out, was the luckiest break of my life. As I was passing Grand Island, I saw a large, crudely painted sign beside the road. It read: to anyone left alive, welcome, and below was an address.

I stopped the RV and just sat there and stared at it for a long time. I had been planning to bypass Grand Island. Now I decided it would be worth checking out. I wrote down the address on a note pad I kept on the dash.

Before I could search for that address I had to gas up the RV. Getting gas in rural areas wasn't easy. It had to be pumped from the underground tanks by a hand-cranked suction pump. It was tedious and arm cramping. Once I got the gas flowing, I didn't stop until the RV was topped off. It was a pain in the as, but it had to be done. In most areas, electricity had only lasted a few days after the end. But in areas serviced by nukes, and hydropower, the electricity is still flowing.

By the time I finished pumping gas and purging the pump, it was almost sundown. I decided to wait until morning to go looking for the address. I started the engine and drove out to open country for the night. I had learned early on not to stay in any town at night. It was too unnerving. I quickly realized I was making an excuse to put off going to that address. I had to come to grips with reality. I might finally face what I had been searching for so long. Another living person.

Believe me, after being alone for so long, it was not easy to think about such an event. Christ! I had been alone for so long, gotten so used to it, I was afraid. Now that I might meet someone scared the shit out of me. I know that doesn't make much sense, but that was how I felt. And with night coming on, I had no urge to go groping around in the dark and get my ass shot off. To help steel-up my nerves, I sat on the steps of the RV and downed a couple of stiff doses of whiskey.

I tried sacking out for the night. One of the things I haven't gotten used to, even after being with Phyl, is the silence. Except for insects and prowling night animals, the silence of no civilization is the one thing that still affects me.

It seemed, that night in particular, to descend on me like a heavy blanket. I couldn't sleep. It was not only the silence, there was no real silence, but the night sounds.

Nocturnal animals sounded loud skittering around the RV. They seemed to amplify in my mind. Some began to sound like someone walking up to the RV. But the reason I couldn't sleep was because my mind was in turmoil. Filling with pictures of what it would be like to come face to face with a living person. Hell! I wasn't sure I could still speak understandably anymore.

Until dawn, I dozed fitfully; awake then dozing. Slowly, it seemed to me, the sun lifted above the horizon into the clear blue sky. The first things I did was brush my teeth and shave. I continued to shave when I found how uncomfortable it was for me to grow a beard. I sat down and had a couple of cups of coffee and smokes. I had butterflies in the pit of my stomach because of an unreasoning fear of meeting another person. I had been alone too damned long!

It took a couple of hours before I was able to convince myself this was something I wanted to do; something I had to do. Just to talk to another person would, no doubt, be the oddest experience of my life. Resolutely, I got behind the wheel, started the engine, and headed into Grand Island.

I had no idea where the street I was looking for was. I drove up and down streets looking at the rusting street signs. I had been cruising for sometime when hunger began to creep into me. Not eating breakfast had caught up with me. I stopped the RV in an intersection and fixed myself something to eat I took the plate from the microwave, poured myself a cup of coffee, and sat down on the steps to eat. I looked around as I ate.

The weather beaten houses stretched along the streets with windows staring like dead eyes. I noticed some of the houses had doors standing open. There were some rusting cars setting in drives. The idea that people used to live in those houses, and might still be there, gave me a sudden electric shiver up my spine. It was then that I became consciously aware that the wind was rustling the dry autumn leaves and whispering softly through the tall grass that had once been neatly kept lawns. I was surrounded by decaying houses with sidewalks that were cracked and overgrown. Then came the goddamn silly idea. From nowhere, it struck me that the sound of the wind might be ghosts talking about the good old days.

IN DARKNESS AROUND US

I dropped the paper plate, Climbed into the RV, and pulled the door closed. I set my coffee in the tray and resumed my search. I was determined that if I couldn't find that address by sundown, I was sure as hell beating it out of town. I just couldn't understand how someone could have continued to live in a dead town. It always gave me the willies, especially after dark. It was the idea of no lights, no sounds, and no people. I could deal with that in the country.

A short while later, I came across the street I was looking for. I drove slowly along looking from side to side until I saw a sign in front of a house.
It had been painted by the same person who had made the highway sign. I stopped in front of a peeling, two-story, yellow house. The grass and weeds were almost as high as the fence that stretched across the yard. This sign read: if you are in time, I'll be alive.

I pulled the RV to the curb and cut the engine. An unnatural silence settled in. Even the noise of birds was gone, and the wind calmed. The heat wasn't all that bad, but I was sweating like hell. I sat there a good fifteen minutes, not moving, just staring at the house. I saw no sign of anyone being alive inside. Maybe I was too late. Or maybe the person inside was feeling the same sort of anxiety that was surging through me.

Hesitantly, I got out of the RV. The door closing sounded awful loud. I slowly walked around to the front of the RV and stopped by the gate. The palms of my hands were so sweaty I had to keep wiping them on my pants. As I stood looking at the front door, I suddenly thought, what if this is a goddamn psycho's trick and he's got me in his sights? But for the life of me, I couldn't really believe that. It was a paranoid idea from a long dead world.

I started to turn back to the RV since there had been no response from the house. I heard a deadbolt click. It was so damned loud I nearly jumped out of my skin. I turned back to the house. I saw the door was open an inch and I could see, in the bright westering sun, a blue eye gazing at me.

"I saw your sign by the highway, then this one. I guess I made it in time, huh?" I guess it sounded kind of stupid, but it was all I could think of.

There was no reaction for so long I was certain the person hadn't been able to understand me. I knew I had spoken understandable English. At least, I had understood it.

Then from behind the door came a muffled voice.

"Do you have a gun?"

"I've got a shotgun in the RV. In wooded country, bears get nosy at times. But I can't see much need for a gun these days." Another period of frozen time while the blue eye bored into me. Finally the door opened and my jaw dropped.

I was looking a real pretty woman. She was about five-six with long, silky brown hair hanging half way down her back. And I saw the twin of that blue eye that had watched me so intensely.
She had on a white pullover sweater that accented her breasts, a pair of yellow shorts from which emerged shapely legs that ended with feet holding things. In her hands, she held an aluminum ball bat.

I sure as hell never expected to see a woman. Shit! I hadn't even thought about women since I thought they were all dead. But there stood an attractive woman. What goddamn luck!

"What's your name?" she asked, seeming to gain confidence at my surprise and immobility. I couldn't remember my damn name.

"Hell, I can't remember," was all I could say, scratching my head. I really had to concentrate on remembering my name. It took a few minutes to dredge it from memory. I hadn't used it in an awful long time.

"I know what it's like. I've had to keep writing my name over and over so I wouldn't forget. My name is Phyllis. Phyllis Costa." She spoke softly, her lips breaking into a smile of understanding at my continuing struggle. I finally remembered who the hell I was, or had been, whichever.

"My name is Kenneth. Kenny Webb. Glad to meet you Phyllis Costa." It was really weird hearing my name after so many years. Especially hearing her say it.

"That's how Phil and I came together. By my reckoning, we've been together for over a year, and she talks of having babies, trying to get human race started again. Since we've been together, she hasn't gotten pregnant. Lately, she's become very pressing about getting some medical books to see what we've been doing wrong. Believe me, we've been doing nothing wrong. We've sure as hell tried making up for all those years without sex. I just keep telling her it's only a matter of time and luck until she gets pregnant. That line is beginning to wear thin with her. But I sure as hell don't have any intension of telling her that my ex-wife insisted I have a vasectomy after the birth of our third child.

THE END